The Road Sharks
Ghost Wind Chronicles #1

www.clinthollingsworth.com

Printed in the United States of America

ISBN: 978-0-9909952-7-2

Cover illustration by Clint Hollingsworth and Jeanine Henning
Interior art by Clint Hollingsworth

CHAPTER ONE
Followed

Yep. I'm being hunted.

She had been training in awareness since she was eight years old, ten years now, and there was no mistaking the feeling on the back of her neck. Someone… something was following her with intent.

One of my former friends, fellow scouts of the Clan of the Hawk looking for revenge? If so, they certainly took their time. It's been six months. That didn't seem likely.

One of the Yakama Nation?

Less likely. The Yakamas were friendly people, both natives and their adoptees. A Yakama medicine woman had nursed her back to health.

She gazed over the sagebrush landscape, letting her eyes wander the dust covered interstate highway to her east around to the slope of the Cascade Mountains to the west.

Nothing showed itself. She didn't believe it would until it needed to.

Maybe not hunted. Maybe haunted.

CHAPTER TWO
The Rock Pile

Damn it, my face aches!

She touched the livid scar that ran from the side of her nose to the outer edge of her once flawless left cheekbone. The cold wind, blowing though the miles of sagebrush made the half-healed white scar throb. There was precious little area to block the weather until she hit the trees again.

I should have listened to Lila Whitefeather. It's too early in the spring to have started my...journey.

She laughed inwardly. Journey. Why not call it what it was? Banishment. Why not call her what she was? Ghost Wind, the exiled scout.

Should have listened to Sifu.

She looked longingly at the old, broken and unused road. The rocks of the open sagebrush country were not kind to her feet, softened by a four-month convalescence, and the moccasins she wore needed the soles replaced fifty miles ago. She would have liked to have walked down the relatively flat middle of the crumbling former highway, but it was not the way of the scout to follow roads.

I'm not a scout of the Clan of the Hawk anymore, so what does it matter if I take the easy way?

She knew better.

The Way of the Scout was the only thing that would keep her alive in the deserts, mountains, dead cities and in the unclaimed lands. Twenty seven years after The Great Die-off, twenty seven years appropriately named "The Crazy Years", it was hard enough to survive as a group.

She was a lone-wolf, and lone wolves rarely survived long.

Skills and knowledge were the only thing between herself and an early grave. That and the few items she had accepted from Lila for survival.

Maybe it was best to just lie down here, out in the sagebrush where no one but the coyotes would find her. Maybe it would be good to just lie down and let the cold claim her. The clan always preached fairness and justice for all, about not making the mistakes of the Beforetimers, but they'd dumped her out to die, wounded and sick without even giving her a chance to defend against what they charged her with.

Some family.

No. She would not let being depressed lead into being dead. She wasn't going to give them that satisfaction. A lot of them obviously wanted her dead, and they'd almost gotten their wish. She felt the old burning anger start in her chest again, like embers coming to life.

Screw them.

Out of the haze of falling snow and wind, she saw something looming. As she approached, she saw it was a semi-tractor trailer, a good fifty feet off the road. Looked like it had been there a long time, the trailer canted at a forty-five degree angle. She could still see the ancient ruts of its path off the main highway.

She crawled up against one of the huge wheels, screened from the wind and sat down to rest. The dancing snow wafted in, touched her face but she barely felt it. She had trained long and hard to stay in the present moment but since the banishment, her rebel mind seemed to take off on its own like a bee-stung horse.

They should have given me a chance to at least defend myself, laying on the ground, tied and bleeding. Where was their much spoken of justice then?

By chance, she looked up at the faded lettering on the side of the old semi, and she laughed a short sharp laugh. It was a Mav-Tech transport.

At least there's someone more hated than me, at least I didn't unleash a plague on the world, wipe out eighty percent of humanity and plunge civilization into barbarism!

Small consolation, but you took what you could get these days.

CHAPTER THREE
Ah for the Old Days

Darwin Shell looked over what had been a beautiful riverwalk in the Beforetime. The memories of how nice things had been back then, over twenty years ago, always made him a bit melancholy. Bend had been a beautiful city. Sitting in his office in the old municipal building, he sighed. Now the city was a slowly crumbling ruin, trying its level best to return to nature.

The riverwalk was choked with willows, the coffee stands sitting there with small trees growing out of them. It seemed all great civilizations eventually fell to their own apathy and stupidity. Having it too good for too long dulled people's wits, made them sit back and assume someone else would take care of everything.

"Well, someone sure as hell took care of us, that's for damn sure," he growled more to himself than to the younger man sitting in an old leather easy chair.

"Thinkin' 'bout the old days again, boss?" Axyl, his second-in-command asked.

"Now why would you ask that, Axe?"

"Whenever you start sighing or growling like that, you're most likely dippin' into your nostalgia fund."

Shell let a slight smile curve his bearded lips. "You'll never understand, young man. You were born into this miserable existence, but I was raised in something far better, far more refined."

"I've lived a lot rougher than this, boss. We've actually got a pretty sweet setup. You get all the best pickin's here and are generous enough to share with me, thank you very much." Axyl grinned. "Seems pretty cushy to me."

"Axyl, I lived in a time when you could fly to any place in the entire world. Now, I haven't even left this area in over a decade. I lived in a time when if you needed to know something, you just typed it in to a search engine and you could find an exhaustive amount of information on your subject. Now, I have to rely on our less-than-reliable scouts to bring me knowledge that is at best, four or five days old." Shell sighed again. "Back then, we had dentists." Shell looked into the mirror, noting the black holes where some of his teeth had been lost.

"I'll take your word for it, boss. But answer me this, didn't you used to have a shitload of rules back then? And a lot of people who made sure you followed their rules or they'd kill you, or chain you in a deep dark building someplace for most of your life?"

"Yes. Yes we did."

"They'd have probably not approved of your having that skinny girl chained up there in your bedroom, just waiting for you to show her who's boss. They'd most likely a'been pissed about all the people we been yankin' off their farms and shipping to those clients of ours back east."

"Actually, you'd be surprised what you could get away with back then, if you had money and power, but I take your point. It's good to be the one making the rules. It's good to 'be da king' out here."

Shell turned back towards the window, thinking about the girl and smirking slightly. She'd been brought in with the last batch of round-ups, and he had taken to her instantly. He pondered taking off early so he could... No. The anticipation was part of the fun and he and Axyl had plans to make.

"Enough chit-chat, Axyl. It's time to decide what to do about New Hope." He spread an old, dogeared map of the area on the table. "That much fresh food would be an asset in the short term, but we really need to control its production. One of our biggest problems, as our Road Shark group grows, is feeding the troops."

"I'm tellin' you," Axyl said, looking down at the map, "if we keep sending all our slaves back east to the Empire, we're not going to be able to get our own food supplies tended to. We need to hold some of them back. The Beforetime supplies that they send us are okay, but fresh food is much better than those old military meals."

"I'm starting to come around to your way of thinking," the older man replied, "so my idea is to make New Hope a designated compound."

"Meaning?"

"Instead of sending its inhabitants back east, we keep them as farmworkers. Once we take the village, we use their children as a lever to keep them in order and productive. We can even let them return to their families in the evenings, reminding them what's at stake."

"Well, that's pretty damn generous, considering all the families we've sent to our 'clients' in old Montana."

Shell looked up from the map to stare at the younger man. "Axe Man, here is a lesson you need to put in your little notebook. If you take everything from a man, then that man has nothing to lose. If our new slaves-to-be perceive they can lose even more than their freedom, as in their loved ones, then they are less likely to get ideas of rebelling or escaping. The cost is simply too high."

"I guess that's all well an' good, but first we gotta take the compound, and you hav'ta admit, it's pretty damn well fortified."

"With enough manpower and a little C-4 supplied by our friends, it can be done. I sent our scouts up to take a look and they should be back any time."

CHAPTER FOUR
The Rock Pile

Ghost Wind squinted in the fading light and lessening snow. It was there, thank the Maker, the three-sheep rock. A large trio of boulders brought there by a mega-flood so long ago that humans probably didn't exist on the continent when it happened.

She was still in Yakama Nation territory, and she was sure they wouldn't bother her. If they did, dropping Lila's name would get her out of trouble, at least until she crossed the Columbia into Oregon.

As she expected, the small cave the slanting rocks made was unoccupied. She had a place to camp.

Hopefully her ghosts would leave her alone tonight.

****

C'mon baby! Light!

The wooden stick twirled in her hand. In warmer weather, she could perform the hand drill fire making method and have a flame in less than a minute. The cold had robbed her hands of their dexterity and now this simple thing was seeming beyond her. She thought longingly of flint, steel and char cloth. If only.

She stopped for a moment to rest, and placed her hands under her armpits to warm them. She could hear the wind whistling around the rocks and thanked the spirits of this place for the windbreak they provided. She checked her tinder bundle, painstakingly scraped from the bark of the surrounding sagebrush, putting it lightly against her upper lip. It was dry.

I should be able to do this in my sleep!

She performed the calmness mantra in her mind.

I am the scout.
I am quiet within and without.
I am made of the stars.
My skills are impeccable.
My mind is clear.
My mind is here.
I will prevail.

The breath. It was the breath she needed to watch, not the fear. It was the now she needed to be in, not the then. Slowly, briefly, temporarily, all her difficulties faded and there was only the spinning hand drill. She repeated the mantra in her mind.

The smoke appeared in the baseboard, and in a few moments, she had the ember she needed. Carefully transferring it from the bark it formed on, she gently placed the smoldering dust in the bird nest of dried grass, shaved bark and wood fluff she had created. It began to smoke and as she gently blew on it, she saw flame glowing in the tinder bundle's heart. She quickly placed it with its mate in the small pyramid of sticks that would be the start of her fire and watched the ember grow to a small blaze.

Oh great Creator of all things, thank you for this warmth!

As her shelter began to warm, she reached into the leather shoulder bag she carried and pulled out the blackened Beforetime coffee can she used for a cooking pot along with two battered stainless steel water bottles. She then began making a dinner of parched corn powder and jerky.

As the meal cooked, she untied the leather cords on her most precious possession, a heavy wool blanket Lila had gifted to her. She pulled it out of the elderly USGI Beforetime poncho she used to keep the elements off of the blanket and laid the poncho on the earth with the blanket on top of it.

I should have wrapped up in the blanket while out there in that frigid cold, but if anything happens to it, I'll be up the brown creek, paddle-less.

A small stuffed bear rolled out of the blanket.

"Hello there, Go-Go. Hope the journey wasn't too bumpy for you," she said. "If you'll remember, Lila told me that you volunteered for this mission." She smiled grimly.

The warrior scout Ghost Wind, relying on and talking to a plush toy for company. It didn't seem quite as insane as it did when Lila first forced Go-Go bear on her. Now it just seemed mildly insane.

The hot meal and the blanket allowed her to finally relax for the first time in the day. "It's unlikely the glow from the fire will be seen from the road, Go-Go. Scouts of the Clan of the Hawk choose their hideaways carefully. And we... they've... been using this one for years." Even though she was deep in Yakama Nation territory, she knew her former fellow scouts used this spot whenever going farther south to scout the "Indie" territories.

That gave her an idea. She pulled out one of the odds and ends she carried out of her bag, a greasy chalk pastel stick. Ghost Wind looked at the rock wall ahead of her.

No, this is foolish. Don't be stupid. Don't leave a trace.

She reached out with the chalk and extending it to the rock face she wrote: GHOST WIND in large off-white letters. She knew it was unwise, but the scouts were the only ones of her people who would ever come here, and she needed to say… something… to them. She continued, I WAS DUPED, I LOVED MY SIFU.

And yet, she was at the very least, a large part of the reason Jannelle Longwalker was dead.

She reached out again, trying to write with vision clouded by unwanted tears. I AM SO SORRY.

But I'm not the one who should be most sorry. The lying bastard murderer who fooled me, who betrayed me and murdered her should be sorry.

She wrote one last line: I WILL FIND THE AXEMAN. I WILL MAKE HIM PAY! I SO SWEAR! Wise or not, she found the writing gave her comfort.

It also gave her a purpose.

****

The scout warrior woke in the dead of night, the small stuffed bear clutched tightly in her arms under the blanket. Even after her convalescence, her senses still were sharp and they were telling her she was not alone. She glanced at the embers of her fire, and threw a little more sagebrush on to warm the shelter up but it didn't seem to help. It was cold! Looking at the far wall of the rock pile she slept in, Ghost Wind saw why.

Her earlier graffiti was barely visible through her guest. Jannelle had come to visit, perhaps, to torment.

"Hello, Sifu." Ghost Wind sighed. "You are one persistent hallucination. Always showing up when I'm half awake. Probably not a coincidence."

The visitor said nothing, but simply looked at her with sad eyes.

She held up the toy. "I travel with a new class of friend now, Sifu, much harder to get him killed. Also he's much less inclined to make a snap judgment about who is guilty and who is not."

The visitor seemed to have a slight smile. She seemed to be saying something, but Ghost Wind couldn't hear her.

"Oh, Sifu, I know I say it every time you show up, but I didn't know… I thought he loved me. I couldn't know… but you told me didn't you? Clan scouts don't get involved with strangers, especially handsome ones who tell you everything you want to hear." Ghost Wind's heart started to burn with her anger. "Especially lying dogs who want to remove a thorn in the side of all the bandits and slavers in the area, who wanted to remove you."

She looked down at the fire "As he did remove you."

The apparition seemed to look at her sympathetically, as Ghost Wind's eyes came back up, blazing with anger.

"I swear to you Jannelle Longwalker, I will find Axyl, and I will kill him. You will be avenged!"

The spirit suddenly looked even sadder. Its lips moved but Ghost Wind, trained from a young age to read lips, still could not make out the words as her visitor faded from sight.

"Oh, Go-Go," she said, "Even if my life is as short as I expect it to be, I still hope I won't have to go through that many more times. It tears my heart out."

The warrior woman gazed out over the snow covered sagebrush, "And worse, I don't know if I'm really seeing her, or if I'm just going crazy."

She crawled back into her blanket and did her best to fall asleep once more. She thought that would be pretty much impossible, but her exhausted body said otherwise. She was asleep in minutes.

CHAPTER FIVE
A Bunch of Screw Ups

"This plan is coming together well, Axyl! In a few days, we'll have the information we need from the scouts I sent out to…" Shell began.

Axyl looked at Shell, nonplussed.

"What? Why are you giving me that look, Axyl?"

"I guess no one told you Porter and his guys got back about two hours ago."

Shell was silent for a moment, then said oh-so-calmly, "They are supposed to be my scouts. If I may be so bold as to ask, why the FUCK haven't they reported in!?" His voice rose, and his second-in-command prepared himself to withstand a hurricane level rant.

"I'm guessing, they're afraid to talk to you, boss."

"And I'm guessing that means there's a snag." Shell's voice was that of a man trying to master his temper, "Axyl, my dear fellow, would you be so kind as to invite these gentlemen to make an appearance? Before I have them strung up by their balls?"

"I'm on it."

"Oh, thank you so much."

****

"Boss, we was just getting there, on the road, ready to set up at New Hope when around the bend comes you know who! He jacked Smitty, cut off his freakin' head with some kinda stick sword. Smitty's head just went bouncin' down the road and the rest of us hauled ass outta there!"

"Porter," Darwin Shell said, looking at him with a frosty stare, "You are supposed to be one of my smarter lieutenants, but Axyl tells me this happened on the main highway!"

Porter looked down, afraid to admit his screw up.

"On a mission of this nature, a so-called smart man might think it would be best to stick to the back roads and dirt tracks of the area. I take it you didn't think that was a good idea?"

"Boss," Porter whined, "a lotta them old back roads is gettin' so overgrown in the last ten years, you wind up havin' to chop your way through half of 'em!"

Shell's voice grew soft. "For your plea to move me, sir, I would have to give a shit whether you had to work a little harder or not. Let me assure you, I do not give the prerequisite shit. Now, man up and do your job!"

Axyl had to work to keep himself from smiling. "So boss, I'm guessing…"

"Yes, goddamn it," Shell said, "send them right back."

****

Once outside Shell's office, Porter asked "Axe, what we gonna do about that damn Eli? He's messing us up at every turn, man."

"Don't worry about that, Porter. I got a couple boys, indies, that I'm usin' as bait. Gonna give ol' Eli a bit of a surprise. And that ol' boy ain't gonna like this surprise."

CHAPTER SIX
The Bridge

The bridges were the worst.

Ghost Wind's foot went out on the old girder laden bridge, and she could feel the wind making the once solid structure sway and vibrate slightly.

This bridge was huge and looked like it had been built well before the last millennium. The sixty or seventy intervening years, particularly the last twenty or so, without any maintenance, had not been kind. She bet the Yakamas would never take one of their "wobbly" tanks across it. They'd probably think twice about driving a truck across.

There were two cars on the bridge. One, formerly a small fusion-powered sedan, leaned precariously over the Columbia River. Even from a distance, she could see the energy generator had been scavenged. The other, an old-school gas pickup held a skeleton sitting semi-upright behind the drivers wheel of his dust rusty tomb, as if he had just pulled over and parked there, forever.

I can certainly think of better places to leave my mortal remains.

None of these things were the cause of her nervousness however. Not the height of the road over the huge river below, or the slight swaying caused by the constant bitter wind blowing down the river. And it certainly wasn't the mortal remains of the people who had been sitting here dead for over two decades. Ghost Wind had seen plenty of decades-old corpses, and not once had one ever threatened her.

The nerve-wracking thing about bridges was the choke point.

There's no way to get across this river unless I use the bridge. She sure couldn't swim a half-mile of icy river in February. *If I was going to set up an ambush, I'd stage it at a bridge like this one. With a decent rifle, you could pick off just about anyone who wasn't wearing some sort of battle armor.*

This was the reason she hated the idea of crossing it. Someone could snipe her just as easily. She might have to wait 'til darkness fell to make the attempt to cross.

She moved down the bank of the river to get a look at the bottom of the bridge. Leaving her gear in a clump of bitterbrush, she carefully followed a deer trail. She moved into the shadow of one of the toppled giant wind-harvest power generators, lying there like some sort of huge alien machine.

Once out of the scant sunlight, the wind chill seemed to drop another ten degrees. As she moved below the bottom of the bridge, she saw a rusty catwalk extending beneath it.

That looks promising! There are a few sections that look questionable, but I can get to the other side of the Columbia without exposing myself to being ambushed. I think...

From the sash she wore around her ratty gray wool and deer skin coat, Ghost Wind pulled a carefully padded small package and unwrapped the contents. The monocular she kept hidden fogged slightly as she put it up to the warmth of her skin. Looking at the catwalk, she could now see some of the sections were very rusty and a few looked as if they had separated from the bridge during one of the heavy winds in the canyon.

Maybe a little less promising than I thought. She stood a moment, considering. *Guess I need to flip a coin as to which is the more dangerous way to go.*

To go over the bridge invited, if not instant death, certainly the possibility of being discovered. From what she had heard, that was a very undesirable outcome.

The clan scouts who came this far told us of a complete breakdown in morality and law. They saw acts of human depravity to leave one shuddering in one's boots.

She looked at the catwalk again with the monocular.

I sure as hell can't fight off a large group of men bent on rape and murder, no matter how much Kung Fu training I have. I need to use the Scout Way, the way of concealment, the way of survival.

She climbed back up, and retrieved her gear. Moving to the beginning of the catwalk, she found her way barred by a rusty metal mesh gate, secured with an even rustier padlock. There was barbed wire hanging limply above the chain links that she might be able to climb over. It was, of course, rusty. Looking closely at the lock, she saw it was in very poor shape.

Ghost wind reached into her haversack, and after rummaging around for a moment, drew out a bit of craftsmanship she had created while staying with Lila. It had once been a ball-peen hammer, but using a small makeshift forge, she had beaten it into a hatchet and hammer combination tool.

Carefully aiming at the old padlock, she waited for a strong and loud gust of wind to rush though then struck with all her strength with the hammer. The ancient padlock's shackle shattered like poorly fired ceramic.

There now, that wasn't so hard. Things are looking up!

Carefully, slowly she pushed open the creaky gate, wincing at the noise it made. The catwalk stretched ahead and through its metal grid flooring, she could see the ice chunks floating down the river. She ventured tentative steps onto the elderly walkway, and when it seemed solid, began her crossing.

She was halfway across when bolts started snapping.

The first one sounded so much like a gunshot that she thought her imagined sniper had found her under the bridge. When she heard the second, the entire catwalk lurched and she knew she was in trouble. Ghost Wind began to run.

She heard Jannelle's voice in her head. *Move from the hips, glide! Up and down motion will tear the catwalk loose even quicker!*

The warrior scout moved as she had been trained from a young age, not wasting motion, gliding forward with her hips as she ran, keeping low. It wasn't enough. The walkway lurched under her again, as more bolts snapped and began to separate from the bottom of the bridge.

Jannelle's voice came again, *Go girl, go! GO GO GO!!!*

She was fifty feet from the end of the bridge when the section she had just moved onto tore loose. The snapping of bolts above her was like a twenty-one gun salute and her section slowly began to separate from the bridge, like a loose thread. The end she was on began to dip towards the river, forcing her to scramble using both hands and her feet to keep moving forward. In a few short moments, she was clawing at the deck, climbing towards the next section. Ghost Wind could see only five bolts still held the entire weight on the section she was on.

Great Spirit, please don't let me die here! I'm not ready!

As if to mock her, the wind began gusting again, and the broken catwalk began to sway. She climbed, hanging on with hands covered in only light leather gloves, her moccasin-covered feet barely able to find toe-holds in the grid floor. She had almost reached the edge of the next section when a particularly vindictive gust of wind hit the bridge and she heard the remaining bolts of her section part all in one loud explosion of sound as her perch began to fall.

Shiiittt!!

Ghost Wind threw herself toward the next section, landing on her ribs and breasts as the section she was on began its terminal descent into the cold Columbia River. Breathless and in pain, she turned her head to see it plummet end over end, hammering down in a huge wave-making splash that sent small tidal waves towards the riverbanks.

So much for the way of stealth. I wonder how much attention THAT will attract.

She inched her way onto the new section and carefully ran the remaining distance to the end. There was a door on this side also, but no lock and Ghost Wind was through and into the tall grass and brush without hesitation. Once into concealment, she waited, watched and listened for the inevitable surge of enemies looking for her.

Nothing.

She sat for an hour, senses on high alert and no one came. Finally boredom drove her to climb up to the pavement to find where the snipers might be hidden.

No one.

It seemed that when 80 percent of a world's population was destroyed by a man-made plague, keeping someone in ambush on a bridge in the middle of nowhere, was not an effective use of time. The area was deserted.

The wind carried a groan to her as if to prove her wrong. It was faint and for a moment, she thought she had imagined it but as she scanned the southern horizon, she saw some sort of structure, roughly a half mile away. Carefully pulling out the prized monocular, she glassed the area. The structure seemed to be a big wooden X, out in the empty sagebrush lands.

And there was a man hanging from it.

CHAPTER SEVEN
Hanging in the Wind

Don't get involved.

For all she knew, the man hanging on this X-shaped implement of torture was a mass genocidal murderer, and helping him might be the biggest mistake she ever made.

She dropped to the level of the sagebrush and moved in closer.

He looked awful. He was a muscular dark-skinned man, but he was covered in bruises, cuts and what may have even been a few stab wounds. If he hadn't moved feebly a few times as she approached, she would have assumed he was dead and passed by him.

He was supported to a slight degree by a board that his feet would just fit enough on to keep him from tearing loose from the cross, but it was probably small comfort.

A crosswind came up, and Ghost Wind realized they were not alone out here, the tortured one and herself. An overpowering scent of body odor came from the southwest, near a small hill and she also caught a whiff of campfire smoke. She decided to see if she could shed light on the situation. She dropped her gear into concealment, taking only her big rough-hewn knife, and wove through the sagebrush.

The camp contained two men, both as filthy as she had ever seen. She was very thankful she was no closer than the top of the small hill, as she knelt in the tall sagebrush.

Oh, I know your kind.

Had she been nearer the two men, she was quite sure the smell from them would have brought tears to her eyes. Men like this often formed the slavers and kilabyker gangs her people had been so invested in keeping at bay.

"I'm tellin' ya, Lester, we should've just gutted that fucker. He's dangerous as hell, man, and we've been tryin' to get Mr. Boy Scout dead fer a damn long time!" One of the men was gesticulating wildly at the other, obviously in a passion over what he was trying to get across. "It was fun as hell to hammer him to that cross, man, and fun as hell to beat on him for a hour or so with the rebar, but he's strange. He still might come back an' get us somehow."

"Fat chance o' dat, Benny," the other replied. "But let's finish makin' these spears, and we'll use ol' the law dog as chuckin' practice. That oughtta give us a bit more fun and make things final for our dear Captain Shit Head. Good by you?"

"Yeah. Good. I owe that guy, and paybacks are a bitch."

Ghost Wind had heard all she needed. Now, should she help, or just keep going and mind her own business?

****

He had been hanging for what seemed like years.

I wish I could flippin' die, already. Soon though...

His hands and his feet throbbed from the thick rusty nails driven through them, and the other wounds he had suffered at the hands of his captors weren't helping him manage the pain.

To think I'm going down at the hands of those two dickheads.

Eli stared down at his leg. As horrific as the wounds from the bear trap were, they were trying to do their thing and heal, at a rate that would astonish the common man. But the sheer number of injuries he had sustained at the hands of Lester and Benny had drained even his ability to heal. If he didn't escape soon, the great experiment would end very badly.

I think this might be it.

Unfortunately, he was far from his peak performance level. Usually, he might have been able to pull out the nails securing him to this god-awful Greek cross, painful as that might have been. Usually he was a lot stronger than he looked, but now, he was weak with pain, injury, dehydration, hypothermia and hunger.

He looked over the landscape of sagebrush and juniper toward Mt. Hood to the west. Maybe when he died, his spirit would wander over its snowy slopes, free from this pain, free from duty, free from worry.

Assuming he had a soul. There had been a lot of debate about that.

As his head drooped, he saw the woman standing right in front of him.

"What...? Who? Where the hell did you come from?"

She didn't answer. He was sure she hadn't been standing there a few moments before, and he saw no way she could have come through the knee-high sage and bitterbrush to sneak up on him.

He began to laugh weakly. "Oh, I get it. Hallucinating. And wow, did I come up with a wonder."

He looked his fever dream over. She was tall, looking vaguely Native American and was wearing an outlandish outfit that looked half wool and half skins and fur. To top it off, she had some sort of coyote-hide draped over her shoulders and his imagination even managed to provide her with a livid scar over one side of her otherwise beautiful face.

She continued to stare at him, not saying a word, as if making a decision.

"Oh, criminy. I want to get off here so bad, I'm imagining rescuers." He laughed.

"Be silent!" she hissed. It was a rather cheeky thing for a hallucination to say, he thought. He watched her bring out what looked to be a small hatchet married to a hammer head and a small wooden strip that she carefully worked under the spike driven through his right foot. He began to feel a little nervous.

Looking up at him, with her intense blue eyes, she said, "If you scream, those men will come back, and I will slip away and leave you here. Do you understand me?"

He nodded uneasily.

"Do you need something to bite down on, to stifle the scream?"

He wanted to tell her it would be a cold day in hell before this torture would make him scream.

But this sure seems like hell, and I'm damn near hypothermic.

He nodded again, and she took a small limb she had been carrying, reached up and gently placed it between his teeth.

"Prepare yourself."

The jolt of pain that shot through him as she began to lever out the spike with the hatchet quickly convinced him he was NOT hallucinating. He managed to choke down the involuntary scream to a strangled high-pitched gasp. Tears started from his eyes, and he tried to remember if it had hurt this much when the bastards had driven the spikes in.

It took her a while, using her crude tools, then there was a squeak as the first spike pulled out, followed by blessed relief as the pressure on his foot ended. The spike fell to the ground with a muffled *plong* and he breathed rapidly for a few moments while the wolf woman waited for him to master himself. She looked at him questioningly, then looked at the spike through his left foot.

He nodded. She went back to work.

The next two spikes were not any easier, but she methodically kept working at them and soon he was supporting his own weight on the two by four Lester and Benny had used for a platform to nail his feet to. She was working on the last spike, when her head suddenly turned to the west and her gaze swept over to the hill his captors had their camp behind to get out of the wind.

"What is it? Did you hear something?"

She reached out a finger, flecked with his blood, and put it to his lips.

Message understood; going silent.

She dropped back to the dirt without a sound and snatched up the three spikes. Moving like a gust of wind, she ran to the sagebrush, crouched down and within a few seconds seemed to simply disappear.

A few moments later, he heard his captors returning from their campsite. Though they had left him fully exposed to the wind and elements, they had seen to their own comfort by setting up a couple hundred yards to the south, in the lee side of a small hill. And why not? They certainly didn't think he was going anywhere but to a shallow grave.

No, scratch that. They certainly weren't even thinking of going to the effort to pull him down and bury him. That would be too much like work. No, they'd just leave him for the turkey vultures, to just stay where he was 'til his empty skeleton collapsed to the dust.

Gonna be a little surprise for you boys.

He carefully moved his feet back where they had been and hoped that Lester and Benny wouldn't notice the spikes were gone through all the blood left on them. From the little the young woman had said, he doubted she was going to get any more involved than she already had. Hopefully, what she had done would be enough. Had he been at full strength, he knew he could rip out the last spike with pure brute effort and no tools. The way he felt now, he wasn't quite so sure.

His ratbag tormentors walked up, and Eli's heart sank. Both of them carried makeshift spears, made out of saplings, cordage and pieces of sharpened rebar. They could lance him, or maybe they had decided to have a contest. Either way, they could do it from a distance.

"Betchew I kin hit him, first try." Benny laughed.

"Sure, yer barely fi'teen feet away," Lester drawled, "Any pusseh could do that. Try it back there another ten feet, by where the brush ends. Hit 'em from there, an' I'll be impressed. Not that I think there's a bat's chance in hell ya could do it."

"Fuck you. Watch dis," replied the ever eloquent Benny.

Lester moved to the side and looked up at Eli. "Sadly, boy, this is gonna have to be the end o' our fun. Me an' Ben got a meetin' to make with the Sharks down near LaPine. But I do want ta thank yas for comin' after us and steppin' in our bear trap. It saved us a whole lotta time and worry that you might catch us when we wasn't prepared."

"Fuck you, Lester," Eli rasped out.

"That's whatcha get when ya try to be Mister Boy Scout. Bye, Eli!" Lester smiled an awful smile. "Give 'im yer best shot, Ben!"

Eli looked from Lester back to Benny.

Benny was gone.

The spear he had been about to throw lay in the dust, and its owner was nowhere to be seen. Lester's mouth dropped open, and he moved toward the last known location of his friend.

He wasn't watching his captive and Eli wasn't one to let an opportunity pass. Pain bursting through his hands and feet, he braced himself, reached up with his free hand and pulled. The spike holding his remaining hand came loose with a loud shriek and Eli fell from his perch to the dusty ground.

"What the fuckin' hell?" Lester snarled turning back to his now free captive. "I dunno what you did to Ben, but youse gonna get a spear up yer ass for yer trouble!"

Eli had just reached his feet, when a wave of dizziness took him. For all his advanced abilities, he barely avoided being skewered, grabbing the spear as his attacker missed. Normally he would have turned Lester into goulash by now, but he had used the last of his strength pulling out the spike. The spear was ripped out of Eli's hand and he stumbled. His enemy raised the crude weapon to finish the kill.

Then Lester's eyes grew very wide. He stood a moment, looking vaguely confused and then fell face first into the dust. His body lay twitching, and Eli saw a very large, very crude-looking knife sticking out of one of his assailant's kidneys. He pulled it out of the still shuddering soon-to-be corpse, and noticed it seemed to be a crude version of a design he had seen before. It looked like it had been hand hammered on a forge, and sharpened with files and stones.

"That is mine." He looked up. The wolf woman was standing a mere three feet from him.

"How in the hell do you do that?" he asked, the faintness of his own voice surprising him. "Here, you might want to wipe the blood off on ol' Lester's shirt there…"

"I have already soiled a good blade with his blood. I have no interest in touching him further." She walked over and began cleaning the blade with dry grass.

Eli watched her for a moment. She moved with the fluid grace of an athlete but she was standing oddly, at a forty-five degree angle.

No… wait… I'm standing at a forty-five degree…

The dusty ground came up and slapped him in the face.

CHAPTER EIGHT
Try Again

"All right, Porter," Axyl had said, "I think the problem was that you didn't have enough backup last time. I'm sending seven more guys with you this time."

Porter snorted, looking back at the "soldiers" Axe Man had provided. This bunch wasn't any of the smarter guys in the Road Sharks. It was just some of the more stupid (and expendable) dumb asses, just like before, only more of 'em. At least Axyl personally made it clear to them they had to keep quiet and out of sight of the farm compound. The problem was that called for stealth, and stealth called for subtlety. Most of this bunch was about as subtle as a thumb in the eye.

"Oh, one more thing, Port," Axyl told him, a big shit-eating grin on his face, "we need to have a map and some drawings made."

Porter's belly clenched. He knew where Axyl was going with it before he saw the kid coming, pushing papers and half worn pencils into a shoulder bag.

"Oh hell no, Axe," he'd protested. "You cannot be serious! You want me to take Durpee with us? Why don't you just shoot me now?"

"Okay, Port. If that's what you want." Axyl reached for the back of his belt where he kept his old model 1911.

"Wait, goddamn it!" Porter raised his hands, "Axe, you're sending me out there, with the dregs, and now I've got to babysit the idiot too? That's crazy!"

"Durp can draw anything he sees Porter, whether right there, or three days later and he draws it real good. Shell's a little less than inclined to think you guys will do a good job of recon, so it's my idea to send Durpee along as kind of a human camera. And like all cameras, you got to take care of it. So, you'll take good care of Durp, right?"

"Yeah."

"I'm not shitting, Port. I want him back here unharmed. You lose the others, I don't care so much, as long as you bring back the kid so he can draw us some pics. Clear?"

"Crystal."

And that had been that. As they drove out of the garage, Porter glanced over his shoulder, and could see the kid huddled up against him, arms wrapped tightly around him. Dupree had his eyes closed and his legs had the fusion cycle in a death grip.

Porter sighed, and drove up the highway.

CHAPTER NINE
Nurse Ghost Wind

Ghost Wind had just decided she had her hand-made khukri knife clean enough when she heard a *plumpf* behind her. Turning, she saw the man she had helped land face-down, limp on the ground. She face-palmed herself.

"Just wonderful," she snarled. "If I leave him here, he'll likely die." She had put all that effort into getting him off the cross, and leaving him to expire on the ground went against everything she believed in.

She looked to the east. She could just make out a streak of green, far back from the road. Water was rare in sagebrush country, and the green, probably spruces she guessed, said there was enough water to support them, a rarity in this place. She carefully moved in that direction, hoping she would find something that might help the wounds of the fool lying in the dust.

There were spruces all right and out from them, a number of desert junipers. A farmhouse sat well-hidden among them.

The farm itself was looking none too great, having been left to itself for the last twenty-something years. There were no signs that anyone had been there for a very long time. Weeds grew through the porch, dead Arbor Vitae surrounded the lawn but in one corner of the yard several birches were still flourishing. By all rights, these trees should have died long ago, and the fact they had not confirmed her earlier assessment. Water.

She moved past the remains of a rusty e-car and saw what she was looking for. Her quick search showed an old hand pump, and bubbling out of its base was a small but steady stream of water. She assumed it was a natural spring, the pump left there for the former owner's convenience.

Near the pump, she found Yarrow and Broadleaf Plantain. "Ah. Just what I needed. At least now, I have something to put on his wounds."

****

Eli awoke to the sound of water dribbling in the distance. Holding his hand up, he saw the wounds in his brown skin had almost closed, but they were covered with some kind of greenish goo. To his left, he saw his own pack and realized he was lying on his sleeping bag. Above this was a latticework of limbs and sagebrush forming an igloo shape and juniper boughs covered the floor.

To his right, the wolf woman sat, tending a tiny fire in a place scraped down to the dirt. She was cooking something in what looked like a blackened and battered coffee can with a wire handle.

"How did you figure out which gear was mine?" he asked, his voice a barely audible croak. "Benny and Lester must've been ransacking my pack for whatever they wanted to take."

She looked coldly at him for a moment, as if trying to decide if she really wanted to engage in conversation with him or just maintain a stony silence. Finally, she spoke, "Your equipment was only dusty. Everything they owned was filthy, and it stunk of them." She went back to tending what she was cooking.

Ah. Woman of few words.

"I want to thank you for... rescuing me. I was pretty sure I was done for."

She nodded slightly, never taking her eyes from the fire. Her dark hair was arranged under a head band, and the forwards sections on the outside of the band formed wings that partially hid her face.

"You're a long way from nowhere, you from up north?"

"We are not discussing me." She looked up. "Instead, let's hear how you managed to wind up on that big cross out there. And I'd like to know how those horrific wounds healed over so fast."

Careful, Eli, this one doesn't miss much.

"Well, it's a little embarrassing," he said, looking down. "I've been hunting those two for about a month, now. I work as sort of an independent... lawman, trying to bring some civilized behavior back to this area."

"A vigilante."

"If you want to say it like that. Right now, several small settlements are being attacked by slavers. People are kidnapped and taken way off to the northeast to some outfit called Farnham's Empire. Don't know much about them, but they sound like nothing but trouble."

She looked up again at his mention of the Empire and her hair fell away to reveal the terrible scar on the left side of her face.

Shit Eli, don't stare at her scar! Were you raised by badgers?

Too late. She had seen him looking. She looked down again and moved her hair back over that side of her face.

"Ahhh so, anyway, I have been tracking down those two in hopes that I might not only take them out of circulation permanently, but also learn something about where these goddamned slavers are. Slavers been workin' with the Road Sharks and that's trouble for everyone."

She looked at him and the message was clear. *Tell me more.*

He sighed, "Unfortunately, when I found Benny and Lester, I thought to sneak up on them in the dark. They were a little smarter than I gave them credit for, and they had trapped the area around their camp. I found their one and only bear trap, the hard way."

She looked at the medium brown skin of his leg. "Yet, that leg doesn't seem to be broken, and the wounds I saw on it yesterday are much less prominent, only one day later."

"Yeeaah… funny story there, but enough about me. What brings a lovely young woman such as yourself out here to what has become a deserted wasteland." He smiled winningly as he said it, which only seemed to make her expression more stony.

"I don't know you, so don't presume to ask me personal questions. It was a hard decision to help you in the first place, and now I'm stuck here trying to make sure you don't die." The haughtiness in her voice reminded Eli of certain scientists and administrators he had known decades before. She didn't look like the administrator of much, but she had the proud voice.

But something in her manner said that pride had been damaged lately.

"Okay, but I've always felt that information exchange should be *quid pro quo*, y'know? You give a little, I give a little," he replied, eyebrow raised, "I'm not asking for your life story, but this is hard country, few travel alone yet here you are. And I've never seen anyone as good at staying hidden or disappearing as you are."

"I understand Latin, you needn't explain it to me." She sighed. "You also travel alone."

"It's not by choice young lady, I…"

"And why do you keep calling me young? You can't be more than a few years older than I am."

"Sorry. As to why I travel alone, I'm trying to help people out here, and that is a very foreign concept in this area." He smiled slightly. "Everyone here is just scrambling to get by and helping others is not something most would go out of their way to do. They sure as hell have no interest in joining me to hunt down dangerous men and women. So, I'm on my own with my Quixotic quest."

She looked at him.

"Sooo, your story is….?" he said, eyebrows raised in question.

She looked at the sagebrush bough wall for a moment, considering. Then she climbed out of the small door of the shelter and walked off into the night.

Okay, then. We'll just have to take that a little slower, he thought.

****

Ghost Wind stepped out and walked away from the wigwam she had constructed over her strange guest. His questions had made her want to escape the narrow space for a time, and the night sky was clear, unlike her thoughts.

In the Beforetime, there would have been lights everywhere, or so she had been told, even many in a remote area like this. They would have made it difficult to even see the stars, but now artificial light out here was non-existent. As her eyes adjusted, her heart filled with a brief joy looking up at the Milky Way, Orion and the wanderer's friend— Polaris, the North Star.

"Hello old stars. Thank you for coming with me. At least you are familiar, like family, in this place so far from home." She felt tears rise.

She didn't need to meditate to know what was wrong. She was afraid. The warrior Ghost Wind had rarely been afraid, but now, it seemed she was always living in fear. Not necessarily fear of death, but fear of the future, fear of loneliness and fear of trusting anyone ever again.

CHAPTER TEN
Decision

Ghost Wind sat and watched him as he slept.

Her own mind was a roiling cauldron of turmoil and part of her thoughts screamed that she should quietly pack her things and leave. Trusting this man could be a huge mistake, just like her trust in Axyl was.

The other part of her was so lonely that she could barely stand it.

The scouts were trained to be alone at a young age, and Ghost Wind had spent weeks, even a month completely by herself and had never had a problem with it. It was different now. Then, she had people to return to, a home, such as it was, and a purpose that helped make the long hours on scout easier, much easier, to bear.

Now, she was truly alone, no one cared about her survival, how she felt, what she was doing. She was in effect, a non-entity. That seemed it would be the course of the rest of her life.

But what if he's just like Axyl?

What if he isn't and I throw away my only ally down here.

Creator Spirit, please help me.

****

Eli woke around four a.m. This was pretty common for him, usually he didn't need much sleep, but his aches and pains made him want to turn over and go right back to dreamland.

He looked over and saw the woman staring down into the dying embers of the tiny fire, the light orange-red on her face. Her scar was in deep shadow, and though she had bags under her eyes, she looked very young, very vulnerable.

"Can't sleep?" he asked.

"I'm on the run," she blurted out,

It took him a moment to realize she had never left the conversation they had been having hours earlier. His sleep muddled mind worked on that briefly before he replied, "You are? Who you runnin' from?"

"I am fleeing the Clan of the Hawk," she said, as if he should know what that meant.

"Okay, I.. think…hill people? North of the Yakamas, right? They're your enemies?"

She looked at the tiny fire, "They were my family."

"Oh." He noted the past tense. He waited for more but she simply stared at the fire. "So then, since we haven't been formally introduced, my name is Eli. Eli Five."

"Five? That's an odd name."

"It has significance. And you are...."

She hesitated, but after a moment, in a very quiet voice she said. "Ghost Wind. My name is Ghost Wind."

"What a wonderful name! Native American then?"

"The Clan of the Hawk is not a first nation group, but my father was of the Nez Perce." She paused. "And it is not such a wonderful name anymore. It is a name of shame and sadness."

"How so?"

"What part of banished did you not understand?" she snapped at him.

"Hoooookay, sorry."

"Since you are awake, you should drink more of this. It will help you regain strength."

He took the offered canteen cup, noting there seemed to be some kind of meat in the broth, cut fine and several plants, some of which he recognized, some that he didn't. It was actually quite tasty, particularly to a body that needed a lot of protein while healing.

After a few moments, she rose, pushed aside the poncho covering the door and went outside again. He couldn't help himself from watching her backside appreciatively as she went.

So young to be in that much pain. He shook his head.

He'd had his times of pain himself, and not the kind that he had experienced at the hands of Lester and Benny. Speaking of those two, soon he needed to go through their gear, filthy or not, to see if there was anything more to learn about this meeting they had set up in LaPine. He wasn't hopeful, he wasn't even sure if his former tormenters could read, much less write anything down, but he still needed to check.

He figured they were meeting with the Red Slavers. He hoped to hell they weren't meeting with the Road Sharks.

He finished his broth, and set the can aside. That could wait. Right now his biggest needs were sleeping and eating 'til he was back to 100 percent.

CHAPTER ELEVEN
The Old Farm

Dawn came with varying degrees of pink and gold. Ghost Wind watched as she sat against the shelter, carefully running an abrasive stone over the lawn mower blade Lila's son had forged into the shape of her old war knife.

The original had been taken from her when she had been banished, but Lila's son had hammered this shape out without losing the metal's temper. She had been giving it an edge one stroke at a time ever since. She had a passible edge on the last six inches and the point, but the four inches closest to the hilt had only the barest of bevels.

"That's kind of a ragged looking chopper ya got there."

She turned and saw Eli half in and half out of the doorway of the shelter. She had come out to let him sleep and heal.

"What are you doing, you fool?" she yelled. "How are you supposed to heal if you get up and move around! Get back to your bedding!"

"You're worried about me!" He smiled at her as he stood. "I'm doing pretty good now, just a few fading scars and bruises."

He was wearing only an old pair of olive drab army pants, and looking at his well-muscled frame, she saw he was right. All of his injuries looked weeks old but it had been only two days and nights since she freed him. It was freakish, and she worriedly wondered if he was one of the old spirits in disguise, playing tricks.

"Pull up your pant leg. I want to see the bear trap wounds."

The horrific tears on his leg had scabbed over, and were turning to scar tissue also.

"How…" she whispered, astonishment lacing her voice. "Your wounds shouldn't even be closed yet, much less scarring over. How is this possible?"

He looked down at the ground, somewhat sheepishly, "Well, some folks heal pretty fast. Guess I'm one of that sort."

"That doesn't explain anything. People just don't heal that fast, it's impossible!" Ghost Wind's voice rose.

"Empirical evidence points to the contrary of your hypothesis, miss."

She stared, until it became evident he wasn't going to say more on the subject. She turned back to the knife, and returned to the slow task of putting an edge on it.

"It's none of my business," she said. "I guess we all have things we'd rather not talk about."

"Well, of course I'll probably need a few days before I'm ready to travel. Thanks again for looking after me, Ghost Wind. I appreciate it."

She was silent.

"Look, I don't mean any offense. There are some things that are a bad idea for me to talk about. We're getting along pretty well, why spoil it?" He said to her back.

"It's no concern of mine," she said, without turning. "If you're doing this well, it is probably time for me to pack my things and be on my way. You obviously don't need any help."

"Wait, I never said that," he said, frowning. "I surely can't hunt for myself yet, and those two cretins ate or defiled most of my foods. I do need your help!"

She looked off the east. "No one needs me."

She glanced up at him and she noticed his dismayed expression. "Don't look at me like that. The world has taught me the lesson I needed to learn. It's simple. We are all on our own; don't depend on anyone else."

"Guess that depends on the glass you see through," he said, "Still, I'd appreciate it if you'd stay and help me. I'll try not to depend upon you, but I'm stuck 'til I heal up. Shouldn't be that long…" Eli looked to the east, toward the abandoned farm. "Why'd you set us up here, and not in that old house?"

"If someone comes by, they won't be looking for a camp out in the sagebrush. A house, even one as hard to see as that one, might still be a place to check out for scavenging. It didn't look like that place had been broken into. In other words, it has a much higher likelihood of visitors."

Eli continued to look. "I dunno, we're a long piece from the main road, and I could use a little exercise. How about we saunter over there and take a look?"

"The scout way is to travel light. I doubt there is anything I really need," she told him. "Extra 'treasures' would just weigh me down."

He looked at her half-finished knife and ragged moccasins. "Well, I respect that. It's a good philosophy, but instead of taking extra stuff, you might find some things to 'trade up' some of your less than perfect equipment."

She looked at the farm speculatively. "I… I need a firearm. The Clan of the Hawk took mine when I was banished. I plan on making a bow and arrows, but if someone comes after me with a gun, I would have to be very lucky to survive with archery."

"Let me get my walking stick then, and we'll just mosey on over and take a look."

Ghost Wind watched him crawl back in the shelter, and emerge with a short wooden staff. She had looked it over while he was sleeping. The last section where his hand rested was intricately carved in some sort of braid pattern: the remainder below was smooth.

"That is a pretty staff you have there," she said as they walked towards the farm.

"A gift from a teacher of mine."

"What kind of teacher?" she asked, her curiosity getting the better of her.

He looked at her, feigning surprise. "What? A personal question?"

"Never mind," she said, face coloring. "I have no right to ask you anything of your past. Unless one is to count saving your life."

"Just givin' you a hard time." He laughed, "It was a gift from a martial arts teacher. We've become friends."

"My teacher…" she started, then stopped. She noticed he didn't press her this time which was a blessing. She certainly wasn't going to discuss Jannelle with someone she had met such a short time ago. "I have had some training in the fighting arts also. All of the scouts are well versed in empty hand and weapons."

"Good to know, in case I need rescuing again."

"Eli," she said, looking at him intently, "you seem to be doing very well for someone who has just been horribly tortured. Were I even to survive something like that, I am sure I would be scarred inside and out for life. Yet you're able to laugh."

He looked directly at her, and the wisecracking Eli was gone. "I've been around a while, and I have seen some shit and had some shit done to me that would boil your brain. You have the choice of dealing with it as best you can or going mad."

"It seems you've dealt with it."

"I think it would be in everyone's best interest if I stayed sane."

****

The farmhouse was not in the best shape, but it had a metal roof and hopefully some of the contents had survived years of neglect.

Eli always approached such places with a mixture of apprehension and anticipation, worried that someone else had been attracted to the possible scavenging and hoping that no one had been here before. He expected Ghost Wind to move extremely carefully, considering her stealth abilities, but to his surprise, she simply walked up to the farmhouse as if she knew no one was there.

"You seem pretty confident that we're alone here."

"I've spent most of my life learning the ways of the tracker. The only sign that anyone has been here are my own tracks to and from the spring. No one else has been around in a long time, unless you count deer and coyote."

He looked at the ground. Eli had basic tracking experience, most people these days did to survive, but that was in dirt. The farmhouse was surrounded by tough springy grass and he couldn't honestly say he even saw her tracks.

Was she that good, or was she just showing off?

"Well, be careful anyway, sometimes the owners of these places put traps around them, if they were die-off survivors," Eli said. "If you think things are crazy now, at least the people today have some degree of self-reliance. Those who didn't expire from the bio-plague back in '35 found themselves in a whole new world of hurt, where everything couldn't be found in grocery stores."

"So I've heard."

"Most didn't garden, few could hunt, instead they relied on huge corporations to feed and clothe them. Take that away and the only way many saw to survive was to go after what their neighbors had."

"Yes, the Crazy Years. The teachers of the Clan of the Hawk do include history in their lessons."

"Thing of it is, down here, the Crazy years never ended. The only saving grace around these parts is that people are so spread out, it's more difficult to do harm to each other. Still, you need to be careful."

"If I can see there are no tracks in this environment, other than animal, I seriously doubt I will miss a hidden bear trap."

"Ouch. Point taken," he replied. "Well, just be careful."

She looked at him, one eyebrow cocked. They moved on.

The house was sealed up. windows were filthy but not broken, garage doors firmly shut, with a wall of vines and grass in front of them. A rusty car sat in the weed-choked driveway. At the front door, Eli pulled out a small set of lock picks and noticed his companion watching intently.

"One of the things one needs for wandering the wastelands," he told her. "You'd think after this long, every home would have been scavenged, but I find out of the way spots like this on a fairly regular basis, and I prefer to open the lock if I can as opposed to kicking the door down. I might need to crash here someday."

"It is not a skill I have learned."

"Schtick wit' me, kid. I'll learn ya all sorts of bad habits." He grinned as he said it, and was gratified to see that ghost of a Ghost Wind smile for a moment.

"I will watch, oh my guru."

It took him close to eight minutes before he heard the satisfying click of the latches disengaging, but when he pulled, the door didn't budge. He gingerly gave a few light yanks, standing well clear of the door frame itself. Nothing happened.

"You're not being forceful enough!" Ghost Wind said, "Here, let me try." She had just given the door a hard yank when it began to slip in the frame. Eli grabbed her and whirled her to the side of the door as a loud bang sounded from within. A half moon shaped hole appeared, smoking, just above the lock and splinters extended onto the weed strewn porch for several feet. They stared at the new porthole, and Eli saw Ghost Wind looked shocked.

"Never, ever, ever throw a door open out here," he told her sternly. "That goes double for a house that hasn't possibly been opened since the Crazy Years. Back then, homeowners often left a weapon rigged at the doors so they could get a night's sleep without worrying someone was going to break in and murder them. I'm just guessing that if there's a back door, it's either barricaded or booby trapped. From the hole, I guessing there's a twelve gauge shotgun hooked to the door here."

"After twenty-two years?" She looked horrified at how close she had avoided death. "How…"

"Old stuff lasts pretty well in this climate, particularly in an intact house. Now, let me just take a look… ah. Yep. Remington 12 gauge 2025 autoloader." He pulled out a worn multi-tool, reached in the door and snipped the trip wire. Looking through the hole in the door, he saw no other traps and gave the knob a hard fast yank. The door swung open with no further protest.

She stepped in after him, and looking around, she observed, "I always find these old homes quite eerie."

The home had not suffered the indignities that most places had. No scavengers had broken in and ransacked or salvaged everything useful. Except for a thick coating of dust and cobwebs and a few plants growing through the floor, it was all intact.

"It always gives me the heebie-jeebies to come into one of these old places that's never been opened," she said. "I always wonder if the ghosts of the original owners are watching in anger as we invade the space they used to live in."

"Afraid they'll pop out and spook ya?"

"I wonder if they can somehow retaliate."

He looked at her, letting his eyes go big and his lips formed a silent "O". He set off towards the kitchen, chuckling.

The place had once been a very nice, tight little home, in the middle of what had once been farm country. Even under all the dust he could see that the house, for the most part had been orderly. However, in front of the rusting washing machine, there was a pile of rotting sheets and clothing, all stained, waiting to be washed by owners long gone. Ghost Wind came in and looked at the pile.

"You think they're still here?" she asked, "Their bodies, I mean?"

"I'd say it's highly likely that in some of the upper bedrooms you will find bodies in the beds, where they ended their days too sick to rise anymore. That was pretty common, since the bio-plague usually took a couple weeks to kill someone. If not, then someone who wound up immune to the plague may have dragged them outside and hopefully buried them."

"Let's hope it's the latter."

"Yeah."

"What exactly are we looking for?" she said, studying his tracks in the dust. She seemed very intent on them and he wondered what she could find so interesting about footprints in fine dust.

"The boys out there were on a drunken spree when they went through my stuff. Some of my gear is either broken, or befouled to the point where I'd prefer to replace it. And, no offense intended, but some of your gear is pretty... marginal." He looked over, to see if she was taking umbrage at his words, but she seemed to be pragmatic about it. She just nodded.

He continued, "As this is your first B and E, I'd just take a look around and see what you can find that might be useful."

"B and E?"

"Henh. Breaking and entering."

"You assume much," she said with a slight smirk on her face.

Ghost Wind wandered up the staircase, and Eli had to admit, it was enjoyable to watch her climb as he followed. At the top, they went in opposite directions, he turned left into an end bedroom, while she went to the opposite end.

Eli saw dusty blankets on the bed, but he was hoping to find a sleeping bag to replace the one that Benny and Lester had torn so badly. It was okay to lie on and use a blanket, but he didn't want to trust it in really cold weather. He was opening the closet door when he heard a clattering and a soft, almost inaudible gasp. Moving faster than he should in his painful condition, he came out in the hall to see a small skull bouncing down the stairs.

He looked up at Ghost Wind, dust settling around her feet and a stiff look on her face as the skull came to rest on the ground floor.

"It was leaning against the inside of the door," she said. "I wasn't... expecting..."

He realized she was embarrassed at having a human reaction. "Well. I would have screamed like a little girl child, so I don't know what you're worried about."

She frowned. "Did you note the size? So small..."

"A lot of children died in the plague, anyone who wasn't somehow immune died. It's sad, but..."

She looked up at him, stricken. "Wait. I want to check something." She moved to the middle remaining bedroom, and opened the door carefully. No shotguns or skeletons were waiting, and she looked in at the bed. "Were there bodies in the room you chose?"

"Nope, quite empty."

"It's as I feared."

"What?"

"There are no adults here. Unless there are bodies downstairs in the kitchen or den, she died here alone, maybe not even from the plague. Maybe... maybe she starved."

She looked terribly sad, and something about that reaction made him like her even more. But it was time to get down to business.

"We need to scavenge these rooms. We can grieve over dead people from long ago back at camp." Her lips tightened, but she nodded and they separated to different rooms.

Forty minutes later, he came down the stairs with several items wrapped in a sheet slung over his shoulder. He saw she had been there ahead of him and left her new belongings on the dining room table. There was a wood handled carbon steel kitchen knife, a stainless steel cooking pot, army surplus mittens and cloth to be used for who knew what.

The prize was a matched set of a .44 caliber Henry lever-action rifle, with intricate engraving on the box and the stalk and a finely detailed .44 magnum revolver. They were obviously show pieces, but the rifle was a Henry and he felt a slight twinge of jealousy. There were also four boxes of cartridges for the rifle (that would also work in the pistol) and they weren't reloads either.

The cartridges alone were worth more than their weight in gold. You couldn't shoot gold unless you made it into bullets.

The surprising thing in the pile was two elderly books. One was *Sisters of the Raven/Circle of the Moon* by Barbara Hambly, the second was *The Wanderer* by Kahlil Gibran. The wolf-woman was evidently a reader.

So much for not wanting extra things to slow her down.

"Now where have you gotten to, wolf lady?" He headed into the kitchen, and looking down, saw a drag mark coming from the stairwell. "No way... she didn't..."

****

He was right, she was outside. The trip-wire on the back door had been snipped, and the door was slightly ajar. He walked into the backyard and saw her.

The sky was overcast as Ghost Wind tossed the last shovelful of dirt out onto the long-dead lawn. She set the rusty shovel aside and dusted off her dirty hands. He watched her smell the scent of the far off mountains in the coming rain and for a moment, she looked at peace. She got out of the three-foot deep grave she had dug and walked over to the small bundle wrapped in a dusty sheet she had dragged from the house. She picked it up and ever so carefully lowered it into the hole.

"If you do that with every skeleton you find out here, you're are going to be spending the rest of your life doing little else but digging."

"She was just a child; she died all alone. Look closely, there are two other graves over there. She probably had to bury at least one of her parents. I think the plague killed them and left her out here with no power, dwindling food, and no help to fend for herself." She sighed. "It's an awful way for one so young to die."

There wasn't much he could say to that. He had seen such an amazing amount of death since the Die-Off, much of it brutal, and he realized he had become callous to most of it. If this wolf woman could show a little kindness to a long-dead child, the least he could do was help. He bent over and picked up the shovel, but a wave of dizziness overtook him.

"Stop that, idiot!" she barked at him. "A day and a half ago you were crucified on a makeshift cross. Don't try to do any heavy labor, you'll just hurt yourself again. What's wrong with your head?"

"It seems to be very,… spinny," he replied, sitting down carefully under an old pine tree. "Please, carry on."

He watched her begin to shovel dirt into the makeshift grave.

"So, this Clan of the Hawk, I'd guess not an original native group then?" he asked.

"It is a group of all races, who do not hold with the technology of the twenty-first century. They believe the Die-Off was caused by the makers of that technology and have decided to have a simpler life. The only ones who use the new tech are the members of the warrior society."

"And your scouts are part of that society."

She stopped digging for a moment. "No. The scouts, with the exception of a few items, make most of their equipment from nature."

"But why? There's still a lot of perfectly good stuff lying around rusting or rotting. Why would they do that?"

"The rationale is that the scouts should be able to be left anywhere out in the world with almost nothing and still be able to thrive. It's the philosophy of the scout society, and while I'm not saying the rules are never bent, for the most part the scouts try to stick to that credo. I personally think it might well be the reason I'm still alive."

"Oh?"

"Yes. We are tested before we leave our apprenticeship and we are tested hard."

She took off her strange hybrid coat and a deer skin blouse to reveal a sleeveless hemp undershirt and even feeling dizzy, he was well aware that she had a very fine figure. He also watched the muscles of her upper arm, corded like metal cable when they flexed.

Strong one, this girl. She'll need to be, out here, all alone.

She looked like a good candidate, but he was hesitant to say anything about inviting her to be part of his own Mountain Folk. She had, after all, been banished from her own group and there had to be a reason for that. Maybe it was just some sort of religious persecution, there sure as shit were plenty of weirdo cults out here since the Die-Off.

What if she's one of those strange ones, predisposed towards chaos and craziness?

He didn't think so. She was cool and calm in dangerous situations, and his conversations with her told him she was very intelligent. But the thing that really convinced him at a gut level was happening right before him. Ghost Wind was trying to give a little dignity to a long dead-child in a world where most people were used to stumbling over and ignoring skulls and bones.

She had just tamped down the earth of the grave, then added a little more, tamped that down. He watched her take paving stones from the garden and lay them in an oval around the grave, then put the remainder over where the child's body lay. She finished by stacking the last few at the head of the grave.

"Go, little one," she said, lowering her head. "Leave this sad place and be with your people. Do not stay here, go where the light is." He saw her eyes glimmer with tears, and after all these years, even with all the bodies he had seen, he felt his own sting a little.

Jesus, have I really become this unfeeling? To forget this simple emotion?

Ghost Wind started toward the house, shovel in hand and he called after her, "You don't really need to put that back, Ghost Wind, these folks are done with it."

She looked down at the shovel for a moment, "Someone may need it someday. I find it... offensive to leave a good tool to rot and rust," she continued into the back door.

He carefully got to his feet and followed.

CHAPTER TWELVE
The Offer

At the shelter, listening to a light rain, they were going through their scavenging finds. Ghost Wind had been almost silent since finding the small skeleton. Eli had made his decision.

"Ahhh… so…" he started, carefully, "what are your plans, if I may ask?"

"To hunt, wander, rest when I can," she replied, suddenly intent on the cleaning job she had started on the revolver.

"That's it?" He knew he was pushing it, but he hoped she might loosen up, at least a little.

"I don't know where I'm going," she said, her hands finally stopping their work. "I have no idea what I'll do, or how long I'll live on my own. I plan on searching for my teacher's murderer, but how I'll ever find him in all this vastness, I have no idea."

She looked at him with intent eyes. "One thing I'm not going to do is roll over and die, just because I was judged unfairly by my people."

"I'm very glad to hear that," he said. " There's an alternative to the lone wolf future you're planning."

"Planning," she said, bitter laughter creeping into her voice. "Oh yes, some plan I have there."

"Ghost Wind, are you willing to listen to what I have to offer?"

She looked at him suspiciously. "This had better not have anything to do with shucking me out of my trousers. I've sworn off men, particularly smooth talkers such as yourself. Nothing but pain and trouble."

He might have been offended by her words at one time, but the experiences of a long life, much of it harsh, had blunted such tender sensibilities. "That is not what I want to talk to you about."

"Then let's hear it."

"I actually am not as much of a lone entity as you might think. I have people who, to some degree, help me, and we've formed a community up in the mountains. Originally, it was made up of ex-slaves, many of whom I rescued from their captivity personally." He paused to see her reaction. Her face had become a mask, giving away nothing. "They've found some peace, away from the roads and they're making a life for themselves. We still scavenge on occasion, but we mostly grow our own food and some of the people have become halfway decent hunters."

When she finally said something, he could barely hear her soft reply. "And what do you want from me?"

The softness of that reply hurt his heart. It was the voice of someone who had given up hope, someone who couldn't trust that anything good would ever again come to her in life. He hated the thought of her wandering the wastelands alone and friendless. He hated that she couldn't trust anyone anymore.

"What do I want? Ghost Wind, I want to offer you a place with us. Is that so hard to believe?"

She didn't say anything, she just sat, head bowed. The wings of her hair obscured all but the end of her nose and the edge of her lips, but it was enough for him to see she was trembling. He hoped it hadn't been too much, too fast. He was usually pretty good at subtle, but this offer had been made on the fly.

He probably should have built up to this. He didn't mean to overwhelm her, but community was obviously a painful button for her, and he had pushed it.

"I'm going to give you a little while to think on this. This is not a one-time offer, it's open-ended and you don't have to make a decision right now, or tomorrow or a week from Tuesday," he said. "You savvy open-ended?"

She didn't look up, but nodded.

"Here, I found this in the man's den," Eli said. "Maybe you won't have to keep sharpening that monster blade of yours." He handed her a fine stag-handled hunting knife in a leather sheath. "It was in a display case, out of the sheath, so there's not much corrosion."

"Hmmm." She took it, looked at it and smiled. "It will make a good hunting knife, but the blade I am working on is a war-blade. It is intended to be used in self-defense. But thank you, I'll take this with me."

"I made quite a find. Found a Saudi-Syria War era sleep set, sleeping bag and waterproof bivy. I'll stuff that in my pack, strap it all onto the Terror and I'm set."

"The Terror?"

"I'll introduce you later. I'm going to rest a bit, then I think I'll saunter on over to Lester and Benny's camp to see what I can find. Will you think about what I said? You don't have to make a decision right now. I understand you don't know me well, but I hope you can eventually learn to trust me."

She nodded again and said, "I'm going for a walk. I need to think."

"Okay then," he wrapped up in his new sleeping bag, and put a fatuous look on his face, "But come back soon, 'cause I'ma gonna be hongry."

He saw that ghost of a smile, then it was gone. She rose and moved through the doorway.

I hope you won't get in the way of your own best interests, lady.

****

The rain had stopped and the freshness of the air and the smell of wet sagebrush pulled a deep breath from Ghost Wind. Her heart pounding, she took another. She had no idea how to deal with what had just happened, she was confused by…

Confused by kindness.

She had reached the point where she was ready to accept the notion that kindness, friendship, and all the other good things in life were of the past. She had accepted from the point she had left Lila's home that her life would be one of simple survival, day to day. This acceptance allowed her to maintain a strong attitude, to not show weakness, to not BE weak and remain strong in the face of her trials.

It seemed that strength was rather fragile in the face of simple human kindness.

I need to be doing something.

She began walking towards the makeshift cross she had found Eli on. If he wanted to see if his two captors had known anything useful, perhaps she could find something he could study while he convalesced. The half-mile walk helped her regain equilibrium.

She came to the point where she had left Benny. The strong single-knuckle reverse punch she'd sent to the base of his skull had severed his spine, killing him instantly. Her active life outdoors had made her strong, and the Kung Fu training she possessed had made her deadly in a crunch.

Benny lay face down, head turned to one side, and as she walked up two turkey vultures flapped off into the distance to avoid her. The man's stupid gap-toothed face hadn't been much to look at while he was alive, but now, with help from the vultures, it was truly hideous. The scout woman had seen enough death in her life that she was unmoved by the sight, but the smell was another matter.

"I thought he smelled bad when he was alive…" she said, trying not to breathe through her nose. She took out the pair of leather gloves she carried, slipped them on and began to search the corpse. She found a small poorly maintained (dull) one-hand opening pocket knife, a well-used snot rag, an old style lighter with a faded picture of a naked woman on it and a few .357 cartridges. Nothing was of particular interest, and she had no desire to carry around the personal effects of someone devoted to evil.

Dark energies clung to such items.

She left his things piled on the small of his back, taking only the four cartridges. Moving out of the sagebrush, she walked over to Lester, who also was no prize to look at. His face was at least turned downward into the dust.

"Well, Lester, do you have something to share with us?" For some reason, the dead man decided not to answer her. Ghost Wind searched him. Lester's ratty pants had no useable pockets but he wore a grimy old vest that was covered with them. The scout simply lifted him at the collar of the vest, and shook the body until the kilabyker's arms slipped through and his corpse fell facedown into the dust.

"Now, what do you have for us, dead man?" She rummaged through the pockets, finding odds and ends, but nothing of use. "Ah ha! What is this? Holding out on me are you, moldy?"

The exterior pockets had given her nothing useable, but an interior chest pocket yielded a folded piece of ragged paper. She looked at it carefully.

"This may be what Eli's looking for." The folded note stated briefly: MEETING AT THE OLD MUSEUM, SOUTH OF BEND, TUES. FEB 27. WAIT. Cryptic, but maybe all her wounded charge needed.

"Great Spirit's eye, I have no idea what day it is." She had lost count. "February twenty-seventh could be today, yesterday or five days from now!"

A quick search of Lester and Benny's camp found little that she hadn't seen in her previous foray to retrieve Eli's supplies, but it reinforced her disgust with their habits and embracing of filth. She could only imagine what their minds would be like. She shuddered.

She left at a trot, before she became somehow contaminated. She was almost back to camp, when the old feeling came to her once more. The feeling of being watched, hunted. She scanned the horizon but saw nothing. Nature gave away no clues, and she wondered if it was the spirit world watching, maybe Jannelle, maybe the owners of the farm, maybe Lester and Benny.

Or maybe none of those. Jannelle had taught her when one tracked an animal, for a time, your spirit and that of what you tracked were linked. Maybe she was being tracked by the living, tracked by someone very good.

Either way, she didn't want to stay here much longer.

CHAPTER THIRTEEN
Riding the Terror

Eli hadn't lied to her. There was a Terror, though she was none too glad to make its acquaintance.

They had packed up at first light under a drizzly gray sky. Ghost Wind was still amazed that Eli could even move, much less walk five miles. He limped a bit and had to lean on his walking stick the whole way but eventually they came to a small grove of juniper trees. She saw something in the shadows, but couldn't make it out 'til she realized it was an object covered with a hand-painted camouflage tarp. Being something of an aficionado of camo patterns, she was impressed.

"Here's my faithful steed," Eli said, breathing a bit heavily from the walk.

"It's an impressive paint job," she said. "Hopefully what it conceals is impressive too."

Pulling off the tarp, he grinned at her, "If you think the tarp has an impressive paint job, get a load of my baby!"

Underneath was a very disreputable looking motorcycle.

"That," she asked, "is the Terror? Do you mean terror from riding it?"

"This," he replied flatly, "is one of the finest cold fusion battery motorcycles to come off the Mav-Tech showrooms in the year 2031. She'll still do a good eighty miles per hour on a straightaway, assuming you can still find a road that you'd care to trust that much. We have a fusion charger back home that will give my baby over 2,000 miles of running distance."

It was a truly amazing amalgamation of parts. The front wheel faring was painted with a garish bright red and white shark smile, with a pair of fierce-looking eyes glaring straight ahead. The wheels didn't match, and some sort of strange carrying rack had been welded on the back, making the cycle a good foot and a half longer. A sawed off shotgun scabbard had been added to the left side, and Eli shoved the newly shortened Remington into it.

"Okay, GW, hand me your gear, and I'll lash it on."

"What?" she said, wide eyed and taking a step back, "You don't seriously think I'm going to ride on that thing with you?"

"Um, yeah. What did you think I meant?" She took another step back, and with one eyebrow raised, he asked, "Oh, mighty scout, are you afraid?"

Her chin went up, and her back became ramrod straight. "Just because I am not suicidal, does NOT mean I am afraid!"

He looked skeptical. "Prove it."

"I.. do NOT have to prove anything to you!" she sputtered. "I have never ridden on one of these monstrosities, and I most likely never will!"

"Never say never." he said, grinning evilly.

****

In the end, an old song her mother used to sing to her about 'Rock and Roll Dreams,' coming to her out of the blue, convinced her to get on the bike. She couldn't run away forever, but she could regret her decision the minute they rolled out on the main highway.

"Too fast!" she yelled over the light whine of the fusion engine. "Slow down!"

"What? We're barely doing twenty-five, woman!" he yelled back, "I haven't even gotten near cruising speed!"

"It's s-so fast!"

He twisted and looked back at her and saw her eyes were wide with fear she would never admit.

"You've never ridden on a motorcycle, have you?"

"I've only ridden in a horse-drawn wagon, and it didn't go even close to this fast!"

"Well, we're going to be going a lot faster in a sec, so put your head against my back and close your eyes."

Ghost Wind, normally not one to submit to being ordered around, meekly complied as she felt their speed increase. Her eyes squeezed tightly shut, her thoughts went back to what one of the senior scouts, Black Dog had said whenever they dared to complain about comfort in their training exercises: *You can get used to anything if you give it enough time.*

"This is cowardice. This is not how I live." Ghost Wind muttered quietly into Eli's jacket.

Open your eyes. Jannelle's voice spoke in her head.

The thought made her tremble, but Ghost Wind forced her eyes open and saw the sagebrush rushing by. She almost closed them immediately, but she forced herself to see her surroundings.

No scout goes about with their eyes closed. Now raise your head up like a warrior.

With all the grit she could manage, she slowly eased up from Eli's back and, heart hammering, forced herself to see the road and the landscape going by at an amazing speed (for one who had never ridden any kind of motor vehicle before).

And she did get used to it.

The first ten miles were nerve-wracking. By the time they had ridden twenty-five miles, Ghost Wind was leaning into the turns with Eli, complimenting his driving rather than fighting it.

"Hey! Not too shabby, noobie! You're riding like a pro!" he said over his shoulder. "We're gonna have to find you your own bike!"

"Don't get crazy!" she shouted over the road whine. "I may never do this again!"

"Bull," he shouted back twisting around to look at her. "I can see in your eyes that you like it. Bet you never got to try anything like this, livin' with the Clan of the Hawk! We'll be turning off the main highway just ahead, so be ready when we slow down."

"Why are we turning?"

"We're coming into Road Shark territory, if we stay on SR97, chances of being ambushed go up to about 99 percent!"

In the terrifying thrill of riding behind Eli, she had forgotten the world she lived in now. Glancing behind them, she saw the Terror's trail in the dust of the road, standing out like the clouds on a clear day. She had hoped no one would follow them, but those tire tracks would be impossible to miss.

As they started to make the turn, she tapped Eli on the shoulder. "Wait! Drive down the main road for another 100 yards, then circle back."

"What? Why?"

"Try to trust ME just this once, if you will."

He nodded and did as she asked, going past then coming back to their turn-off on the other side of the highway, then cutting across their trail onto the side road.

"Pull off here, in this brushy area," she said. As they came to a stop, she swung down from her seat and realized her legs had gotten a little stiff from sitting. She stretched for a moment, then, pulling out her small hammer/hatchet, she chopped off two large sagebrush fronds.

Moving to the rear of the bike, she began a rhythmic erasing of the tracks they left on the side road. Two swipes side to side, then two fast vertical swats, and as Eli watched, he saw she was making a half-way decent imitation of the rain pocks from the earlier downpours. He began to follow.

"Eli," Ghost Wind brought him out of his reverie, "If you are going to come with me to do this, then please get behind me, so I can erase all our tracks at once."

She watched as he looked behind him. The tracks he was leaving were almost imperceptible compared to what the heavy bike and its passengers had been leaving, but they stood out like a Beforetime neon sign to her. He stepped off the road and went to a thick stalked sagebrush. Grabbing a limb almost an inch in diameter in one hand, he wrenched it loose with a loud snap. She looked at him, astonished.

"I'm... ah... feeling better."

Ghost Wind was strong, but she had to hack at a similar sized limb with her hatchet to get it loose. Many of her male fellow scouts with the Clan had been bigger and stronger looking than Eli, but she was quite sure none of them would have been able to break off that branch with one hand. Certainly not without a lot of wrenching back and forth.

Eli walked alongside her and began helping her erase the trail. It was all Ghost Wind could do to let the incident go without comment.

It took them almost a half an hour to reach the spot where they had turned the Terror around on the main road and come back to the smaller road. They erased the return trail, leaving the first line of travel untouched until only the original track on the main highway, before they had looped back, remained. Eli hadn't argued with her method, he seemed to be watching what she did carefully and trying to emulate it. It now looked like no one had ever turned off on the side road.

"Okay," she said. "From this point it gets a little tricky. If you will move off the side of the road between those two large bushes, I'm going to practice a little scout magic."

"I can't wait to see this!" he muttered, stepping to the side of the road.

Ghost Wind moved forward fifteen feet and very lightly began to run her brush-broom over the end of the remaining track. As she progressed back towards the end, she increased the pressure, making sure to erase her own tracks as she went. When she reached the end, she moved off the road, continuing to obscure her own trail.

"What do you think?" she asked, as they surveyed her handiwork.

"You've made it look like our track just fades away. But where is the 'magic'?"

"The magic is making someone see something, and getting them to believe what you want them to believe. The scouts of the Clan of the Hawk are well trained in psychological warfare. We're the DDT."

"You're what?" he said, "Scouts are the clan's pesticide?"

She had no idea what he meant, "DDT, The Department of Dirty Tricks. We bring terror and confusion to the minds of the enemy. What did you mean?"

He sighed. "Never mind. Information no longer relevant. So what is the purpose of fading the track like that?"

"The enemy follows the track, but it just fades away and vanishes. Did the wind blow it away? Did the riders just vanish? Did angels come and take them away? This far from settlements, the imagination can have quite an effect and ghosts can seem quite real." She paused for a moment, a frown coming momentarily to her face. "Er... anyway, perhaps it will be distracting enough, they won't think to go back to that overgrown little side road and find our real trail."

Eli nodded. "I've done a little DDT work myself," he said, "Someday we can swap secrets."

"Perhaps. It looks like a rain squall is coming. That should make our counter tracking look perfectly normal."

Eli turned and headed into the sagebrush and junipers. "Let's get back to the Terror."

CHAPTER FOURTEEN
Seeking New Hope

"All right Durpee, you and I been all around the compound now. Izzat enough for you to do your drawin' thing?" Porter asked.

"Yeah, Port! I seen it all, an' I can draw it when we get home!" The boy seemed excited just to be someplace new.

"Good, then. I need for you to sit tight in this little spot back here in the trees. I gotta go take one more circle of this place and look for weak spots. Then I'll go get the others and we'll get on home. All right?"

"Sure! I'll stay hid back here and maybe I can take a little nap. I had ta get up pretty early this morning." The boy yawned as he said it. "Hey Porter?"

"Yeah, Durp?"

"How come we hadda bring Pid and all them other guys? They don't seem to do much except sit and play cards."

"Yeah. I got a lot to say on that, but we don't have time. You just stay here 'til I come get ya, 'kay?"

"Okay."

Porter carefully made another circuit of the farm complex, doing his best to stay out of sight of the guards on the wall. Those guards weren't really looking too alert, and one guy seemed to be nodding off at the south quadrant, but Porter did not want to be seen. It wasn't just to avoid trouble here, but mostly to avoid trouble back at HQ with Shell and Axyl.

He noted a spot near the southeast section that didn't quite look as sturdy as the rest of the sheet metal walls. Not that it probably mattered with as much C4 as they had, but you never knew. There was no success like excess.

"Just let this go smoothly…"

Shots began cracking out in the morning air. Coming from the area of the front gate.

He really should have known better.

CHAPTER FIFTEEN
Horace

The backroads went on forever.

The Terror, which had seemed to be going faster than the speed of sound when they started, was actually going down the dusty tracks at 35-45 miles per hour, and the journey was long and bumpy. One moment they would be cruising through miles of pine and juniper, the next through long forgotten and overgrown backstreets of the many small deserted towns along the way.

Ghost Wind's early gut clenching fear had gone from fear to exhilaration to familiarity to boredom. When Eli finally pulled over her stiffening body was glad for the break.

"Not that I'm complaining, but why are we stopping? I thought your enclave was up in the mountains somewhere."

"We'll meet up with Highway 126 later on, but right now, I'd like to take a detour to New Hope. It's a small community of farmers, our closest real neighbors and Kita asked me to see if they had any apples left to trade."

"I thought you had to be south of Bend by February 27th, Eli."

He looked at her. "It's only the 25th. Unless a huge snow storm moves into the area, I have plenty of time to get there and cause mayhem. Right now, I'm going to have a snack."

She sat beside him on a bed of juniper needles. There was snow packed lightly in the shady spots in the mini forest they were in, but they had chosen a spot where the sun warmed the ground. She noted that even when they just sat, the silences were comfortable. That was rare in non-scouts. Most of the outsiders she had met in her travels tended to want to fill the air with small talk.

Don't get too comfortable. You don't really know this man, and the Scout Way says to keep your guard up.

The truth was though, even after her experiences with Axyl, she still felt instinctively that Eli was a much better man. Maybe that would be her undoing. Just thinking about it made her head hurt. But Axyl wouldn't have been able to let the silence lie, he would have had to fill it.

They were sitting on a high spot in relatively flat country and the view was superb. The low-lands, filled with a flowing forest of smaller high-desert junipers and sagebrush gave way to pines and firs as the Cascade Mountains climbed to the west. Clouds sat, sluggishly approaching from the way they had come.

Eli looked up from his canteen, "Did you hear that?" he asked her.

"I don't think I heard…" Ghost Wind listened for a moment, then cupped her hand behind her ear. "I might have heard gunfire, but a long, long ways off. Someone in a running gun fight?"

"Doesn't sound like the dustup's moving. It's coming from the direction of New Hope." He looked at her. "I think you'd best wait here a while. I'm going to see what's going on."

"I'm going."

"There's no need for you to get involved in this," he said, "You have no stake in this, and you don't know these people."

"I saved your life. I helped you regain your health, which, by the way, I am not convinced that you HAVE regained fully." She looked at him with raised chin. "I have a stake in your continued living."

She expected an argument, but Eli looked toward where the sounds had come from. "Pull your gear off the back, hide it in the brush, and get your firearms out to take with us."

"Why pull my things off?"

"Because," he turned back to her, "there are no guarantees. This could go bad, but if you can get out in the bush, I'm confident you could get away if things go to shit. If you can get away you can eventually find your way back here, and have your gear intact."

She nodded and pulled her bag and bedroll from the Terror, and placed it thirty feet from the road. She had just pulled her rifle out when she heard the motorcycle engine, quiet as it was, start up. She ran back to the road only to see Eli driving off down the road in a plume of dust.

"I'll be back! Wait for me!" he yelled back over his shoulder.

The people of the Clan of the Hawk believe habits influence life, and they didn't tend to swear often because of that belief. Ghost Wind, however, never one to enjoy being tricked, almost turned the air blue with the rapid fire comments about Eli's parentage, personal sexual inclination towards farm animals, and general habit of having a cranium filled with excrement. She did NOT like being lied to.

"I will be damned if I'm going to be here when he gets back!" she said, after realizing she had begun to repeat herself. Grabbing her things, she started to move cross-country, then pulled up short. This hadn't helped increase her trust in Eli, but the thought of having a people, a home again grabbed her around the jagged edges of her broken heart.

"If I go, there a chance I will always be an outcast." The lure of having a tribe to live with swayed her decision. She thought again how lonely she had been since leaving Lila's place.

Dammit. I want to know if I could fit in with…

The gunshots couldn't be more than a few miles away…

"Damn you, Eli!"

****

She was sweaty when she arrived, but not tired. Ghost Wind was used to covering vast distances on foot, often trotting and she would have felt right at home with the trail runners of the Beforetime. She realized she was not quite fully recovered from her convalescence though, when her breath was shorter than it had been for many years.

The gunshots had died down, but she wasn't going to be less cautious because of that. She hadn't wanted to use the road, but the last few miles, she had realized that she needed to follow Eli's tracks if she was going to catch up with him. Ghost Wind hoped she wasn't too late to help.

She was sure she was getting close and as she moved along the edges, the wind shifted to blow into her face.

Oh Great Spirit! What stinks?

As the wind shifted, she realized it was the scent of unwashed men blowing down the road and moved off into the thick junipers, readying her engraved rifle. The six-gun at her thigh was an afterthought, needed only as a backup, but she was glad to have it with her.

She had barely settled in when a troop of eight men began filing past. They were unkempt and from the look and smell, filthy. They wore dirty jean vests, though some were obviously jackets that had been cut off at the arms and each vest bore a hand-painted picture of some sort of cartoon shark. She was sighting on the third man in line when she realized that none of them seemed to be armed. She was almost thirty feet away, but she clearly saw empty holsters and knife sheaths and none of the group was carrying a rifle.

They're all injured! All unarmed.

Each man that passed was limping, holding an arm or ribs and all seemed to have been battered around their faces. One man was softly sobbing and holding his jaw, which seemed either broken or dislocated and another was patting his shoulder, trying to help. They all occasionally looked behind them, either in fear or hatred but none of them seemed willing to return to whoever had done this to them.

After she was sure they had all moved on, Ghost Wind moved from her hiding place and paralleled the road for another two hundred yards. Trying to remain alert with all her senses, she eventually heard raised voices ahead and gripped her Henry rifle tighter. Moving with the stealth of a wolf, she came to a point with line of sight to the argument. In front of a large wall, made mostly of concrete, rusty sheet metal and various kinds of barbed wire, Eli stood yelling up to a big hairy man with an old M-24 army rifle who stood on some kind of rampart behind the wall.

"Damn it, Horace! I've been working with and trading with you folks for the last four years! Why in the hell would you stop trusting me now!"

The big man spit off to Eli's left. "A'cause you didn't kill them bastards when you had the chance, Eli. Ever' one o' them Road Sharks that bites the dust is a little more peace o' mind for decent people. The fact that they're still breathin' makes me wonder if you don't have some sort o' deal with 'em."

"You saw me come up behind 'em and kick the shit out of them, isn't that enough? I have their weapons, and a couple of those men have injuries that'll take a lot of time to heal, if they ever do," Eli shouted. "I think that's enough to send them back to their HQ and report this is a place best left alone."

"The less of them around, the less brave they are."

"We could sit here and argue all day. Bottom line is, I didn't feel like killing anyone today that I didn't have to." Eli, obviously quite angry, began to pick up weapons from around the area. "I'll just take these with me, if you're not interested, or if you really think I'd have a deal with those pukes, go ahead and shoot me in the back."

Even from her hiding spot, Ghost Wind could see Horace hesitate.

"Now wait a second there, son. I mighta been just a little hasty, about that deal remark. I know you ain't with that bunch. Let me see them guns and such, and let's see if we can come to some sort o' agreement."

"Okay, but I gotta hurry, Horace," Eli said, his voice slightly cold. "I'm keeping a lady waiting, standing here jawing with you."

Ghost Wind's eyes narrowed.

Ah, yes. Thanks for reminding me that I am really irritated with you, trickster. The little woman has decided not to stay hidden in the brush!

Eli began holding up rifles for Horace to see, and as they started to haggle, more heads popped up from behind the rampart.

Ghost Wind calmly and methodically set down her rifle and pistol and moved forward. She kept to cover as she had been taught, emerging into sight fifteen feet behind Eli. She knew the people on the rampart could see her and she carefully raised her hands to show she was unarmed, and put a finger to her lips to signal silence. Eyebrows raised, but the farmers decided to play along and watch to see what would happen. There wasn't that much to do in these parts, so any entertainment was appreciated.

She thought about slapping him on the back of the head like a misbehaving apprentice, but decided on something a little less violent. As Eli vocalized the benefits of one of the salvaged rifles, Ghost Wind leaned close and blew on the back of his left ear. What happened next astonished her. One second he was right in front of her facing away, the next he was six feet away, looking towards her, hands in a combat position. She had barely seen him move.

"Gawd'amighty woman! You about made me jump out of my skin!"

Laughter poured over the rampart.

"This the gal you said was waitin' for ya, Eli?" Horace cackled. "Appears she grow'd tired of it!"

Eli lowered his voice so that the spectators couldn't hear. "Ghost Wind, don't ever sneak up on me like that! I could've overreacted and hurt you, which is about the last thing I want to do!"

"You tricked me," she replied, equally quiet. "Somehow you think I can let that stand? You want me to trust you, but I was ready to take off cross-country and you could've kissed my fading footprints!"

"Heweee!" Horace called down, "A couple starts talkin' all quiet like that, you know there's a storm on the horizon."

"We're not a couple!" Ghost Wind and Eli replied simultaneously.

"I'm dang glad to hear it, seein' as how our little community is three quarters men and one quarter women. Anyone who can look that good and can sneak up on Mr. Sharp Ears there, would be mighty welcome here!"

"Do you want these weapons, or not?" Eli yelled up.

"I think you two best come in for a little stew and tea, and we'll discuss it!"

"I don't think—" Eli began.

"Accepted!" Ghost Wind cut him off. "Thank you for the hospitality!"

Horace laughed, and the metal gate began to move.

CHAPTER SIXTEEN
Road Sharks

"Porter," Axyl said. "Please tell me Eli didn't do this."

Um…" From the hangdog look on the man's face and the lack of the rest of the battered-looking crew's ability to raise their gaze from the ground, Axyl knew that was exactly what had happened. Again.

"Fuck, man, how the hell am I supposed to keep Darwin from just shooting you, Port? This is twice you've screwed up a simple recon!" Axyl looked at Porter, shaking his head.

"Dammit, Axe. You keep sending me out with the stupidest guys in the gang, and they are just not good at being slick or quiet." The other men looked at Porter with hard stares. "Sure as shit, them farmers heard some of these yahoos talkin' in the brush, and the next think I know, firefight."

"You'd better not have lost Durpee," he said. "Or I swear to God, I'm gonna beat the boss to the draw in blowing your brains all over this nice wallpaper."

"No! No, Axe, Durpee was hid when the shooting started, I had to go back an' get him! He ain't got a scratch, man! Wish I could say the same for the rest of us."

"Where's Stanley?"

"Ol' Eli dislocated his jaw so bad, I don't think even the doc could'a helped him. He was hurtin' something' terrible, boss, so… I popped him when he weren't lookin'. It was a mercy, honest!"

"All right, Porter," Axle cut in, sighing. "Just tell me what you learned about New Hope so I can have an idea what went down before we tell Darwin."

The meeting upstairs with Shell went just about as Axyl expected, badly.

****

"Honest to fuck, boss, it wasn't our fault!" Porter Dell had a note of hysteria in his voice.

"You come back here," Shell started quietly, volume increasing with each word, "beat to hell, missing men and not bringing me the information I needed! Tell me, Porter, you're supposed to be one of my lieutenants, but what the HELL good are you?"

Porter flinched and subconsciously tried to protect the shoulder that Doc Mullins had just put back in the socket. Shell was tempted to punch the man in that shoulder, but knew that getting information from people while they were sobbing was tedious at best.

"Tell me," he said, "what exactly happened, Porter."

"Boss," Porter looked at him with a pitiable expression, "It was that goddamned Eli again! He snuck up and jacked us from behind!"

Shell closed his eyes and massaged the bridge of his nose. When he opened them again, Axyl was leaning over Porter shaking his head. "Porter," Shell said, "you were supposed to just recon the compound, why in the hell were you exchanging valuable bullets with a bunch of farm boys for no damn reason?"

"Uh, well, sir, you know Pid?"

"Pid. He's the guy that always has that vague smell of urine about him, right?"

"Yep. That's Pid. Well, he.. um.. kinda let himself be seen."

"Exactly what we told you not to do."

"Yeah, well, ol' Pid wasn't really too bright and he couldn't seem to shut up. Anyway, the farmers started shooting at us, then we had to shoot back and--"

Shell interrupted in a fury, "The one thing we wanted you to do, to bring back information on their set up, you didn't manage to accomplish, but you did manage to do the one thing we least wanted, which was to get them more alert to possible attack. Does that about sum it up, Porter? Do I have the lay of the land correct here?"

Axyl watched his employer start to reach for the gun in his shoulder holster and calmly stepped between Porter and Shell.

"Whoa, boss," he said, looking Shell directly in the eye, "you're trying to build an army here, let's not be offing the troops less'n we have to. Ol' Port here is one of our smarter guys, let's not waste him."

"God help us if he's one of the smarter ones." Shell dropped his hand, then his expression became perplexed. "Porter, you say it was Eli who nailed you? And he just beat the crap out of you?"

Porter nodded miserably.

"Did he kill any of you, this time?"

Porter shook his head.

"Then how, if you don't mind my polite inquiry, did you lose two of my men?"

Porter looked down at the carpeting.

"Porter," Axyl said, a warning in his voice, "you'd best answer the man."

"Well, y'see... like I tol' ya, Pid let 'em know we was there, and on the way back to the bikes we was all in some pain. Pid kept moanin' and all he had was a few bruises, far as I could see." Porter hesitated for a moment. "Well, I was already purty damn pissed at him anyway, and finally all that moanin'... well... I just hauled off and shot him in the head. Stanley, on the other hand, wasn't even gonna make it back on his own, and I kilt him as a mercy."

Now it was Axyl's turn to massage the bridge of his nose in exasperation.

"Get him out of my sight, Axyl, before I shoot the stupid ass."

"C'mon, Port. You and me are gonna step outside and see if we can figure out how to make this right."

****

"Oh, damn, Axe," Porter turned to him, a relieved grin on his face, "I got to thank you for..."

The Axe Man's right hand struck as quick as a rattlesnake, grabbing Porter's crotch, getting his subordinate's testicles in a death grip.

"Porter?" he said softly, "do I have your complete fucking attention?"

"Yeeeggg!"

"Good. Now, as you and I know, you are an incredibly useless piece of shit, and it was just luck and me that have kept you alive to this point. Is that a fair assessment?"

"Y-Yeeeesss?"

"All right then, you had better not EVER fuck up this badly again, or you are going in the ground. Am I clear?"

"Y-y-yyeess." Axyl let go and Porter collapsed to his knees.

"Porter, when you can walk again," Axyl's voice had turned conversationally friendly, "go get Durpee and bring him up here to me. I want him to show the boss something. Don't take too long, okay?"

"Okayaaayyyy."

CHAPTER SEVENTEEN
Local Hospitality

The stew must have been very tasty to one who had been living on dried meat and foraged plants for the previous several weeks. Eli was amazed and impressed to watch Ghost Wind pack it away. She ate with a gusto that he found refreshing.

The women of New Hope tended to flock around Eli when he came to visit, and knowing their matrimonial structure he was always a little careful to be circumspect in his flirting. Alice Ann was squirming her way onto his lap and Horace had to shoo her off so they could conduct their business.

"I'll gladly trade you a full bin of apples for them rifles, Eli, though how you're gonna get 'em up to Yama no Matsu is beyond me. Certainly ya cain't carry that many up there on the Terror, even if ya was to leave this lovely young eatin' machine here with us." Horace looked over at Ghost Wind fondly.

"You're not going to believe this, Horace, but Tengu found a matched pair of draft horses, I think actual Clydesdales. He has a wagon now that we can bring down here and do some proper trading, not just these pieces and bits we're always exchanging back and forth."

"Where is the hell didja find draft horses, much less a wagon to hitch 'em too? Such things weren't that common in the Beforetime."

Eli's face darkened, "We found them on a patrol. The original owners had run afoul of the Road Sharks."

"Surprised they left the horses alive."

"The horses were smarter than the owners."

Looking up, Ghost Wind wiped her mouth and said, "Who are these Road Sharks? Are there really so many that everyone is afraid? Can you not drive them out of the area?"

"That's a lot easier said than done, Miss Ghost Wind," Horace said. "You only rarely catch 'em in small bunches like today. Usually it's twenty or thirty at a time, and I got ta tell ya, they are a mean bunch. Most folks don't want to attract their attention, 'cept maybe Eli here."

"We can't seem to coordinate a big enough group effort to drive off or exterminate the vermin," Eli said, looking pointedly at Horace.

"Now don't start. Dammit, Eli, me and my people ain't fighters. We just stick to what we know, farmin' and defending these walls. Anything else would most likely be the end of this place."

"And so, they just get a little stronger every year."

Both men were silent for a moment. Horace looked at Eli, "That's why I wished you'da just taken them boys outside the wall outta the picture. The less men ol' Shell has, the less power he has."

A sharp reply came to Eli's tongue, but he swallowed it.

"Horace, there's some days when killing others, even when they deserve it, just sits poorly on a man's mind."

"Well, hope that high-minded liberal idealism don't come back to bite ya in the ass, Eli."

"Yep."

"Oh dearie me," Horace said, and Eli looked where the big man's gaze fell, "It appears to me your Miss Ghost Wind is talkin' to Marilee. Kinda wish that could'a waited…"

Eli stifled a laugh, watching Ghost Wind's eyes suddenly go as big as saucers. "Well, let's be honest, Horace. There's no one here who will talk as frankly about your mating setup than Marilee."

"Yeah," Horace sighed sadly, "I know."

****

"You have more than one husband!? Two men?" Ghost Wind said, her provincial morals deeply stung.

Marilee looked at her with mild amusement. "I would never be so thoughtless, girl! The ratio of strapping men to women here is almost three to one. I would never be so rude as to only love two men."

It took Ghost Wind a moment to absorb the implications of this, but when she did, her eyes, already quite opened, grew even wider. From the age of eight, she had been trained by the tracker scouts of the Clan of the Hawk and she had not had a lot of romantic interaction other than occasional flirting and kissing with the male apprentices.

Then Axyl had come along and besotted her with "romance." He had been her first and only lover, and his betrayal left her not even wanting to think of the sexual interactions between men and women. But now her curiosity wouldn't let her drop the subject.

Marilee could see the young woman calculating in her head, and waited for the inevitable questions.

"But," Ghost Wind started, the hesitated a moment, "does that mean you sleep with all the men here?"

"Not all at once!" Marilee laughed. "No, silly girl! Of course not, Shorty and Lem are my first cousins, that's a no-no."

"But the rest?"

"I've had four children since I've been here, and have one on the way," Marilee told her. "Eventually, we'll have to find more young women, but for now, everyone understands the needs of our community. And though the men are the muscle here, I want you to know the women run this show."

Marilee looked at Ghost Wind pointedly. "And for harmony's sake, we don't let any of our men go too long without sex."

Which, Ghost Wind thought, *is another way of saying "yes, many husbands".*

"Which brings us to you…"

"Me!?" Ghost Wind's eyes again grew huge.

"Young, strong obviously, and very feminine build. Be a great plus for us, and if you understand your genetics, a very good decision, biological diversity-wise. The more women who join us, the sooner we can all take a break. I don't know who you're with now, but we can offer a lot. No shortage of food, good people and a target that's hard to take for any raider group."

But still an obvious target. Ghost Wind thought.

"And I would have to…?"

"Oh, not at first, sweetie. We're not barbarians!"

"But later…?"

"Well, the needs of the many must be met." Marilee looked to her left, and a slight smirk came to her face. Ghost Wind followed her gaze and saw three bearded men watching her. They quickly smiled, in an attempt to be disarming, but she knew desire when she saw it and was sure they were all hoping she would join their "service agreement."

"I… um… need to talk to Eli for a moment," she told her hostess.

"Oh, certainly, sweetie, see if you can get that handsome rogue to join as well." Marilee looked toward the vigilante. "We could definitely use some of those genes in the mix!"

"Ahhh… yeah," Ghost Wind said, moving away.

As she approached Eli and Horace, she noted they were drinking out of a quart jar and both were laughing and acting a bit less formal. Ghost Wind took Eli's jar from his hand and sniffed. The burn in her nose told her all she needed to know and she handed it back to him.

"I am going back to where we left my gear. If you want to meet me there, I will see you then. If not, then good fortune to you and perhaps I will see you at a later time," she said, picking up her rifle.

"Ghost Wind, wait!" Eli stood a little unsteadily. "Horace and I have just about finished with our haggling. Give me a few minutes and I'll come with you."

"Young lady," Horace chimed in, "no matter what Marilee may have told you, no one is forced to do anything they don't want to do around here, with the possible exception of helping to weed the fields. I just want you to know that, and to know you are welcome here."

Ghost Wind looked over her shoulder at him and nodded. "Thank you."

                              ****

She had barely walked a quarter of a mile, when she saw where Eli had hidden the Terror. She hesitated a moment. Should she do as she said she would, and walk all the way back to where she had left her gear, or should she just wait by the motorcycle for his return?

Eli hasn't done anything wrong, if you don't count running off on his own. Why am I mad at him?

She sat next to the battered cycle, watching the multi-color sunset to the west and pondered her question.

We're just traveling together, no strings, and certainly no obligation to each other. So why am I having this urge to be angry at him? It's not his fault Marilee freaked me out.

Eli had been kind and solicitous to her since he had awoken in the shelter. He had been generous and concerned with her wellbeing.

A dark inner voice spoke, *Just like Axyl.*

Yes, Axyl had been kind, gentle, concerned with her happiness and had treated her like a little wilderness princess. Right up until the time he had convinced her to set up a meeting with her teacher, Jannelle. Her first understanding of the enormity of how she had been fooled came when Axyl drove his tomahawk into Jannelle's subclavian artery.

And of course, when her own sister, Ravenwing had opened her face with her knife, thinking that Ghost Wind had been a willing accomplice.

She had not shown her emotions since then. Not during her "trial," not when she spent the time living with Lila, not even when she was alone, trying to survive, but she could feel them down there, trying to reach the surface like an underground river pushing to reach daylight.

Grief, and the demon, FEAR.

Eli was kind. Axyl was "kind." She was attracted to Eli; she had been attracted to Axyl.

The longer I sit and mull this over, the closer I am to losing it. I need to move.

Ghost Wind rose to her feet, and walked into the twilight to find her gear.

****

Eli returned to their camp an hour after sunset. Before he had taken off, he had driven a juniper wood limb into the ground on the opposite side of the road from where he had originally dropped Ghost Wind off and driven a rusty aluminum can onto the top end. It would have been very easy to miss the spot in the fading light.

Not that darkness bothered him much.

Pushing the Terror up the hill a ways, he pulled out the tarp and carefully covered his baby then moved uphill to where he hoped Ghost Wind was. He picked up a hint of woodsmoke, and after following his nose for a short while, saw a flicker of flame in the dark.

"Hello, Eli," she said, not looking up from the stave she was carefully carving on. "Glad you didn't spill that thing off an embankment in your current state."

"I tend to metabolize alcohol very fast, even that paint remover Horace calls whiskey."

"Another one of your mysterious talents?"

"Yep. Whatcha workin' on?"

"I found this piece of dead vine maple, near that creek down the road. It looked about perfect to make a bow out of, since mine was… lost."

"Lost?" Eli gently said. "I wouldn't think anyone who can track like that would ever lose anything."

She looked into the flame. She was trying to keep her face a mask, but he could see that she was upset.

"Broken," she replied, "When I was banished, Shining Moon broke my bow over a boulder, cut the string in several places, snapped all my arrows and threw my war knife into a deep river. I was bound at the time."

"Holy shit! He had a serious mad on at you."

"She. She looked at our teacher, Jannelle as a mother. We all did. She had raised and trained us since we were eight years old, but Shining Moon really loved her and that love turned into hatred for me. No one stopped her. They might have just stepped aside if she had decided to kill me." She paused. "No, that's not right. Black Dog, one of the most senior scouts, actually stepped in when she started to make threats. He had known Jannelle even in the Beforetime, but he still kept the hot-heads off me."

Eli saw the memory of that act of kindness made tears well up in her eyes.

"Ghost Wind, I will never share anything about this subject that you tell me. Maybe you need to let someone hear your side, even if it can't change things. I'm a pretty good listener, and I can keep secrets when it's important."

She hesitated, looked at the fire, and seemed to come to a decision.

"I fell in love with a man. His name was Axyl and he was… gorgeous. He smelled… good. I was a foolish virgin girl and he played me like a fiddle." Her voice went from soft to bitter. "He told me sweet lies and when I could sneak away, he set my body on fire with need for him. He… was good at that."

Eli had never met the guy, but there was an Axyl with the Road Sharks. Could it be the same asshole?

"After three months," she took a deep breath, "he began his campaign to meet with Jannelle. He told me he was part of a group of traders that had buyers of Beforetime tech up in Canada and they needed a direct route through Clan of the Hawk territory. The scouts of our people carry a lot of weight regarding who gets in to our… their territory and Jannelle's word carried more weight than most."

"They couldn't go up to Canada on old I-5? On the west side of the Cascades?"

"He told me the Western Alliance put a huge tax on anyone bringing items through their lands. I had no idea if that was true or not, but surely this man

I loved so much wouldn't lie to me." The tone of her voice could have melted lead.

"So, I'm guessing he wanted to meet with this Jannelle lady?"

She looked up at him, her expression so wretched he wanted to reach out to her but he sensed she needed to let this out without distraction, or it would never be told.

"I was so in love. I would have walked off a cliff for him if he'd asked me to. I organized a meeting between them on neutral ground and Jannelle, myself and my little sister Ravenwing went to meet him at the appointed place. Axyl was sitting on his fusion cycle, all smiles and Jannelle told us to wait on the hill above, then went down to parley with him. We watched them talk, and I could tell by her body language that Axyl's charming gestures were not impressing her."

"Then what happened?"

"I remember being angry with her. Wondering why she couldn't see how wonderful he was. And then…"

He waited.

She took a deep shuddering breath, "And then, I saw him gesture up the hill at us, and Jannelle turned our way. As she turned, he pulled a tomahawk that must have been hidden under his jacket, raised up and drove it down in a powerful chop to my teacher's neck where it joined the right shoulder. It bit deep, she was dead in sixty seconds."

"Gaw'damn!" Eli said. "That's horrible!"

"The horror didn't stop there. As I stood there, frozen, he sauntered to his bike, got on and made kiss noises at me. Then he laughed like a maniac and drove off in cloud of dust."

"Shit."

"I realized how much of that very thing I was in, when my darling little sister, Ravenwing, with tears and hatred in her eyes called me a traitor." She paused again, looking into the fire. "Then she gave me this scar with the knife she carried."

Eli, wincing, decided to keep quiet and let Ghost Wind talk.

"I woke up at my trial, covered in my own blood. No one had even bothered to cover the wound, and some of them were advocating executing me as a traitor. It was at that point I realized the depth of Axyl's betrayal. Not only had he lied to me about everything for the opportunity to kill her, but he had left me holding the bag. If Black Dog hadn't taken charge and told everyone I was to be banished, I'd probably be dead now. If it hadn't been for Lila Whitefeather of the Yakama Nation taking me in, I'm sure I would be."

They both sat silent for a while, lost in their own thoughts.

Eli broke the silence first. "Tomorrow, we'll head up to our little hidden village, Yama No Matsu and I will introduce you to the people we've gathered up there. They've all come from different backgrounds, and I'm not gonna try to tell you that everyone there is perfect, but that diversity tends to make them more accepting."

"Do you think they will accept me?"

"Yes. I wouldn't take you up there only to be rejected. However, you are a strong-willed person, and we have a few very strong-willed folks up there already, so you'd better realize there's probably gonna be some conflict. Kita is, for lack of a better word, 'mayor' of the place as well as being my sword teacher. She can be... how to put this gently..."

Ghost wind raised an eyebrow, and waited for Eli to continue.

"She can be a bit of a hell-bitch on wheels occasionally. I'd advise not takin' her on too early, though I am sure you two will eventually clash, but you might want to put that off 'til you're established. And if she busts your chops, try not to take it too personal and storm off. When she warms to people, she can be one of the most caring individuals you'll ever meet. Sometimes concerned with others wellbeing to the detriment of her own."

"And whatever she dishes out, I should just stand and take it?"

"Might be better, at first."

"I can't promise that."

"Well," he half laughed. "tomorrow should be interesting."

CHAPTER EIGHTEEN
Drawing Away

"Do you want to tell me why you sent the half-wit on that mission, Axe?" Shell asked.

"Boss, no offense but," Axyl looked at his employer, once again staring out the window towards the river, "I know the men a heck of a lot better than you do. I drink with 'em, bullshit with 'em and ride with 'em."

"A leader must keep a certain distance from his underlings, if he is to be respected, young man."

"And that's why you have a brilliant, handsome, and likable second-in-command. I can mingle with the troops and report back to you."

"The half-wit?"

"Ah yes, Durpee. Our pal the Durpster may be an idiot, but he's also one of them idiot…ah… saviors?"

"Savant?"

"Yes! Savant! Damn Beforetime word. Anyhow, Durp is a savant. He has a photographic memory. But he can also do one extra thing." Axyl gestured towards the used copy paper and honed-down pencils on the large table. "Dupree can draw anything he remembers, and draw it incredibly well and in detail."

Shell's eyebrow raised. "I see. And you believe he may be able to draw the compound for us?"

"You know all those office supplies down on the first floor? There's one of those empty books and a packet of unopened pencils that I promised him if he could do that very thing. Compared to all this used stuff and pencil stubs, that's a treasure to him."

They were interrupted by a knock at the heavy wood door and Porter stuck his head in. Shell's face instantly darkened, and the man looked very distressed.

"Axe, I brung Durp like ya asked. Here he is."

"Thanks, Porter. Now, make yourself scarce." Porter was only too happy to comply.

"Durp! Howya doin' buddy?" Axyl said, white teeth shining in a huge friendly smile. "You ready to earn that sketchbook?"

"I did what you told me Axe. I went up there and seen it all, but them people shot guns at us! I was scared."

Axyl's expression became tragically sympathetic, "I know, brother, and I am SO sorry about that. I had no idea those people up there were so mean! So, I guess you were probably too scared to remember what to draw, hunh?"

"I can draw it!" For a moment, the young man's dull eyes flashed with fire.

"Whoa! Sorry, my friend, didn't mean no offense. I've got some pencils here and a bunch of recycled paper for you to work on. So why don't you sit down and show the boss here what you can do?"

Durpee's eyes went greedy for a moment. "I'ma still gonna get that drawin' book, ain't I?"

"Depends on how good a job you do, Durp."

"An' the pencils?"

"Show me something good, brother, and they're all yours."

****

It took the boy almost two hours of furious sketching, and several of the half used pencils to get his images down on paper. He worked with a strange, almost trancelike intensity and Axyl set a sandwich by him when it appeared he was close to finishing.

As Durpee wolfed down the venison and homemade bread, Axyl and Shell began to sort through the stack of drawings, some twenty in all.

"My God, these are amazing!" Shell said, "They're almost photographic!"

"Told you, boss," Axyl said patting the boy on the shoulder, "we had no idea what a resource we have here in the ol' Durpster. He's gonna be very…"

Shell looked up at his second-in-command as Axyl's words died away. The younger man was staring at one of the last few drawings, and his face had gone deathly pale.

"What is it, Axyl? I don't like that look on your face."

"Look at this, Darwin! For fuck's sake, look!"

Shell moved to the younger man's side and looked at the drawing that had turned Axyl's face pale. It portrayed in very tight detail a young woman, dressed in rustic clothing and moccasins, carrying a rifle. The drawing showed her running down a road, and Durpee had captured her athleticism perfectly, with a subtlety that he didn't possess in his own life. The young woman's face in the drawing was a clear as daylight, and showed a terrible scar on the left side.

"Hmmmm. Someone of your acquaintance?" Shell asked.

Axyl looked at his employer with a haunted expression. "Boss, you sent me north to deal with the leader of the of those hill people bush ninjas, remember?"

"I could hardly forget. They kept interfering with our slaving up that way, 'til it got to the point we could hardly do business up there. They'd sneak into our camps, free our slaves, destroy our equipment."

"Yeah, they were being a grade-A pain in our asses."

"As I recall, I had you seduce one of the females up there and you managed to get close enough to their leader to get the deed done and eliminate her."

"Boss," Axyl said shakily, pointing at the drawing, "this is the one. This is the one I tricked. She's the one I seduced,and now she's down here!"

"Hmmm. Interesting."

"Interesting? Boss, she's can only be down this way for one reason. She wants to find me!"

"The ladies just can't get enough, can they, Axyl?" Shell smirked.

"Okay, you're not gettin' me here, so let me spell it out," Axyl said, his voice tight. "If she's down here lookin' for me, it's so she can come up on me in the dark some night and cut my throat before I even know she's there. She's good, boss. During our little love meetings, I usually never knew when she showed up until she stepped out of the bushes, or dropped out of a tree. Her type start their training as little kids, and by the time they get to be her age, they're damn dangerous!"

"You seriously think one girl can cause us trouble? You think she can challenge the Road Sharks? Come on…"

"Look, man, our troops here ain't exactly elite forces. These scouts of the Clan of the Hawk…"

"Clan of the Hawk? How melodramatic."

"These scouts of the Clan of the Hawk can move as silent as them ninjas in the old vids. I'm gonna have to sleep with one eye open while she's anywhere in the vicinity."

Shell leafed through the stack to the last drawing in the pile. "Oh, this is interesting."

Axyl moved to look at the drawing in Shell's hands. It showed the same woman again, but this time she stood facing and apparently arguing with a tall dark skinned man wearing a long duster.

"Eli," Axyl said. "She's knows Eli."

Shell looked at his subordinate. "That might mean she knows where that son of a bitch lives."

CHAPTER NINETEEN
The Mountain Folk

The ride up into the mountains was cold. The late February day was sunny, but the farther into the Cascades they went, the more snow was along the single rutted path that ran before them.

Though it followed a Beforetime road, the path through the snow had obviously been worn by passing vehicles, not plowed. It was bumpy and rutted and a few times Ghost Wind's heart went to her throat each time Eli slewed the bike around in a particularly slushy part.

Even though he had reduced speed, the cold on her cheeks was brisk, but Ghost Wind wasn't afraid of cold. She spent most of the ride looking at this new country of pines and sagebrush. Most homes along the highway, showed signs of being broken into along with years of neglect. The houses had been beautiful and had probably cost much of the "God of the Beforetime," but now, nature was slowly starting its reclamation.

Eli slowed the Terror to a stop, and to Ghost Wind's surprise, began to let it slowly roll backwards. She looked behind them and saw that he was unerringly keeping the bike in the track they had just ridden up.

"Hold still, please," he said, "This isn't as easy as it looks."

She held her head and body still, amazed when they kept rolling downhill. What she had assumed would be only a hundred feet turned into a quarter of a mile before he applied the brakes and shut off the engine.

"Okay," he said, "this is where it always gets a little tricky, but it's a good workout. You've shown you're quite good at obscuring tracks, so if you'd help me out with that, I'd appreciate it."

"Aren't you going to need for me to help you push, like earlier on the way up?" Following Eli's gaze, she saw the barest trace of a trail off the side of the road.

"Not this time." He gave her his toothy grin reached under the frame near the front and the back. With a grunt, he lifted the fusion cycle into the air and began to shuffle down the faint path with it.

Ghost Wind began to think there would be no end of amazing things she would witness. She had helped push the Terror through a snowdrift on the way up, and was surprised at how heavy it had been. She was strong, but the motorcycle weighed at least six hundred pounds. If Eli hadn't been pushing also, she probably wouldn't have succeeded in moving it by herself.

Now, he was carrying an object that she was sure three men couldn't easily get off the ground, and though he was straining, he seemed nowhere near the limit of his endurance. She stared at his back for a moment, then began to attend to her job of obliterating the trail into the forest. After a short distance the main road disappeared behind the trees and she turned to find Eli covering the Terror with his homemade camouflage tarp. He had carefully positioned the bike in a brush patch, and even with the leaves gone, the tarp made it almost invisible.

"How can you possibly carry that much weight?" she asked, taking her bedroll and haversack from him. "You're barely breathing hard! You hardly broke a sweat but you didn't even unload our gear from the bike."

"I gots me some secrets, girl." Eli shouldered his own pack. "Stick around, and maybe I'll share a few with you. For now, though, we walk."

Shortly after they left the fusion cycle, Ghost Wind realized they were walking down an old road, the entrance now hidden from the highway. In places they waded through knee-deep snow, in others, they walked on cracked pavement, heated by the sun. Her gear was light for the most part, but it was unwieldy when the snow was deep.

She had repaired and greased her moccasins, but she began to wish she had been able to make a pair of winter mukluks. After a mile, even with the bare stretches, the wet from the snow began to soak through her leather shoes and felted socks. At the two mile mark she felt the warmth draining from her feet.

"We're gettin' close, Ghost Wind," Eli said. "See that bridge up there? That's the old hatchery and it's where the road to the village starts."

"How much farther?" she asked.

"Getting tired?" he said, looking at her with concern.

"No. Not tired, but my feet are soaked and they're getting cold."

"Damn," he said, looking at her soaked moccasins. "I should have noted that. I'm sorry. I could have gone on and retrieved some decent winter footwear from the village. I wasn't being mindful."

"I am... was... a scout of the Clan of the Hawk. I am not a wilting flower who cannot deal with the cold. I have stood in the Icicle River in January, up to my neck and controlled my body temperature while doing so..."

"Okay, okay. No knock on your skills or toughness was intended. But cold wet feet just plain suck. We keep a guard house at the old hatchery, and I'm sure Kenji will have his little hibachi set up to stay warm. You can dry your feet there while I go on to the village and retrieve a pair of boots for you. It'll give me a chance to tell everyone we have company."

****

Kenji was probably around sixteen years old and male enough to try not to be caught staring at the new female in town. He wasn't entirely successful. As Ghost Wind hung her socks over a small dowel by the hibachi, she set her moccasins a little farther back and pointed the bottoms of her feet at the tiny stove. The heat was wonderful!

"So, do you always run this lookout, Kenji?"

He blushed. "Um… I'm, like… here on Mondays and Thursdays. Old Mr. Palmer is here on Tuesdays and Fridays, and Gramma Jones is here on Wednesdays. On the weekends, others rotate in." He shyly looked back towards the coals.

"Ah. Well, your people have done a good job of hiding the road in here. Unless one has a Beforetime map it'd be unlikely someone would wander in here."

"Yeah, but Kita says we have to be 'always vigilant' or slavers might raid us and take us away again." Kenji's face grew dark.

"You say that like slavers took you away before."

He hesitated for a while, and Ghost Wind waited.

"I was a little kid. Back then, my name was Jimmie Franks. My mom and me had gone to try and find my dad, 'cause he'd like… disappeared. We was just a day or two away from home when them bastards caught us. Chained us like animals and started marching us north. Eli rescued us and even gave us a ride on the Terror back to our farm, but someone had emptied it out. There was nothing for us to live on. Turned out our neighbor down the road had told the slavers where we were so he could pick our place clean." Ghost Wind saw hate flare up on Kenji's young face.

"What did Eli do?"

"Nuthin'. The guy had five kids, an' all the food we stored was eaten. We were lucky to get some of our stuff and our two horses back alive. Eli talked Mom into comin' up here with him, and we joined the village." He looked up at her, his eyes warm again. "It's good here, we ain't gone hungry. Are you gonna join too?"

His hopeful expression put her at a momentary loss for words. "I… I don't know. We'll have to see how things go."

"Just so you know, I don't got a girlfriend. Just… just sayin' y'know." His face turned bright red and he looked back at the hibachi.

Well! You silver-tongued devil, she thought.

"Good to know," she said, "Didn't you say your name was Jimmie though? Why are you now Kenji?"

"Oh! I changed it in honor of Sensei Kita! She's been teachin' me naginata-do and Iaido. Several of her students have changed to Japanese names."

"That's very interesting. She seems to command a great deal of respect."

"Eli may be the rescuer, but it's Mamma Kita who holds us all together and makes thing work at home." He lowered his voice conspiratorially. "Eli is a great dude, but he gets the urge to roam a lot. I think he wants to bring law and order to this area, but that's a pretty big order, what with the Road Sharks and the Red Slavers owning so much o' the area."

"So he's not at home much?"

"Oh! I don't wanna make it sound like he's gone all the time, he ain't! But most of us like to stay hidden here in the mountains and only go down the hill when we need to scrounge something, or trade with New Hope. Eli though, he likes to get on the Terror and ride."

"Hey, Kenji," a voice called from the door. "You're not supposed to tell her all my secrets!" Eli entered the guardhouse through the narrow door.

"I have a feeling Kenji here barely scratched the surface," Ghost Wind said. She noticed the bundle he was carrying. "For me?"

He unloaded the package to show her a pair of Beforetime boots, with an inner felt liner and a pair of homemade wool socks.

"Got a little somethin'-somethin' here," he said, smiling. "Try 'em on!"

"These socks are SO soft!" she said, pulling them on.

"We got alpacas!" Kenji exclaimed, "Most of the ladies are pretty good on the looms, and some of us men, too!"

"Nothing like wool, and this is some fine wool."

Eli watched her enjoyment as she put on the socks. There was a sensuous smile on her face as she put them on. He found his heart beating a bit faster.

"Do you ever use your wool for trade?" she asked him.

"We trade some loomed wool to the folks down in New Hope, but there aren't that many communities out this way to do business with, and we're sure not going to try and trade with the Road Sharks. Maybe someday the area will be less like a war zone and we can actually start an economy."

She thought about that for a moment. "Is that why you're trying to bring law and order to the 'badlands,' Sheriff Eli?"

"Part of it," he smiled wryly, "and also I just hate vermin that prey on their fellow human beings. I've seen enough of it that I want to put as much of an end to it as I can."

"I've heard worse goals, Eli."

"Yeah, well, don't get me on my soapbox. If you'll put these boots on, we'll go meet Kita."

"Do you think I'll make a good impression?"

"Lady," he grimaced, "nobody makes a good first impression on Kita."

CHAPTER TWENTY
Kita

"Well, this is home," Eli said. "What do you think?"

The village of Yama No Matsu was bigger than Ghost Wind had thought. Almost fifty small homes, made from a combination of stone, raw lumber and scrounged materials from Beforetime structures, dotted the landscape with muddy paths joining them all.

Though the construction of each was pretty eclectic, she was impressed by the sturdy-looking buildings and the elaborate metal and stone chimneys that extended from sheet metal roofs. Though the village was warmed in winter by wood, the chimneys were designed to stunt the raw smoke going into the air, and she hadn't smelled them 'til she was almost to the township itself. She also thought she saw a few solar panels at various points.

"I... I haven't lived with this many people for over a decade, but it's very impressive. You've gone to a lot of effort to make this place hard to find"

"Considering the state of things in the world, I doubt anyone could blame us for that."

"I wasn't complaining."

Eli stopped at a snug little cabin. "This is it, my little corner of the world."

It was very well built, with a small porch with three old wooden chairs sitting on it. It looked like a nice spot to sit and listen to rain ping off the slightly rusty sheet metal roof.

"I like it; it looks warm in the winter," she said.

"Would you like to take a look inside? You can leave your gear here while we go do the meet and greet with Kita."

****

Kita lived in a nicely appointed cabin almost at the end of the village. It was small but sturdy, with a trickle of smoke coming from the stove pipe sticking out of the green and rust colored roof.

"Where did your people get all the building materials, Eli?"

"Well," he looked back at her as he stepped on to the porch, "if one were to take a survey of the Beforetime homes in this area, one would find a lot of empty foundations lying about. Our villagers make a pretty good reclamation team and if you look carefully, you can see most of the cabins have solar panels nearby. We keep looking for a fusion charger, but so far, we've only found a small one, fit only for motorcycles and carts, but we're doing pretty good up here."

"Yes," she said, a speculative tone in her voice, "and you're far enough up in the mountains that you're probably not bothered much."

"That was the idea. Continued experience shows this is a time when it's best not to let strangers know your home address."

Eli rapped gently on the wooden door, and a few moments later, a senior woman opened it. She appeared to be in her early sixties, compact and muscular for one so short. Her black and steel gray hair was cut close and her face was quite smooth for one her age. It was set in an emotionless mask until she saw it was Eli standing there, then the mask slipped away and was replaced by a pleased expression, sub-texted with mirth.

"So, wandering one, you have finally decided to grace us with your presence again," she said.

"Ah, Kita, you know me. I was born under a wanderin' star…" He started to take a deep breath, and the woman raised one finger.

"Please, no singing. That is NOT one of your many talents."

Eli assumed a tragic expression, "Kita, really. I'm gone two weeks, and this is the reception I get?"

"I have heard you singing with the men when a new batch of 'shine' has cured. It is not to be endured by anyone with a reasonable sense of tone and pitch."

"Okay. Fine," Eli said with a wounded air. He gestured towards Ghost Wind, "Kita, I would like to introduce you to Ghost Wind, former scout of the Clan of the Hawk up there to the north."

Kita looked at the younger woman, the emotionless mask fell back into place. "You brought her here, directly to the village without taking her to the waiting house first?"

Eli seemed surprised, "We've traveled a while together, I've gotten to know her and I vouch for her. My word should mean something, as co-founder of this place."

Kita looked back at the scout. "And why, girl, are you a former scout of the Clan of the Hawk?"

Ghost Wind flushed slightly, but she stood straighter and said, "I was banished."

Kita turned to Eli with a 'what the hell were you thinking' look, then, turning back to the younger woman asked, "Why exactly were you banished? Tell me the entire story."

"I… I made a horrible mistake." Ghost Wind could no longer hold her head high and found herself looking at Eli's boots. "I was seduced by a man. We met on the sly and he… he… seemed wonderful. I fell in love with him."

For a moment, the iron haired woman's face softened. "That seems like a small thing to be banished for."

"That was not the reason." Ghost Wind's face grew more red. "He did not love me as he said he did. He was using me to get close to my teacher. I took him to meet her and he murdered her. She had been a formidable thorn in the side of the kilabykers and slavers of that area and he used me as a tool to remove her."

"And you were banished," Kita said, matter-of-factly. She reached out and raised Ghost Wind's chin, "Was that scar part of your punishment?"

"Not officially." The young scout's voice quieted as she pulled her chin from Kita's fingers. "It was given me by my sister. She also assumed I had been a willing accomplice to my teacher's murder."

"And were you?"

"I was NOT!" The girl's face came back up, angry, "I loved my teacher! She was like a mother to me from the time I was eight years old. I would have died to have prevented what happened! Instead, I almost died because I couldn't. I cannot return to the Clan lands upon pain of death. I am alone."

"And you are still alone." Kita raised her hand to stop the angry outburst starting from Eli's lips, "Perhaps all is as you say or perhaps you are a skilled infiltrator sent by our enemies to find our weaknesses. If not the latter, then you are simply a warrior with extremely poor judgement. In either case, I can see no place for you here."

****

Kita saw astonishment on Eli's face. He couldn't seem to believe what he was hearing.

He rounded on her, turning his back on the young scarred woman he had brought unannounced into their village. "Goddamn it Kita! What. The. FUCK!!"

The woman had seen her long-time friend angry before, but in their fifteen years of building Yama No Matsu, she had never seen him this enraged. She had a momentary urge to take a step back, but that was not the way of Bushido. She simply gave him a flat look.

It took a moment for the tall dark skinned man in front of her to master himself, his corded muscles unclenching. She took that moment to seize control of the argument.

"You say she is a lost waif warrior alone in the wilderness, but she has already been used to cause the death of one of her masters" Kita said, voice sharp as a sword blade. "Who is to say whether or not she has told you all of the truth of that story, or if she has just woven some truth into a web of lies. For all you know, she's joined the groups we strive to avoid and is mentally taking notes of all our defenses to take down to Shell and his gang."

"The hell." Eli's sensuous lips narrowed to a thin line for a moment and she waited for him to continue, one eyebrow raised. He took a deep breath, obviously trying to control his anger.

"Now you listen to me, little sister, I may not be the great organizer you are, and I may not be the leader of a dojo full of warrior wannabes, but I have been around a LONG time, even longer than you. In those years, I have learned a little bit about people, and this young woman is not a liar. She may be proud, stiff necked, and not always able to see what's good for her, but by God, she is not with those fucks down in Bend."

"It is my place to watch over this place and these people," she said. "I do not have the luxury of wandering all over the region playing rescuer to every lost soul wandering what remains of the old roads." Her own voice began to rise, "You brought this girl here, completely violating and bypassing all the safety protocols we've set in place and expect me to welcome her with open arms? Really?"

"Kita," Eli said, obviously trying to get his anger under control, "Ghost Wind is special. She's already a warrior. She's a tracker and a scout, two things we desperately need and I've never seen anyone who could appear and disappear so damn well, not even in the Beforetime when I was with all the Special Operations people."

"And what if she is playing you?"

"She saved my life. Without her, we wouldn't be having this conversation. In fact we wouldn't ever be speaking to each other again without the use of a séance."

Kita was silent a moment. "Tell me."

"Remember I went to see if I could smoke out Lester and Benny? Well, that didn't work out so well. It was a trap. They'd somehow been expecting me, and left a few well-hidden bear traps lying around. Being a little overconfident…"

"You? Really?"

Eli gave her a flat look of his own. "If you don't want to hear the story…"

"Please! Continue."

"Those two rejects from a pigsty actually managed to get me caught in a rusty iron bear trap, which I might add was one of the most painful things I'd ever experienced until I was worked over with rebar clubs and then nailed to a big wooden X out in the cold, windy, farm area south of the river."

"Dear God!" Kita's expression was one of disgust and horror. "And your… 'special healing powers' couldn't fix you?"

"There's only so much super-genetics can do. I wasn't in a position to consume mass quantities of food. I was too busy trying not to freeze to death. So, guess how I survived?"

"The girl?"

"Got it in one. She appeared out of nowhere, practically under the noses of Benny and Lester and got me off that damn cross. The turds came to investigate, and she disappeared back into the sagebrush. When they were getting ready to use me for spear practice, she managed to kill both of them, with no gun, and they NEVER saw her coming."

"I… did not realize that she helped you that much…"

"She didn't 'help' me, Kita, she flat out saved my life. Then she took the time to nurse me back to health. I'd say that makes her pretty 'vouched for' in my book."

"Think for a moment, Eli," Kita looked up at him, "If you were going to infiltrate us, can you think of a better plan? No one would miss Lester or Benny, numbskulls that they were, not the Road Sharks, not the Red Slavers. This 'warrior woman' just happens to appear, right when you're at your worst and 'rescues' you. Who is to say she didn't betray her people in reality and join with this lover of hers against them? You have only her word how she received that scar. It could all be an elaborate hoax to find Yama No Matsu so it can be pillaged and its people enslaved."

"I see two problems with your theory, Kita. One: I was not born yesterday. In fact though most might not know it, I'm older than you are. I have worked with some of the most devious people in the world and I'm pretty sure, buried bear traps notwithstanding, that I can see through the bullshit of even a seasoned actor."

"I see. And two?"

"Two: What would be the more desirable outcome for Shell? To gain the location and inside info on this village, which does not in anyway impact his day-to-day, but instead is just on his wish list…"

"I sense an 'or' coming."

"Or… to eliminate the biggest thorn in the side of the Road Sharks by killing me, the one who is constantly thwarting him, releasing slaves, attacking thugs, tearing at his infrastructure. Which do you think would be higher on his to-do list? I'm thinking my death would be on top. He'd want, and pardon my hubris, to take the king off the chessboard. But look, here I am. Because of her. Please, explain how that makes ANY sense in the context of your paranoid theory."

Kita looked away over the valleys and mountains.

"All right, I might be willing to give her a chance, under close scrutiny."

"Did you hear that…?" Eli looked back over his shoulder, Ghost Wind was gone.

CHAPTER TWENTY-ONE
Going Downhill

"I should have known," Ghost Wind muttered under her breath. "How stupid was I to think the Creator Spirit would let me off the hook for what I've done. Until I atone by taking Axyl's goddamned head, I will always be alone!"

She had retrieved her gear from Eli's cabin, and was almost back to Kenji's lookout. She opened the door, bringing in a small amount of crumbly snow and surprised the boy, who had been lightly dozing.

"Miss Ghost Wind!" he said, jerking awake, "I wasn't sleeping!"

"Yes," she said dryly, "so I see." Ghost Wind kicked off the borrowed boots and checked her moccasins which were almost dry. She hesitated a moment, but regretfully slid the alpaca wool socks off and put her own damp ones back on. They were clammy, but at least they had dried some.

"Um," Kenji said, "how did it go with Kita?"

"Not well." She pulled on her moccasins and stood, shouldering her bedroll pack. "Not well at all. It was nice to have met you, Kenji. I must be going."

"But... I don't understand! Why didn't Kita..."

"You can ask her, Kenji, but when you see Eli, thank him for trying, will you?" With that, she stepped out of the door and started back toward the main road. As she moved from a dry piece of pavement to snow patch and back, she looked over her shoulder. Kenji was watching her from the doorway. His expression was confused and sad.

Well, at least one person is unhappy I'm leaving. Guess I should be thankful for that.

As she walked, Ghost Wind noted that even up here, where the snow still reigned, the areas under many of the pines had melted, and if they were close together, the bare patches almost formed a highway through the wilderness. There was a lot less brush in this area than on her home range and the going would be easier, even having to cross the large snowy areas still remaining.

Time to go back to the Scout Way.

****

Eli was fuming. "You couldn't have said anything, when you saw her walking off? You should have said something!"

Kita shrugged. "I wasn't going to let her stay. Her walking away was just fine with me, but I knew you'd try to stop her."

Eli glared at her, and started down the street. "Was she heading towards my place?"

"Yes," Kita yelled after him, "So, I wonder, Eli, is your interest in this young woman more than just for a new member of the village?"

"Phht." Eli looked over his shoulder, "No! Nothing like that…"

A slow smile began on Kita's face as the big man stalked off.

Eli walked the length of the makeshift 'street,' watching for the tracks the boots he had loaned Ghost Wind would make.

"I've really got to do a refresher on my tracking," he said to himself. People out and about watched their champion curiously as he went muttering down the street, gesticulating with his arms at no one visible.

When he arrived at his cabin, Ghost Wind was nowhere to be found and all her gear was gone. She hadn't waited.

"C'mon, girl, give us half a chance here. We can make this work!" He cringed when he thought of Kita's words to the proud young scout. It was really no wonder she had been gone when he turned around. He should have expected it and headed her off. When you put one overly proud, stick-up-the-ass woman against another, disaster of one sort or another was usually the eventual result.

He turned down the path towards the lookout point and finally found her tracks, recognizing the slightly overlarge bootprints in the snow. Ten minutes later, he stuck his head in the door and barked at Kenji, "Where is she?"

The boy, not used to this tone from the normally kind and charismatic man he idolized, pointed at the footwear on the floor.

"Is it true? Did she have a fight with Kita?"

"Yes." Eli saw that Ghost Wind had left the boots and the alpaca wool socks, and switched into her probably still wet moccasins and ratty socks. "And obviously, she's not going to take anything from us that might be helpful to her."

"Ghost Wind seemed pretty mad, but kinda sad too."

"Aw… SHIT." Eli looked at the boy. "I'll see if I can find her, and maybe we can get this sorted out. I think Kita might give a little, if I can just find Ghost Wind and keep her from hitting the road prematurely. Later, Kenji."

Eli started out at a brisk pace, assuming Ghost Wind would aim for the road. As he moved over the snow covered areas he thought he occasionally saw her footprints, but they were very faint, much more faint that he would have expected from such a solidly built, muscular girl. As he neared the Terror, he wasn't seeing any trace of her at all. He uncovered and picked up the bike and moved around the tree it had been under, trying to stay off the snow as much as possible. He didn't want to take the time to brush out his tracks, but his conscience wouldn't let him just leave them there.

He assumed that Ghost Wind had started walking down the same road they had come in on, and that on the bike he'd be able to catch up with her in short order. After ten miles and no sign of her, he realized he'd badly underestimated her. She'd gone overland.

He felt a strong loss, the kind he hadn't felt since Jean-Anne had died in the plague.

Weird. I barely know this girl.

He turned the fusion cycle around and drove back up the hill, looking for any sign of Ghost Wind he could find.

****

"This might do, for a while," she said as she came to a small plateau, thick with pines on one side.

Ghost Wind finally found a place to rest. She had moved down the mountainside for most of the remaining day, and eventually, the snow had given way to dirt and the earliest signs of spring. Grass was starting, buds were forming and there were even some patches of ground that she could consider reasonably dry.

Maybe it's time to take a break and just live for a while. I've traveled far enough to be out of the Clan of the Hawk's reach.

It was a pretty place. She could see far out over the lowlands, to where the pine forests thinned out to sagebrush and juniper to the east, and to the north she could see a high mountain, once a volcano. She was unsure if it was Mount Hood, or one of the other old volcanoes in this chain of mountains.

"I wish I'd have been able to take one of the old maps from the clan's libraries with me," she said to herself, setting her bedroll on a layer of pine needles. "I didn't know much about this area before I came here, and I still don't." It was, of course, an absurd thought. The Clan scouts hadn't let her take anything but the clothes on her back.

It was late afternoon, and the sun had already set in the lowlands. She began making a triangular frame of sticks and limbs, then stuffed as many of the sun-warmed pine needles and big-leaf maple leaves from the previous year into the frame as she could make fit. After mashing them down a bit, she made a mirror of the frame on the other side of ridgepole and began to weave smaller limbs into it. Using the old poncho, she poured more leaves and pine needles on top of the shelter until they were almost a foot and a half deep.

Once her shelter was built, she unrolled her blanket, and pushed all her possessions inside, with the tiny stuffed bear being last, sitting and looking out of the shelter at her.

"Well, Go-Go," she said to her verbally challenged friend, "it appears, as I feared, I am not wanted anywhere. That's all right. I can be perfectly content out here away from everyone and living off the land. That's what scouts do, and I am just FINE with that." As she dug a foot deep pit to build her Dakota-style fire, the ache in her heart said otherwise.

Twilight was falling as she dragged a fourth load of firewood to her camp. She had gone a ways afield to find a dead maple, as the pine tended to be quite smoky, something a lone woman wanted to avoid in her fires. The world was vastly depopulated from what it had been in the Beforetime, but it seemed that an inordinate number of assholes had survived.

No sense in taking chances.

She took a thick sapling, and cut it into sections with her big knife, using the two narrowest sections to drive into the ground next to each other at an angle. She then hacked the rest of the stave into shorter sections, and stacked those on each other, tying them together with handmade twine. The end result was a backrest that she could lean against as she sat and watched her steel canteen cup boil jerky and nettle stew.

"As quick camps go, this is pretty comfy, Go-Go," she opined to the bear, "And it'd be pretty damn hard to find. I can hear water down the hill somewhere, and in the morning I can go down and fill my water bottles." She looked across the meadow with new growth coming up everywhere.

Maybe we'll stay here for a while. I can make a bow, and maybe hunt and dry more jerky.

Unfortunately, as she sat in the darkening evening, the quiet also gave her time to think about the day and what had happened. She had probably, once again been her own worst enemy, though Kita was certainly trying hard for the position.

Her face turned red with shame. She had stormed off too soon, Eli had been advocating for her, but Kita's words cut straight to her fears. She had walked off, not in pride, but in fear. Fear of being rejected once again.

"Oh bear," she sighed, "at least I don't have to worry about being a total screw-up around you. Lila was wise to at least help me have one friend in the world."

"Sorry, Go-Go." she looked down at the small stuffed toy, with its scuffed plastic eyes seeming to watch her. "That sounded a lot like feeling sorry for myself, didn't it? I apologize. That's not the way of the scout warrior, I assure you. I hope you'll overlook it."

She looked out at the wide open sky, curving off into seeming infinity over the lowlands. She could see Orion starting to appear to the southeast, and the Dipper was starting to show in the north.

"That's what I need to remember." Her voice was soft in the chilly evening breeze. "Banished from the Clan of the Hawk or not, I have the training of the Scout, I AM a scout warrior and if nothing else, I can devote myself to improving my skills. Maybe someday there will be someone worth using them for again."

The bear, never a great conversationalist, didn't reply.

CHAPTER TWENTY-TWO
The Plan

Late that night, many miles away, Axyl was rallying the troops. He took a deep breath before he began. It was always a test of patience trying to get complex ideas across to the Road Sharks and the plan he had made with Shell was about the most complex plan they'd ever been exposed to.

"Everyone drink up! We've got some good home brew here, and I don't want anyone to not get their fair share!" Several of the men gave loud hoops and cheers. Enough home brew always made them more receptive.

Sitting in the back of the room with his five cronies was Cord. The tall man, with his coal black hair, watched the rest of the Sharks with disdain as they swilled the half cured beer, laughed at jokes a toddler could see coming and occasionally made vomit-induced rushes for the door. The smell of the place testified to the inability of many of the gang to navigate that short distance in time.

Cord and his boys didn't want to be here, but riding north they'd found themselves in Shark territory and before they could make an exit, they'd been given an offer they couldn't refuse, join or die. They didn't participate in most of the excesses that the rest of the bikers did, but they did what they were told.

Axyl nodded at Cord, and the other man gave him the slightest acknowledgment in return.

"All right, listen up you buncha coyotes! This comes from Shell, so, boring as it may seem, you best open your ears." Axyl knew Shell delegated these meetings to him because Axyl had something the older man lacked, charisma. Shell was the brains, Axyl was the voice.

For now.

"We've got something comin' up. Something BIG. Shell says it's time we started to consolidate our holdings."

"Con.. what?" Chimed in a thick browed thug named Grogan, sitting in the front.

"Sorry, boys, I shouldn't of used the old man's fancy words. What I meant to say, is that it's time we, the Road Sharks, controlled all the settlements in our area, starting with New Hope."

"How we gonna do that, Axe?" Grogan interrupted.

"I'm gettin' to that, Grogan," Axyl said, starting to feel just a bit irritated. "We are going to trickle in by twos and threes to the area around their compound over the next day or so, keepin' out of sight, and then blow one of their walls away with some C-4. Our friends to the east have gifted us a generous amount and we can…"

"Oh man!" Grogan exclaimed. "I LOVE blowin' stuff up! I wanna be the one to give them farmers the blow job!" The more stupid members of the crew thought that was the height of humor and guffawed loudly.

"I thought they was supposed to give us one," another idiot chimed in. "I'd sure like to have…" The second man stopped, being aware enough to read the look on Axyl's face.

"Grogan?" Axyl said softly, taking a half step forward.

"Uh, yeah, Axe?" the biker said, trying to hear him.

"Grogan," Axyl said even more softly.

"Yeah, Axe, what is it?" The man leaned forward slightly but several of the more observant Road Sharks had started to put a little distance between themselves and their more mentally challenged comrade. They noted the momentary look on their leader's face before it had become a neutral mask.

"Oh, Grogan," Axyl said, even more quietly.

"Axe, I can't hardly hear ya," Grogan complained, leaning farther forward.

The boot heel that slammed into the spot just above Grogan's nose came as quick as a rattlesnake's strike. Axyl had purposely kicked the man in the head, reasoning that an impact to his brain was the place least likely to cause noticeable damage.

Grogan went over backwards and the people around him did their best to avoid being in the path of his impressive trajectory, but no one moved to help him as he lay there groaning.

"Do I have everyone's attention?" Axyl asked, almost pleasantly. Heads nodded around the room. "Good."

Grogan, however was starting to get to his feet, groaning and it was obvious he was going to protest his treatment until Cord yanked him from the ground in an impressive display of strength. He grabbed the back of Grogan's neck, slammed him into his now righted chair, slapped the back of his head and growled "Shut up. Listen."

Grogan could understand short simple instructions and he shut up. Cord gestured to Axyl.

"Thank you." The Axe Man continued. "As I was saying, we'll blow a hole in New Hope's compound wall, and then flood in and capture the farmers with superior numbers. HOWEVER, listen to this part CAREFULLY. We want to kill as few of them as possible!"

The disappointed looks in the room were many and varied.

"But.." one man started. Axyl silenced him with a look.

"I know everyone here," he looked at Cord, "well, most of us anyway, like to be there at the moment of the kill, but this is different. We need to look long-term. The farmers are a resource, one we don't want to waste. If we get them under our thumb, we won't have these lean fucking winters like we do every year. We'll make them slaves, but we'll treat them better than we do these poor sods we've been sending east to be the Empire's slaves."

"Why for, Axe?" Porter asked from the back of the room.

"Think about it. These people produce something we need, food that we eat. You don't destroy the beehive to get the honey, you just make the bees work for you." Axyl could see, by the perplexed look on many in the crowd, that he was getting on shaky ground with his metaphor and decided to be more literal, "We're gonna make the farmers work for us, but we can't be too hard on 'em or they won't make the food grow. Or some smart ass will put something in our food. We're gonna let them go on pretty much as they have before, only we'll be in charge."

"So…" MacCombie said hesitantly, "what about their women and kids?"

"In this venture, it is HANDS OFF the women and kids. They're our insurance that the menfolk will do as they're told. We only harm them if some farm boy decides he's not gonna cooperate; if so, his loved ones suffer in his place. It keeps 'em from getting creative."

The looks of disappointment from a majority of the crowd didn't surprise Axyl in the least.

"Look, guys. We are building our own empire here. That means we can't just rely on soldiers. We need farmers and we're gonna need hunters, at least better hunters than we have now. Eventually, after we own New Hope, we'll find all the little communities around here and ALL the resources will be ours. Then we can move outward, with more men and take over. Then you'll be able to kill and rape as much as you like while we expand."

Axyl could see most of them relax. As long as they had the promises of future atrocities, he could keep them in line. He hoped.

"Just how are you gonna pull this off, Axe Man?" Cord drawled from the back, "Far as I can see, the Road Sharks only have about forty to fifty guys on their best day. That don't really seem like an overwhelming force when you go after these farmers inside their stockade."

"There are several independents that help us on an occasional basis. Guys like Benny and Lester, the Shucks, and we're gonna try and recruit the Reds. I've sent out messages and called a meeting with them down at the old Desert Museum in a day or two, that could boost us up to eighty, maybe a hundred. When they see what we're doing, they'll want in permanently, at least those who are able to join a group will."

Everyone was silent for a moment. Even the Road Sharks knew there were some crazies out there even the gangs were afraid to be in proximity of for any length of time. Definitely not team players.

"All righty then. We're going to start trickling small groups up into the area that New Hope is in, and needless to say, if they see any of you early, I will PERSONALLY cut your balls off. I'm going to say who the groups are. Now, any more questions?"

There were none, though some of the men put their hands defensively over their crotches.

****

"I can't help but notice me and my boys are stuck here at headquarters, Axyl," Cord said.

He had caught up with the Axe Man as he'd been on the move toward the upper floors. Axyl looked at Cord with a slight sneer.

"Shell still isn't convinced of your loyalty, Cord. Honestly, if he hadn't been so intent on recruitment for the Sharks, you and your boys might well be already dead and your gear distributed," he said. "I'll be blunt, man. You and your boys tend to be absent when there's hard shit to do to people, and Shell's starting to wonder if you're an asset or a future liability."

"I guess that's blunt enough."

"Listen, Cord, you and your boys want a nice long life, free from being crapped on? Simply do whatEVER the hell the old man tells you, as well and as fast as you can fucking do it. Honestly, it'll be better for you, it'll be better for me, if you lose that suicidal squeamishness you've been showing and get ready to roll in the mud with the rest of us. Call it a survival skill. Those who have too many morals and qualms don't survive long in these parts."

"I hear ya. Seems like this Eli character tends to hold an opposite view."

"Yeah. He does. And one of these days it's gonna cost him. You think on what I said, Cord. I want to be on your side, honest."

As Axyl walked towards the stairs, Cord left him, keeping his face blank as he thought, *you're on our side like a sheepdog's on the sheep's side, asshole. Keeping us all in order so we can be sheared later.*

****

"How did it go, Axyl?"

"Boss, I gotta tell ya it's like trying to herd bears. The stupid ones are somewhat obedient, but you can't hardly get an idea across without hitting 'em over the head to get their attention. With the smarter ones, you never want to turn your back to 'em." Axyl flopped into one of the elderly wing chairs of the office. "Maybe we should'a gone into bootleggin' instead."

"I know it's difficult, but eventually, the bootleggers, other slavers, farmers, indies and vagabonds will all work for us, or they will suffer the consequences." Shell said, his tone deceptively mild. "Gaining control over the farmers is simply our first step. Once you control the food, you control the area and your forces are a lot more ready to do your bidding when they are getting decent rations every day."

"It sounds grand, boss. But sometimes I question what we have to work with."

Shell laughed. "They don't have to be geniuses. They just have to be willing to do violence to whomever should be stupid enough to oppose us." He grew serious. "We are building a kingdom here, Axyl, and while I may be the ruler, you are the crown prince. I'm in my early fifties, I've got maybe twenty years to get this all built, and then you will take over when I retire to the good life. But now, we have to be utterly ruthless, willing to do anything to anyone to make our goals a reality."

"Assuming I'm still alive by then."

"What's this? Don't tell me you're still worried about that Ghost Wind, are you?" Shell asked, surprised. "She's only a woman. What can one woman do to us? Seriously."

"You just don't know what she's capable of. I'm sleeping with one eye open 'til I know she's dead or unable to come after me."

"All of the men have been shown the drawing, and they have orders to capture her, and bring her to me, unharmed. If she's as good as you say, perhaps I can recruit her. A gifted scout and assassin could be worth her weight in gold."

"Oh, boss, you don't want her here. Even if by some miracle she ratted out Eli, and decided to work for us, that still wouldn't change one unalterable fact."

"And that is?"

"And that is she wants my balls on a platter. I screwed her over in more ways than one, and the scouts of the Clan of the Hawk don't forgive."

"Well, if we do manage to find her, and I get the information I want, it doesn't mean I have to live up to any promises to her. I'm the boss, remember? I promise you, if we get a hold of her and I have what I want, I may eventually put her head on the block, and you can chop it off."

CHAPTER TWENTY-THREE
A bad day for all

Eli was having no luck at all.

He had crisscrossed all of the backroads a person could possibly have reached in a single day and night and he hadn't found even the slightest sign of Ghost Wind. He had hoped that she would leave some trace of herself that he could find so they could have talked this out. Eli had found the chink in Kita's armor, and he was sure that Ghost Wind could prove herself if given a chance.

He pulled the Terror over at a wide spot he knew, and hiked up to a rock formation that loomed over the road to sit and think a bit. He sat on a huge flat boulder and looked over the morning landscape, stretching away to seeming infinity, much of it untouched yet by the rising morning sun.

"Crap," he sighed, "I am never going to find her in all this unless she wants to be found. I need to let this go, and hope I run across her again someday soon." The thought made his heart feel heavy.

He took out the note she had found on Lester's body.

'MEET AT THE OLD MUSEUM, SOUTH OF BEND, TUES. FEB 27. WAIT.'

"She didn't know where this was when she handed it to me. Just as well, I wouldn't want her within fifty miles of the place when this goes down."

Shit. February 27th was tomorrow.

Eli had been to the High Desert Museum in the Beforetime. He'd been a kid, chaperoned by one of the Mav-Tech staff and he'd loved all the animals and the history displays. He'd known even back then it hadn't been out of any particular sense of kindness towards him and his siblings that the scientists had taken them out into public places. It had simply been part of the *socializing* of the products of the experiment. He didn't need to be reminded of the old days at Mav-Tech and he had avoided even looking in the museum after the Die-Off.

But tomorrow, it would be time to change that.

****

"Quail eggs would be so nice, this morning, if only I had some."

The morning found Ghost Wind stirring the embers of her tiny fire, trying to coax them into a flame. She had placed some slow burning hardwood on the fire before she had crawled into her shelter and now, she saw just the slightest glow from under the ashes. She put scraped bark tender on the glow and blew on it softly. A thin tremulous plume of smoke began to rise and a few moments later, a tiny flame appeared in the tinder. She carefully stacked tiny twigs on it.

"Unfortunately, it looks like it's going to be jerky and pemmican soup, Go-Go. I'll probably need to do a bit of foraging before I work anymore on my bow, or we'll be down to eating dry grass here pretty soon."

She ate silently, looking out at the pinkish morning cloud formations to the east and, quite without meaning to, thought of Eli. No one could pick up a huge motorcycle like that and carry it around. And how had he healed so fast? If she'd had the kind of injuries Lester and Benny had inflicted upon him, it would have taken her three times the length of time he'd healed in, if ever. She would have most likely died instead.

She wished she could talk to him, convince him to tell her about his past.

That wasn't the only thing troubling her, though. It was his smile. It was those muscles. It was the kindness behind his eyes when he spoke to her. It was very unsettling. Thinking about those big kind brown eyes shifted her right back into a place of sad loneliness.

"Dammit. Enough of that!" She sighed. "Go-Go, soon as I eat I need to go down the hill and check out this stream I've been hearing. I just used most of our water to cook this and it's time for a refill."

She ate her food, listening to the birds sing, and when she was done, she used the last of her water to rinse her old stainless steel canteen cup. Picking up her two metal water bottles, she put a piece of cloth between each and cord-wrapped them together to keep them quiet.

It took her longer to find the water than she thought, and she was very surprised to find it across a backroad at the bottom of the hill. She crossed the road and carefully threaded her way down through young vine maples.

Definitely going to have to find an easier way down through these thickets if I'm gonna stay here, she thought, after hanging up for the third time in a row in the thick foliage. *Either that, or I'll have to manufacture an easier way with knife and hatchet.*

When she finally reached the rocky bank of the stream, the climb down was worth it. The stream was closer to being a small river, and a waterfall ran off moss covered rocks less than fifty feet upstream. The noise of the falls had fooled her into thinking the water was closer than she'd imagined, it drowned out the birdsong and other sounds of the forest. She stepped lithely across a line of rocks leading into the river and pulled her water bottles from where they hung on her sash. She had affixed a loop to the bottles so she could dip them in the water, rather than stick her hands into an icy stream that was coming directly off the snowfields in the mountains.

She looked around as they filled.

It was a beautiful place. It made her wish she had someone to share it with and as she gazed down into the clear blue-green water Eli, once again, sprang to mind. She shook her head, capped the now-full bottles and stood.

Stop daydreaming, and be practical, idiot. Hell. You probably should have camped farther away from his village than you did.

She grabbed a vine maple, and pulled herself back up the bank, fighting her way to the road. She blew out a breath, trying to re-hook the two steel bottles to her sash when she heard it. A buzzing whine and the sound of grit being compressed.

To her horror, as she looked up, she saw six Road Sharks coming right at her full speed on their almost-silent fusion cycles.

Couldn't hear them coming over the waterfall!

Her bottles went flying down the hillside as she tried to run but the lead biker was practically on top of her. His leather braced forearm caught her across the face and her feet went flying into the air while her head smacked hard into the antique pavement.

Ghost Wind struggled to her feet, stars across her vision, only to stagger into the faring of the next rider, sending her flying over the pavement. She made it to all fours when another biker, driving by at full speed kicked her in the ribs, sending her flopping down the road.

Have to get up! Have to get in the brush!

She climbed to her feet once again, hunched over with pain and then made for the path she had just come up. The buzzing of another cycle was coming towards her, and she heard someone say, "Damn! She's a tough little bitch!" Then she felt an impact on the back of her skull.

There were more stars, then there was blackness.

****

Eli rode south, sticking to backroads as was prudent these days. He was going to keep looking until he had to leave for his ambush at the museum.

"Small chance I'm gonna find Ghost Wind now. Guess it's time to do my job." As he road south, he didn't notice the steel water bottles just off the road, or the few drops of blood he drove over.

CHAPTER TWENTY-FOUR
Welcome to the Jungle

The throbbing was like waves on the ocean. One moment, the pain would be manageable, the next it would swell to the point she had to grit her teeth to keep from gasping.

Ghost Wind had found herself tied to the rider bar of a fusion cycle, arms cruelly wrenched back and tied behind her. In front of her was the form of a filthy biker who was trying to keep her sedated with the smell rising from his body and blowing back over her.

Fear lanced through her, and she sought the mind calming techniques that had been so strongly drilled into her by her teacher. Her heart began to slow.

They were coming into a large town, a small city, and driving down the dilapidated main street without a hint of wariness. That could only mean these bastards were in their own territory and had nothing to fear.

Calm your fear, watch as you go. You'll need to know how to escape from this place. Jannelle's voice spoke in her head, as if she had been right at Ghost Wind's ear.

Teacher? Is that you?

Silence.

They drove near a river, heavily overgrown with trees and brush along the edge and she knew if somehow she could reach that, she'd be able to make her way out of here before they could find her. If she could escape. If she could keep from being gang raped and murdered. Her captors were filthy, hard men and they probably didn't know what empathy for others even meant, much less sympathy.

Eventually, they pulled up in front of a large building, ivy and brambles growing over the dead cars in the street and up one side of the building. Metal doors creaked upward and they drove into a parking garage filled with fusion cycles in all states of repair, some so ratty and dirty that they probably no longer ran. Many had been stripped and cannibalized for parts to keep other's running. Even the two mechanics tending them looked badly used.

They pulled up to a large pair of dusty-looking glass doors with the words "City of Bend Administration" on them and the smelly riders got off their cycles and stretched stiff muscles. The one she had been riding behind looked back at her, leering.

"Oh, I do like 'em when they's tied up," he muttered. He started to reach for her breasts when another stepped in front of him.

"No mate, we let you have her tied to your bike, Grogan, but the boss was specific. He said if we found her, we's supposed to bring her to him, alive, unscrewed, and able to talk. So just back away, or Axe'll have your balls!"

"Ain't afraid o' that pretty boy, Porter," the brute grumbled.

"He may be a sight better lookin' than you, Grogan, but if you're ever on the receivin' end of those hatchets of his, you'll be afraid enough to piss yourself. Now we're all gonna be goin' back to New Hope tomorrow so we can finally join up with everyone when we hit the place. I'm gonna need you in working order, man, and you WON'T be if you fuck up and really piss Axe Man off."

Axe. Hatchets. They can only be talking about Axyl!

The anger came boiling up out of the depths of her soul, and when one of the men stepped close to begin cutting her loose from the fusion cycle, he took a step back as he looked into her eyes.

"Boys! I think we'll need a few more guys to get this bitch tied in the pen."

By the time they had her off the bike, they realized they should have wired all of her limbs together. Porter had Ghost Wind's arm twisted up between her shoulder blades, thinking there was nothing she could do when she simply counter-spun away from him, stealing the leverage that he thought he had. The spinning crescent kick to his face took him off his feet and he landed hard.

Another biker tried to punch her, and she dropped under the punch and hit him six times in the ribs with punches so fast they sounded like machine gun fire. As he started to crumple, she snapped a hard kick into his groin. Grogan, came in and took a hard round kick to his face, but being too much of a cave man to realize he was being hurt, managed to hit her hard on the jaw. She went down, stunned.

By the time they chained her to the wall in the slave pen, she had been stripped down to her breechcloth and bandeau, and she had taken a few more punches and kicks. Her captors however were worse for wear and most either limped or were pinching bloody noses, and at least one would probably not be sexually interfering with anyone for a good long time.

As the old jail block door slammed shut, and Ghost Wind's eyes adjusted to the gloom she realized she was far from alone. The smell of fear and unwashed bodies wafted over her, and she saw, chained in various places along the wall, other women. They were stripped down to undergarments in most cases, though a few were nude. All looked at her, the newcomer with a mixture of wariness and pity. And hopelessness.

She looked at her wrists, which had been tied together with old baling wire and then wired to a chain in the wall. The wire, while leaving her a little room for circulation was far too tight to wiggle out of, but she thought she might be able to work the wire link to the chain back and forth enough to get it to snap.

A voice softly drifted over to her, "So if you get loose, what then?"

She looked up and saw one of the women, Latina by the look of her watching intently.

"Better to have my hands loose from the wall than be double bound when an opportunity arises," Ghost Wind replied.

"Yeah. Good luck with that." The woman looked away.

****

"They got her!" Axyl said, walking into the room energetically. "I can't believe it. They fucking got her."

Darwin Shell, once again looking over the street to the river, smiled. He turned toward his beaming lieutenant. "Fortune favors the fortunate in this case, Axyl. She evidently wasn't paying attention and stepped right out in front of Porter and his boys as they were going up to get ready at New Hope. Under the circumstances, I could easily forgive them for postponing that to bring our savage little canary here to sing for me."

Axyl's face darkened. "I'm telling you, boss, when you get the location for Eli and his hidden little village, kill her quick. For my sake, for your sake, for everyone's sake, blow her away all business-like, 'cause she is trouble slash death in a curvy package."

"Really, Axyl. Man-up. She's just a woman. She may bare her teeth and kick of few of our more stupid employees in the crotch, but she's not some primal force as you seem to fear." Shell sighed. "She's just a tool at the moment, one that will give us the means to find the biggest thorn in our side, AKA Eli. We have her, and if she doesn't want some extreme unpleasantness laid upon her, she will do what I tell her."

"Yeah?" the Axe Man replied, stung by the accusation against his masculinity. "Let's see how you feel when she gets loose and runs a sharp knife across your throat late some night."

"Yes, yes, I'm sure. Now how has our deployment to New Hope gone?"

"We're trickling our guys into the area, so as to not get 'em suspicious with a lot of activity. By tomorrow evening, we'll have all our soldiers and the C4 in place."

"I love it when a plan comes together."

****

"Too bad we don't get to have the bitch first!"

Four men came into the cell, growling at the other women, telling them to shut up, then concentrated on Ghost Wind. They came with a strange device she had never seen before and there was no preamble, one of them simply put the device to her shoulder and thumbed a button on the thing.

"GAHHHH!!!"

Ghost Wind thought for a moment that she'd been hit by a lightning bolt, then she stopped thinking other than wanting the pain to stop. When the device was pulled back, she shuddered and trembled so badly that she couldn't control her limbs and a part of her was immensely glad she had used the provided bucket next to her before the men had come. Soiling herself in front of these vermin would have been a terrible humiliation.

They didn't even bother to unwire her wrists, instead simply cutting her bonds with a pair of wire cutters, then re-tying them with what looked like mountain climbing rope from the Beforetime.

"Suck it up, Buttercup," the one called Porter said as they yanked her to her feet. She saw her own heavy homemade blade stuffed into the front of his belt, but she couldn't make her arms work to try for it.

"She ain't such a pistol now, is she?" It was the terrible smelling one hanging on to her arm on the other side. He slapped her hard and she saw stars. "Little payback for that kick to my face earlier, bitch!"

"Time to go see the boss man, girly-girl. And I sincerely hope you try that hard-ass attitude with him. The results will be funnier than hell!" Porter said, "Mr. Shell don't take no shit off no one."

Ghost Wind was not a small woman, but the men simply lifted her so her feet only touched the ground every few steps. They fast-marched her up a flight of stairs to the third floor to a spotless carpeted hallway. Coming to a heavy wooden door, they knocked tentatively, and Porter stuck his head in.

"Uh, hey, boss," he said uncertainly, "we brung the chica, like ya asked."

A rich voice, almost theatrical in its tone, called out, "By all means Porter, bring our guest in! We've all been dying of anticipation to meet her."

They half-dragged her into a luxurious office, with several men standing against the various walls, watching her. She was taken to the center of the room, to a chain with a tow-hook on the end that hung down where once a fancy lighting fixture had been. Her tied hands were looped over the hook. The balls of her feet barely touched the floor, and Porter looked at the set-up disapprovingly.

"She's just a tad too tall, boss. Her tip-toes is touchin' the floor."

"We'll just have to make do, Porter. I'd like to get this show on the road. You and Grogan just stick close to her, and discourage any acrobatics she might want to try out."

Ghost Wind had recovered enough to look around the very cold room, but it was all she could do to remain calm. Anything, *anything* could happen to her here, and no one would intervene, no one would help her. She was entirely on her own in a room full of the worst sort of men.

Calm your mind warrior. Jannelle's voice again sounded in her head. *The calm mind prevails. Gather the information you need to escape.*

She didn't know if her teacher's voice was from the spirit world or from her own psyche desperately trying to hold it together, but Ghost Wind began to observe her surroundings in depth. They had let the fire go out in the makeshift wood stove and the room was very cold on her exposed skin. It was obviously to put her even farther out of her comfort zone, if such a thing were possible.

"Now, Miss Ghost Wind… what a wonderful nom de guerre, so… romantic." An older man dressed in a heavy gray wool military trench coat, smiled at her benignly. "I'm Darwin Shell, perhaps you've heard of me? I know you've heard of my associate, Axyl, the 'Axe Man.' In fact, I believe you have a history?"

"Axyyyyll." The growl came from her throat, as her eyes finally came to rest on the man who had killed her beloved teacher. The sound caused some of the men in the room to look nervously at her, but Axyl literally took a step back, bumping into the wall. He saw a hate in her eyes that warned of painful death if she were ever to get him alone.

"Ah! I see my lieutenant's description of your affection for him was not exaggerated!" Shell grinned. "I guess we'll have to take this slowly, so I can get past the deep feelings you have for him. You may be wondering why you're still alive, when Axyl has been advocating a 'shoot on sight' policy where you are concerned. It's really quite simple, I need information."

To her horror, Ghost Wind felt a scaly hand starting to reach up under her top, to cup her left breast. She turned her head and saw the smelly one, Grogan staring at her chest, his face blank and a thin trickle of drool coming from his mouth as he worked his way towards her nipple. She tried to jerk away.

"Oh for fuck's sake!" Shell yelled, "Grogan! Stop! How can she concentrate when…"

Grogan wasn't hearing his employer's irritation, his eyes looking glazed and hypnotized.

"Axyl, discipline that dog." Shell's pique grew even more when he realized his second-in-command had no intention of going near the woman. "Someone?"

Cord stepped from a shadowy spot by the wall and with some malice hit Grogan in the back of the head. "Your boss is trying to talk, ass-wipe. Quit molesting her so she can fucking concentrate on what he's fucking saying!"

Grogan raised both arms to protect his head, giving Cord a look of pure hate, which Cord returned. For a second, the dark-haired man's eyes met Ghost Wind's, and his look was one of deep shame. He looked away quickly, and returned to his spot by the wall.

"Thank you, Cord. Grogan, don't interrupt me again," Shell said. "As I was saying, miss, we can work things out amicably here. I need something from you, and you very seriously need my good will at this point."

The assault on her person should have left her frazzled, but instead, it focused her warrior self. As she listened to Shell, it crystalized in her that her main intent needed to be escape from this situation, not defiance or revenge on Axyl. With that, as she listened, she watched the room, looking for options.

"What do you need from me, other than the usual things men like you want from a woman?"

"Ah. No pleading, no crying. How refreshing!" Shell said amicably, "What I want from you is very simple, young lady. I want Eli. I want his little hidden town amongst the pines. I know you know them both, so let's make this easy on everybody, especially you, and just give me what I need."

For just a second, she was tempted. She still remembered Kita's nasty reaction to her truthful words and the humiliation of walking out of the village, knowing she wasn't wanted there. But then she remembered Eli, his kindness and Kenji and all the other innocents of Yama No Matsu. But even more than that, she remembered that this was the man who had sent Axyl to murder her teacher and ruin her life.

If she died killing him, she could live with that.

No. You must escape. See the way out before you. Remember the wrist dislocation techniques you were taught. Jannelle's voice sounded so close she looked to the side, expecting her teacher to be standing there. *The path to freedom is right in front of you.*

"I barely know Eli, I only met him two days ago," she said. "He mentioned something about a village, but I thought that was the farm village." She noted that the leader, Shell had her engraved pistol stuck in his belt, barely visible under the heavy military wool coat he wore.

"Oh, I am afraid that is not the answer I want to hear. Let me be honest with you, telling me the truth I want to hear is what is going to keep this from being a very long, painful and humiliating night for you. These randy young bucks are more than happy, in fact eager to come at you one, or maybe two at a time while you hang there helpless. After each one has enjoyed himself, I will ask you my questions again. I would guess after a short time, your attitude will be much more… pliable."

She noted the desk Shell stood behind, right in front of a floor to ceiling plate glass window.

"I'll tell you everything I know! Please, just give me a moment to think of everything he said!"

"Why, of course, my dear, I in no way wish to rush…"

Ghost Wind felt the hoary hand on her bare ribs, moving up towards her top and looked to her left. Once again, the idiot Grogan, face blank and drooling was starting to grope her.

Perfect.

CHAPTER TWENTY-FIVE
What Just Happened?

"Why, of course, my dear, I in no way wish to rush..."

Shell stopped his urbane and gentlemanly reply to his captive when he realized that he, once again, had lost her attention to Grogan's Neanderthal pawing. Fury boiled up as he realized the idiot was directly disobeying his orders yet again. Perhaps some soldiers were simply too stupid to be worth keeping around and feeding.

Shell gestured at the cretin. "Cord, if you please, would you mind kicking the living shit out of this imbecile, please?"

As the dark haired man stepped from the wall again, things went strange.

He saw her flex her feet for a moment then Shell heard a popping sound, like one might hear when ligaments were over-stretched, come from her hands. Immediately afterward, the woman fell to the floor. She landed on all fours, her head lower than her butt, which was aimed towards Grogan. The man's face changed from a blank hypnotized stare to the look of a man who had died and gone to heaven.

Heaven however, was not what he received, quite the opposite.

Looking over her left shoulder, the black haired woman's foot lashed up and straight out into some kind of karate mule kick and her heel impacted Grogan's crotch so hard that Shell was sure he heard the man's testicles squish from ten feet away. The imbecile went up and over backwards, making the sound a pig makes when it knows it's about to have its throat cut and he landed hard. Grogan went into the fetal position instantly, rocking and screaming.

As everyone else in the room, men normally accustomed to violence from other men, stood and gaped, she grabbed the knife from Porter's belt with her one still bound hand and ran the edge along the inside of his thigh. The blade was very sharp and it bit deep. Blood spewed from the inner arteries of his leg and Porter screamed, and went down.

Hands dropped to gun belts as she leapt from the floor onto Shell's desk into a coiled crouch, and Shell vaguely noted that neither of her hands were now tied. She cocked back the arm holding the huge knife, and Shell realized she was about to throw it right between his eyes from a distance of a few feet.

"Wait!" he screamed as the shining flash of steel spun towards him.

"No!"

The wind next to his ear as he involuntarily jerked his head away gave him the realization she hadn't thrown her knife at him. She sent it spinning into the floor-to-ceiling plate glass window he'd spent so many hours looking out of. The glass exploded out over the street and dead cars below.

Shell turned back to his desk to see the woman launch herself at him, much like a mountain lion would. Her strong hands grabbed his collar and a half second later her feet jammed into his stomach. He tried to keep his balance, but the momentum carried them both backwards. His arms windmilling, he heard a shot ring out and something hot burned the side of his neck.

"Shit! Don't shoot! You'll hit the boss!" Axyl's voice rang out.

"Help!" Shell screamed as he fell back, trying to keep his feet under him. And then he realized he was walking on nothing.

****

Ghost Wind knew that the chance of dying in this stunt was quite good.

As she drove Shell through the broken window, trying to put his body between her and any broken glass, she knew the landing was not going to be fun. She shifted her weight when she started to roll forward so that her adversary's body once again rotated under her. The fall seemed to take forever, with the terrible anticipation of its ending looming in her mind. Shell's horror-filled face looked up at her, whites of his eyes showing all the way around and he screamed, realizing his predicament.

"Damn you, you fucking b—"

The impact was harsh to say the least, as both of them landed on a 2027 Toyota Seeker, smashing in the roof. Ghost Wind's powerful legs drove down into Shell and she catapulted out into the dusty street into a shoulder roll, trying to absorb some of the force in counter momentum. She came up hard against a derelict van and saw stars as well as feeling a shooting pain in one wrist, the one she had purposely dislocated earlier.

"Oh. Great Spirit!" She gasped. "That was…" She stood, swaying for a moment. There was no time to be lost. Feeling a shooting pain in one ankle, she staggered over to Shell. Ghost Wind grabbed one of the sleeves of his wool coat and began shaking him out of it.

"Augh!" His pained scream told her he had regained consciousness. "Stop! Please! My back, I think it might be broken!"

"How awful for you," she replied, pulling him out of the first sleeve and flipping him face down onto the hood of the car. "That must be really painful!"

"NGHH!" Shell sobbed. "You bitch, my legs just went numb! I can't feel my legs now!"

"Karma's a bitch, and now, so am I." She knew she had to work fast. She pulled the coat the rest of the way off, stripped the man's sneakers off his feet, grabbed her pistol and knife and did what the Scouts of the Clan of the Hawk did best.

She disappeared into the twilight.

****

They all stood frozen for a moment as the woman and their leader backed out into thin air through the broken window. They all heard the impressive crash sound seconds later. Axyl, usually pretty fast to adapt to new situations, took several moments before he recovered enough to run to the now open-air window to look down at the carnage below.

Shell lay face down on a derelict car. Axe could see the dent in the roof where he had obviously impacted and he heard the man groan in pain. He saw no sign of Ghost Wind but he knew she was out there, waiting to cut his throat.

"Listen up!" he shouted, "The boss is in a bad way. I want two of you to get Doc Mullins and a stretcher and get him back indoors where he can be tended to. I want everyone else to get out there and find that bitch from hell, and I want her SHOT ON SIGHT! Is everyone clear on that? Kill her if you have any opportunity. If she's alive I... we all... are in danger. She's sneaky as hell, and can cut your throat before you know you're dead. Understand me. Kill her on sight!"

They all stood dazed, no one moving except Porter whimpering as his blood ran out.

"Move! NOW, damn you!" They broke for the door like a wave. Cord was the only one who didn't hurry.

"Cord! You get a tourniquet on Porter's leg. Let's see if we can keep him alive."

"What about Grogan?" Cord gestured towards the smelly Road Shark now up and leaning heavily on Shell's desk.

"Let me take care of our Mr. Grogan, Mr. Couldn't Keep from Fucking Up." Axyl walked up behind Grogan, reaching between his legs from behind, grabbing him by the crotch in his right and the man's neck in his left. Grogan screamed that pig scream again as Axyl calmly walked him to the edge of the broken window and kept walking him through it.

Axyl had made sure to hang onto the man's crotch a half second longer than his neck to ensure Grogan went head first and was not disappointed. He calmly watched as his former comrade went sailing down, screaming all the way and winced slightly at the sound of a muffled impact.

"Oh dear," he said, looking back at Cord who was affixing his belt to Porter's upper thigh.

"What?"

"I think we're going to have to change poor Grogan's name!"

Cord had no love for the smelly biker, and a good idea where this was going, "Oh?" he asked.

"Yep. Let's remember him by his new name…"

"Which is?" Cord waited, eyebrow raised.

"Lawn Dart!" Axyl began to go into uncontrolled fits of laughter. *Hysterical laughter,* Cord thought to himself.

CHAPTER TWENTY-SIX
Little help here?

Eli was being excruciatingly careful. Riding past the old city was always tricky and he had no intention of giving himself away. Passing the belly of the beast the Road Sharks had made of this area, with all its traps and ambush points, made him not want to make any stupid mistakes. Eli had seen what happened to people when they let the Sharks get the upper hand.

It was close to dark. He was on a backstreet, as far out from the city center as possible and pushing the Terror on foot. Fusion cycles were very quiet in comparison to their combustion engine predecessors but they still made noise, a droning sound that, if listened for, could give a biker away. The enemy had many years to lay traps and ambushes and Eli had run afoul of a few. One or two had been near misses, and his nerves were keyed up.

When the ragged silhouetted figure stepped out of the brush in front of him, he braced his motorcycle and pulled his handgun in less time than it took to blink. It was only the need for silence which prevented him from pulling the trigger but when the person stepped out of the dark shadows, he was very glad he hadn't.

"Hello, Eli." Ghost Wind said. He noticed she was limping, and seemed none too steady on her feet. As she came close he saw her face was bruised and scratched and she looked like she had a shiner on her left eye, just above her old scar. She'd obviously been through the wringer.

And she still took his breath away.

"Ghost Wind! Good God! What happened? Are you all right?"

"I am now. Get me the hell out of this place! These bastards are all insane."

He noted the heavy wool military coat, with her revolver sticking out of one large pocket, and her heavy knife in one hand. What surprised him most though was that she was wearing what appeared to be a pair of Beforetime tennis shoes, the kind that had been nicknamed "Chucks," on her feet. Her legs were bare.

"We're almost through the Shark's home turf. If we can get a little further south, I can fire up the Terror and we can make some time. I can't risk starting it up now." He told her, "You get on and steer, while I push and you're going to have to be the alert one so I don't run us into one of their ambushes or traps."

"They're searching for me, the ones who haven't gone up to New Hope."

That brought him up short. "New Hope? What's going on there?"

"The people they have guarding the slave pens are not exactly the sharpest tools in the shed. They tended to drop bits and pieces of information. They're planning on some sort of attack of the compound tomorrow night."

"I was on my way down to the meeting they're calling at the old High Desert Museum. I would bet the meeting has something to do with this attack they're planning. New Hope is not an easy target."

She was silent a moment.

"Eli? I think I am well enough to ride, if you will take me with you. If I can get off my feet for a little bit, I might even be useful."

"I should just find a good place to hide you until I get back, this is going to be a little iffy, danger-wise and I don't really want to risk you getting captured or killed. Don't think I don't have a lot of respect for you and your skills, but I'm not sure I could stand it if I got you killed."

"When is the meeting?"

"I'm pretty sure it's later tonight, so I need to get my ass a movin' and I can't look after you at the same time." He expected an argument, hopefully a quiet one, but her next suggestion mangled his own argument with a totally unfair dose of common sense.

"I can warn New Hope and possibly tell Yama No Matsu what is going on while you're down there. I just need your help."

"My help? Ghost Wind, how the hell are you going to get back there in time?"

"You are going to help me steal a fusion cycle."

****

"Nuthin' like a warm fire on a cold night," Olaf said to himself.

Olaf was not exactly the prime example of a Road Shark. Oh, he enjoyed the privileges of being one of the gang, but in another far off age, he would have been considered 'shy.' Not the shy that has trouble speaking to strangers, but more along the lines of a complete lack of desire to do anything dangerous. He took a lot of shit for that, but as he often told himself, many of the ones who had called him chicken hadn't survived for long, and he was still kicking.

Not wanting to rely too heavily on his fighting spirit, his leaders had given him a lot of duties that bored the hell out of most of their men. Olaf was fine with them.

He didn't mind sitting for mind numbing hours at a roadside checkpoint-ambush, he didn't mind guarding the bikes, he didn't mind walking half the length of town to scrounge something the boss wanted. What he minded, was being shot at or having to fight people who had a vested interest in spilling his blood. Didn't want that, didn't want to have to try to chase people down, when he could just pick 'em off from the brush and he didn't want to ever have to face that Eli bastard again. He'd wound up with a dislocated shoulder at New

Hope, and even though Doc Mullins had put it back in place, it still ached. He hadn't even seen that son of a bitch coming before he was down in the dirt screaming.

At least he was better off than Pid and Stanley.

No one was likely to be coming down the road in the dark, and he probably should have gone back to the 'barn' to see if they wanted him to do some other bullshit job, but he had built a small fire to keep warm, and was in no hurry.

"Nice night," a voice said.

Olaf looked up, and the devil stepped out of the darkness in front of him. Olaf froze, not even thinking about reaching for the deer rifle next to him and trying very hard not to pee himself.

"Olaf, isn't it?" Eli said. "We've crossed paths a couple of times now, as I recall. Um.... did you want to try for your rifle there?"

"Oh shit, no!" The reluctant Road Shark kicked the rifle hard enough to send it into the brush. "Please don't kill me, Eli!"

"Wellll, I dunno. I mean you are a Road Shark and all, and I DID let you off pretty easy a day or so ago. A smart man might have taken the hint and cleared out, but here you are, goin' about the Shark business of setting ambushes. I will admit, your heart obviously isn't in it. Kinda hard to ambush someone when you're staring into a warm fire."

"I just been doin' what they tell me, man! I don't want trouble, but y'know when you're in the Sharks, you do what Shell tells you. Or... at least we did."

"Make yourself valuable, Olaf. What's the situation there? And if I find out you've lied to me..."

"Shell ain't in charge no more! Axe Man is. Shell's bombed out of his mind on meds since some hardass chick kicked him out a third story window and broke his back."

"Hmmm. Interesting." Eli smiled widely at Olaf, knowing who the hardass chick had to have been, "Say, Oley, I hear there's a meeting down at the old Museum tonight. Brief me."

"Uh, Axe is goin' down there to recruit all the indie bikers in the areas to the south and east...."

"Recruit them for what?"

"Um," Olaf knew he's said too much now and was trying to figure out something to tell this demon from hell. Unfortunately, he did not have the best poker face.

One moment, Eli was on the other side of the fire, the next he was standing next to Olaf and had his right hand in a vice-like grip. He slowly bent Olaf's middle finger until the tip was pressing against his palm, and then pushed down on the joint next to the knuckle. Pain exploded throughout Olaf's world and he went up high on his toes.

"Okay! Okay! Okay! Stop! Please, Eli!" he said, panting for air. "I'll tell you! I'll tell you everything!"

"Good fellow. Now what is the plan?"

Olaf had no idea what, if anything Eli knew, but he wasn't going to take a chance and tell him a lie. The Road Shark's plans were not worth his own ass.

"Shell has been tricklin' guys up into the New Hope area for the last day or so. Tomorrow night, after almost all the troops are up there, hidin' in the trees, they's gonna blow a section of their wall with C4 they got from this "empire" to the east. Then they're gonna rush in while everyone's still stunned and take the place and make the farmers into their own personal food workers." Olaf was spilling his guts so fast, he had to pause a moment to catch his breath. "Then the Road Sharks will control the farm food supply for the this whole region, enough so that we won't have short rations in the winter and the Sharks'll have more clout to take over the whole region."

"Quite a plan."

"Goddamn, I didn't come up with it! That's about all I know other than the attack is supposed to happen around midnight, tomorrow night! AH! GOD! Please, Eli, let go m' hand!"

"Oh," Eli said, absentmindedly, "Sure. So, I have one more question, Olaf, an important one, so pay attention. This afternoon, the Sharks had a young woman trussed up. They beat her and were making some pretty awful threats. Oley, were you one of those men?"

"Shit no! I been stuck out here since sunrise, Eli! I didn't have nuthin' to do with it. When those guys start in on them girls, I make myself scarce. I know you won't believe it, but I hate the screaming. It's just pure awful to hear."

"I see. Well, let me confirm that. Ghost Wind?"

She stepped out from behind a nearby tree and one look into her intense blazing eyes convinced Olaf that if she decided to say she recognized him, Eli would snap his neck right then and there, no appeal. She looked at him for a moment, contempt in her eyes and turned and walked away.

"I didn't see him there," she said over her shoulder. She blended in with the darkness like a shadow.

"Well, I think that's all we need." Eli paused a moment. "You mind if I borrow your bike there, Olaf?"

He gulped, but Olaf was no fool, "Take it if'n you want it, man. I'll figure out somethin' to tell 'em."

"About that... Olaf, you'll agree, I could have killed you this morning, right?"

"Uh.... Yeah?"

"And yet, here you are, still with the Road Sharks. It seems it would be folly to give you another chance, when you didn't take the first one."

"Oh God! Please, Eli! I promise…" Eli held up a hand, and Olaf went silent.

"Ole, you've been very cooperative, and I have to count that in your favor, so, tell you what I'm gonna do. The next time I see you in Road Shark colors, I'm going to tell that young lady there, who by the way makes my skills at stealth look sick, I'm gonna tell her you need your throat cut. And you know what? You will NEVER see her coming until your life's blood is running down your hairy chest. Do you see where I'm going with this?"

"Uh… you're gonna let me live?"

"Yes. I'm gonna let you live. But let me spell it out for you so there's no mistake. I'm going to wipe out the Road Sharks. If I find you with them, you're dead, sorry to tell you, Oley. So, if I were you, I would pack my gear, steal another ride, and quietly get the hell outta here. I think you might live a lot longer if you do."

"Dude, by tomorrow morning, I swear to you I will be a hundred miles from here. You got my promise!"

"Okay, then! I think our business is concluded. Hopefully I won't see you later, Olaf."

"No way. Eli, thanks for not killin' me!"

The tall man waved as he walked away. Eli looked back over his shoulder as he turned Olaf's fusion cycle down the road, the way he had come. "I got your promise, right?"

"Fuck, yes!"

"Good man."

****

Later, after sneaking into the fairly depopulated garage with a backpack and a pair of saddle bags, Olaf found Shell's personal fusion cycle, beauty that it was, unguarded and fully charged. Just before dawn the next day, somewhere near the Nevada border, he thought about his former companions and started to laugh.

He'd never liked those fuckers anyway.

CHAPTER TWENTY-SEVEN
You're Not the Boss of Me

Axyl began to miss Shell in a very short time.

Well, not actually miss the man so much, Shell was actually just across the room in the new office they were moving everything into. He was lying in a portable bed they had scrounged from the hospital, high out of his mind on their precious dwindling supply of Beforetime pain meds.

What he missed was Shell's way of thinking. Axyl was good at short-term planning and keeping the troops in line but he wasn't much good at the long-term big picture stuff. His current question was whether to continue their current campaign against New Hope without Shell's guidance or to abort and pull back.

"Axyl," Doc Mullins peeked around the door. "We've made him as comfortable as possible, and I've got him on Perc 3 to ease the pain. Our meds are a bit past their prime, but a least he's not in agony. His back is definitely broken and with the facilities we have here, I doubt Shell will ever walk again."

"You don't seem to be too broken up about it, Doc."

"I'm here because he gave me no choice, Axyl. I took a healer's oath to help those who need medical attention, but I often wish I was helping a group who was worth it."

"You never know, Doc. Someday maybe we'll be better."

"Or I'll find a better class of patient." Doc walked out the door.

Axyl smiled. Everyone would be singing a happy song if they could get control over New Hope and all the food production, even Doc. And that brought him to the Indies. He had to be the one to go down to the old museum and convince all the outside operators to join in the attack with the Road Sharks. Axyl had always been the one to do the convincing when it came to troops.

He needed to delegate the task of getting the troops in place around the farming community and who the hell could he trust from this bunch? If Cord wasn't such a namby pamby asshole, he would have been the ideal choice, being smarter than most of the Road Sharks, but Axe couldn't trust him.

"Porter is out. Sky Rider? Yeah, maybe." The Rider was the oldest member of the Sharks, and had been a real badass back in the Beforetime. The thing was, he was almost seventy years old now and had pretty much drawn the light duty jobs for the last several years. "Sure, he's old, but he's managed to not get killed during the collapse of the old republic and to survive everything the after times had thrown at him. He's pretty sharp for an old guy."

Sky Rider could also take directions and carry them out, generally without fucking up. Axyl would just have to lay down the law that anyone who didn't follow the old man's orders would be in for a ton of bricks coming down on their skull.

He rose from the desk, carrying the small notebook he had been filling with knowledge from Shell. Axyl realized with a start, that he no longer thought of Shell as his boss anymore.

If the newly crippled man could be of some use with strategy and planning, then he might still be worth keeping around. If he was going to just sit there and suck down their medical resources, well, he was gonna have to go. Maybe Doc could wean him to just pot. Plenty of that around.

Axyl smiled for a moment. By God, he was starting to think like the big boss... he WAS the big boss. And Shell was either an asset, or a liability.

And if it was the latter, he wouldn't be around long.

CHAPTER TWENTY-EIGHT
You've Got to Believe

There was no real reason they couldn't just go back to New Hope or Yama No Matsu. They knew the main gist of the Road Shark plan and with the Sharks you probably couldn't make any plan too complicated. Eli doubted they would learn much more about the plan by sitting in on the meeting taking place at the old museum. He was for turning around and heading back to tell their allies what was up and he was surprised when Ghost Wind resisted.

As he checked over their newest bike, she said. "If Shell isn't the one to address these 'Indies' then as his second-in-command, Axyl will probably be the one to go, won't he?"

"Probably." He looked up at her, "Why?"

"Because then I, for the first time in almost a year, know where he will be, and when."

"And you're sure that the Road Shark's Axeman is the one who, basically, ruined your life, killed your teacher, got you banished?"

"I saw him, Eli," she growled. "He was there in the room when they hung me from a chain and threatened to gang rape me until I told them what they wanted to hear about you. In his defense, he DID plead for his boss to just shoot me in the head, so there's that."

"Fuck." Eli felt anger rising deep in his chest, "What are you thinking about him being there at the museum?"

"I'm thinking of coming up behind him and chopping his head or his balls off so that they all go bouncing across the concrete. Maybe both, balls first, head second."

"Ghost Wind, you're so sore and lamed you can barely walk straight. Besides, you and I, we need to be in two places at the same time."

"What do you mean?"

"We need to warn both Yama No Matsu and New Hope about what's goin' down. I intend to convince Kita we need to get our warriors to sneak up on the Sharks from behind, while you have Horace and his people ready to kill them as they get near the walls."

"I have a better idea. I'll go to this museum, you can come along if you wish, and end this. If I kill Axyl, and the one called Shell is crippled, then these Road Sharks will have no leadership."

He pondered for a moment. There was some merit to what she said, though he doubted in her condition she could deliver on her promises as well as she thought she could.

"Yeah, I see there's some wisdom there, but you're not taking into consideration the variables."

"WHAT variables?" she said angrily. "I kill him, they have no leadership, and maybe the whole gang falls apart."

"You're assuming all the Road Sharks are as stupid as the foot soldiers you've seen. I know for a fact, there are some old wolves in the pack who can think for themselves, and they've probably been deployed to the farming village to keep order. The plan is fairly simple, and there is no guarantee if Shell and Axyl don't show up they won't go ahead and attack. Once they're in, they are in control of the compound and it's going to be very hard to remove them. Who knows how many of the farmers will be killed or injured in the process."

Ghost Wind scowled towards the north.

"There's one other thing," he said. "You're injured."

"I'll be fine."

"Bullshit. You've been trying to hide from me that your ankle is pretty badly sprained, and you keep babying your left wrist. It's obvious to anyone with eyes that you've had quite a beating, and I can't even tell what injuries you've got under that big ol' coat. Right now, I think you'd have a tough time slipping through to New Hope, much less through a multitude of Indies to reach Axyl."

The uncertainty in her eyes was all he needed to see to know he was right. She hid it quickly, and he braced himself for the inevitable argument. She surprised him.

"You're right, Eli." She glanced at the ground, with a look of shame. "The pain in my ankle keeps getting worse, the more I'm on it. But I'm a warrior and if I can't help with this, of what use am I to you, or your people, or the people of New Hope? I must do this or I am worth nothing!"

And there it is, Eli thought, *a need for self-worth. To be useful. And being a warrior is the only way she knows to be useful.*

Eli stepped toward her, carefully and slowly. He gently enfolded her in big arms and drew her to his chest. He leaned his cheek against the top of her head and said in his low rumbly voice, "You are worthy, Ghost Wind, just by being you. As for my people and me, we can be pretty sure that in a short time, we'll all marvel at our luck that you'd stay with us."

He felt her begin to tremble, and he hoped he hadn't overstepped his bounds. She pulled back and looked up at him and the man from the past was surprised to see tears flowing down her face.

"I want to help," she said, wiping her eyes, "not for revenge, but to show Kita I am useful. She said I was unwelcome…"

"Kita and I had a little talk." He said, "After hearing how you saved my life, she said she would give you an opportunity. What you do with that opportunity is up to you."

She looked at the ground, considering. "What can I do then, Eli? I know I can crawl through the vermin surrounding New Hope, without standing on my ankle, but it will take half a day to make it there on my belly. Then how do I get Horace's attention?"

"I don't think that plan of having you go to New Hope is the best way to go, now."

"Then what?"

"I think that you need to go see Kita and convince her to deal, not with the fellows hanging around New Hope but—"

"The indies coming north with Axyl!"

"Precisely, Kita can field fifteen half-trained warriors with rifles. If you all can get a proper ambush set on the main road up from Bend, maybe we can divide and conquer the Road Sharks."

"Eli, she won't listen to me."

He looked at her, not quite certain of what he was about to say, but somehow, he knew if he let it flow, it would come out right.

"Listen to me, he said, "you are the warrior scout Ghost Wind. You were trained by the masters of the Clan of the Hawk. There is very little you cannot accomplish if you BELIEVE that you can do it. I'm not going to tell you how, I'm only going to say what must get done, then I'm getting out of your way. Convince her, Ghost Wind."

She looked at him a little dubiously.

"All right, but you need to teach me how to ride this infernal machine first."

****

There was a certain amount of evidence that Eli was trying to kill her, not teach her to ride a six hundred pound fusion powered motorcycle.

It seemed that for the last few days, her life had been one of fear and flight but when she told the big dark handsome man that she needed to learn to ride this monster, she'd left herself open for a different kind of fear.

He had ridden beside her for a time, as she had learned the basics of balancing the monstrous machine, actually holding onto the cargo bar in back while leaning across from the Terror. He had shown her how to accelerate with the hand throttle, the basics of braking and the foot shifting of the gears, but he couldn't show her how to be comfortable on the big machine.

"AHHH! Hellbats!" she yelled as she dumped the bike for the third time that evening. "Damn it! Damn it! Damn it!"

She had rolled away at the last second, narrowly missing being under the bike and had left a little of her hide on the ancient pavement. If she had still had her deerskin pants, she would have come out unscathed, but the thought of that just made her mood darker. She kicked the overturned machine.

"Impressive road rash," Eli said blandly, "you still up for this?"

She limped around the fusion cycle, feeling like ten miles of very bad road. "It's not like there's a choice, is there?"

"Actually, for someone who's never ridden a bike before you're doing pretty well. You just need to be a little more careful in these sharper turns until you and the bike become one."

"I doubt I will live that long." She wheeled on him "And if you say 'never say never,' I swear I'm going to punch you!"

He raised his hands in front of him, "Okay, time for a break. It's just about sunrise, so you go to that tree there, and I will rustle us up a snack while you rest for a little bit."

Eli walked both cycles off the road a space and rummaging through his saddle bags pulled out a waxed cotton sack. He walked over to where Ghost Wind sat, her hand over her eyes, head tilted back against the tree.

He handed her a stick of jerky, and uncapped his water bottle. He passed it to her and asked "So, how are you holding up?"

"I'm not sure I've ever been this sore and tired, even during my scout trial. You were right, I just need to sit and rest for a bit." She leaned her head against him, and within a few seconds was snoring lightly. He caught the piece of jerky before it slipped from her fingers and she woke slightly to say, "Eli? Sorry… yelled at… you." And she was gone again.

Eli smiled, and watched the sun rise over the eastern desert. He put his arm around her, but she didn't wake up. He sat and lived completely in that cool early morning moment, wishing the sun would take its time in rising.

****

Ghost Wind hadn't wanted to awaken in the short two hours they were there, but she had snapped to consciousness with Eli's light touch on her arm. Sunlight was in her eyes and she needed to stretch to get the blood flowing again.

Everything hurt, the results of being run down, clubbed, beaten and a fall from a third-story window. She'd been lucky on that, if she hadn't landed on Shell's overfed stomach, it would have probably been much worse. She limped slowly towards her 'new' fusion cycle, and climbed on.

"You sure you're ready for this?" Eli asked her.

"Do I have a choice but to be ready? I know how to use the clutch and to shift now, and I'm pretty sure fear will keep me from falling asleep."

"I dunno, for a cave woman, you're picking this up pretty fast. You've had a few spills, but I can see when you ride, that you're instinctively learning to lean and shift your weight correctly. I think you're a natural!"

"I'm sure your flattery will carry me through," she said, giving a slight smile to take any sting from the words. "I need to go now, though. I've memorized the route you showed me. Let's hope the Road Sharks haven't set up any new checkpoints along that way."

"I'd find it unlikely they would. This little plan of theirs is taking most of their forces. They would almost have to pull people from check points and ambushes to pull it off, but be careful anyway."

She started to give a sharp remark but remembered she had been caught flat footed when her awareness faltered earlier. She only nodded.

"Fare you well, Eli Five. I hope we see each other again."

"I feel the same way, miss. Let's just say 'via con Dios' and leave it at that."

****

The trip was not as hard as she feared it would be. As rough as she felt, after riding a while she realized Eli and not been 'shining her on' about her ability to ride the big machine. The farther she rode, the more she and the fusion cycle became one on the turns and twists. Great Spirit forbid she would admit it, she was feeling exhilarated with each lean and recover.

My teachers would be having a fit if they could see me now.

She resolved not to get too far in love with it though. Riding a vehicle down the center of a paved roadway, no matter how dilapidated, was hardly the stealthy Way of the Scout. Stealth, awareness and strategy had kept her alive this long and she didn't want to lose those skills in pursuit of a new toy.

She was alert for choke points, but Eli had called it right. The only other beings she saw were winged or four legged. She learned about slowing down if even a hint of a deer was at the road, and once missed using her cycle as a hunting weapon by mere inches.

"Watch out you nitwit!" she yelled as she just missed grazing a buck. A person from the Beforetime would have been amazed at the number of animals about, but Ghost Wind found them a bit of a nuisance at that moment.

She was just passing through a stretch of backroad when her attention was caught by markings in the dust, and she realized this was where, just twenty-four hours before she had run afoul of the Road Sharks.

"Spirits preserve me." She shivered as she remembered the viciousness of her captors, and her determination to pay them back came back strong. She pulled over the fusion cycle and got off. She could read the story as plainly as she could read printed words. She could see each stagger as she had been struck repeatedly and even her own outline where she had finally fallen. She shivered again.

Remembering what she had been doing, she walked down the bank and found her steel water bottles. Retrieving them, she took a drink.

"Still cold. Now I just need to stay the same way." She looked up the hill. Her gear was still up in her tight little shelter and contemplated if she should retrieve it. "No time. It's fine where it is, and it would take too long to secure it to this thing."

Ghost Wind headed north again.

CHAPTER TWENTY-NINE
Don't Want to Believe

"Train hard!" Kita barked at her flagging students. "You must be able to go beyond your tiredness when you defend yourselves and this village!"

The gakusei, the students, renewed their efforts to make the attacks and block with the heavy wooden swords. They knew their teacher was right and that someday, their lives might be saved by being able to go that extra few inches beyond what they believed they could. Eventually, their sensei, their teacher, said, "That's enough for today. Tomorrow, archery again."

The sweat-soaked gakusei bowed off the floor and went to sponge off with wet towels marked "Hilton." They were used to practicing hard, but sensei Kita had pushed them this session, almost with desperation and their normal hour and a half had stretched on an extra hour. There would be many sore muscles in the morning.

As they began to file out, Kita's demeanor softened, and she talked with a few of her students as she left. Kenji was one of the last to leave, and Kita stopped him for a moment.

"Kenji. You're still falling for that high feint Roger keeps throwing at you. Are those ribs bruised enough that you might consider not falling for it anytime soon?" She smiled at him, but he knew she was serious.

"Sorry, Sensei," the young man blushed, "he just comes at me so fast, I can't seem to see the second attack coming!"

"It will come with time. For now, just keep practicing your cuts, and tomorrow, you can show him up on the archery range." Kita escorted him to the door, and watched him as he went down the path to the main part of the village. He looked back and waved at her, and she smiled and gave a slight wave back.

"He's a good kid. Glad he's learning to defend himself." A voice spoke from somewhere to Kita's left. She whirled, inwardly cursing that all her weapons were in the dojo, and saw no one. She looked around carefully, and finally noticed the shape sitting just outside the edge of the doorway, sitting native style on the porch floor at the far end of the bench that sat there. A familiar face looked up at her.

"You! What are you doing here? Where is Eli?"

"Are your people any good with firearms?"

"Answer my question, young woman!"

The shape on the floor elongated into the shape of a human, and as she walked towards Kita, the sword master could see the younger woman was limping. As she stepped into the sunlight, Kita was shocked to see her face. Ghost Wind looked as if she had gone five rounds with a street brawler and come up short.

"My God, girl, what the hell happened to you?" she said, looking with fascinated horror at the bruises all over the Scout's face.

"I tripped. As for Eli, he's sneaking into New Hope to warn Horace and friends."

"Warn them? Warn them about what?"

Ghost Wind looked at her. "That the Road Sharks are coming to take over New Hope. To warn them that the Sharks have recruited an extra forty or so men to help with the siege and that the bastards have C-4 to blow down their walls, that's what. But that's not the question you should be asking."

The two women looked at each other, locking gazes.

"What IS the question I should be asking?" Kita asked.

"The question," a grim half smile appeared on Ghost Wind's battered face, "is why am I here to talk to you."

Kita waited without asking.

"All right," the scout said, sitting on the bench, "the answer is I'm here to ask you and your students to help me to ambush all these independents who'll be going to New Hope."

Kita stepped back. "You must be joking! These people are trained for the defense of THIS village, I'm not about to take them all over the country side looking for trouble!"

"And what about your neighbors? From what I understand, you trade with Horace and his people on a fairly regular basis. You just going to leave them high and dry?"

"I don't even know you, girl. I certainly don't know if I can trust you, and certainly I don't want to trust you with the lives of my people!"

"Eli told me you would say that." The younger woman looked down the hill, across the small village, "I told him I needed a note because you would never trust an outsider, hopefully you can recognize his scrawling." She handed Kita and note written on the back of an old piece of junk mail.

She read; *Kita, please listen to what Ghost Wind has to tell you. I know you're not going to like the idea of visiting the rest of the world, but there is a time to stay hidden, and a time to come out of your safe place to ensure your future. Have Ghost Wind place your people along the MAIN ROUTE up from Bend and she can help them be invisible. If New Hope is going to have a chance, the indies Axe Man has recruited have to be whittled down considerably, and yours are the only fighters available. We can't hide in the mountains forever. If New Hope falls, it makes it that much easier for the Sharks to come looking for us. TRUST HER! - Eli*

Kita didn't want to trust this strange young girl. Not because she didn't believe her, but because she didn't want to believe her.

"Come inside. I will fix you some soup, and speak with my students."

****

They were all looking at her a little apprehensively. Ghost Wind wiped the last of her stew from her lips with the back of her hand and noted that Kita's student warriors were all ages, from a man in his late fifties to sixteen year-old Kenji. She guessed their apprehension was probably reasonable, as she stood there, looking beat to hell in a big old wool coat, Beforetime shoes and not much else.

Had she been able to get into their heads, she would have known that all of those considerations would have paled next to the wolf-like expression of her eyes.

"I understand some of you have actual experience fighting your enemies, and I'm hoping that you can recognize the need to do it again. Would those people please stand over there?" She pointed to a spot on the other end of the dojo porch and a middle aged woman, a young man and the older man moved. "I want all of you to know, that it is a certainty, that if you come with me you will wind up killing men. If you come with me, and you find you can't, the likelihood is high instead that you will killed instead. This is serious."

"Who are we killing, and why?" a young red haired girl asked.

"Good. Direct and to the point," Ghost Wind said. "The who are a bunch of part-time Road Sharks who are going to reinforce the Shark regulars in overrunning and taking over New Hope. The why is so that the slime bags fail in the attempt, as well as culling the population of said slime bags for everyone's benefit."

The girl nodded. "Works for me."

"You must be mad!" A thirty-something man chimed in. "We're going to go down there and murder these men... out of the blue? With no provocation?"

Everyone looked at him as if he had just gone insane.

"All right, they're a pretty awful bunch, but we can't just stoop to their level and commit murder. Sensei says her arts are to be used for defense." He took a deep breath and stepped off the porch. "I have NO intention of going down there and participating in this, especially under the order of some young ragamuffin girl!"

"What's your name?" Ghost Wind asked.

"Tam." he said suspiciously. "Why?"

"Tam, thank you for letting me know where you stand ahead of time. Does anyone else feel strongly the same way Tam does?"

"This is not a dojo test," Kita said. "This is deadly serious, so be honest."

A smallish woman in the back stepped off of the porch and stood next to Tam, but she was unable to raise her eyes to meet those of her sensei. A couple of the students wavered, but stayed where they were.

Kita stood. "All right, Kenji and Arianna, you will stay here also."

Both Kenji and the red headed girl looked at her in astonishment.

"No arguments!" Kita shouted, "It will be a cold day in hell before I take sixteen-year-olds into a war zone to fight seasoned killers. You two, Tam and Rosie will be the home defense. If this goes wrong, you four will arm the villagers and organize a defense with the people here. If our enemies find this place you will be the ones who must stop them. Do you understand?" They nodded.

"The rest of you, meet us at the armory in ten minutes."

****

"Here is how this will go down, warriors," Kita told her assembled students as she passed out the odd mixture of deer rifles and assault weapons contained in the armory. "Ghost Wind here will help us conceal ourselves at this point on old 97. Eli seems to be very confident that is the route our prey will take and we are going to catch them in the mother of all ambushes."

She looked around at the young scout woman and her own nervous students, wishing there were some way to not have to take these people into battle.

"Does everyone have their sword? Ervin crafted some very good blades for us, and if we can't shoot these dogs down, there's a chance that swords will come in to play. I know we have all trained in the dojo, but there is a world of difference when you are striking at a living being, filled with blood. If we set this trap right, we'll take most of them out with bullets and arrows."

"Sensei, how many kilabykers are we talking here?" asked the oldest man.

"Around forty, Mort."

"And there's sixteen of us, plus you and young Ghost Wind there. Them odds are a little steep in the wrong direction."

"Yes, unless our trap is very well laid, and we can cut the odds dramatically at first contact," Ghost Wind said, looking down at a very fine Beforetime recurved bow. "Some of you will be archers, stationed where the enemy will first come by. After half of them have passed, we will quietly try to take as many of the rear guard as we can without alerting the men in front. The question is, how do we get everyone down to the ambush site in time?"

Kia half smiled. "I think we have that covered."

The rest of the group smiled with her.

****

Ghost Wind stood for a second, in the well-camouflaged doorway and stared. There were almost forty fusion-powered motorcycles in the old hatchery motor pool, and most looked like they were usable. She looked at Kita.

"Eli said you needed to use a horse-drawn wagon to trade with Horace! What is this?"

Kita let her own smug gaze drift over the assorted hardware, "We've been scrounging for fusion powered vehicles almost since the village was founded. Half of our people are experienced riders, but only about a third of these are actually in working condition. We keep hoping we can find an experienced fusion-gen mechanic but no luck so far. But everyone of them we have here, is one less the kilabykers can use against us."

The students began rolling the machines from the shop. Ghost Wind found herself impressed with the cool efficiency they displayed getting the bikes and gear ready to move out.

"You can ride behind one of the men. I want everyone who can ride to have a fusion cycle and—"

"I have my own bike." Ghost Wind interrupted the older woman, then began to chuckle, leading into a full-throated laugh.

"What?" Kita asked her.

"My teacher, were she still alive, would have had a conniption fit to hear those words come from my mouth. The scouts of the Clan of the Hawk are supposed to steadfastly use only ancient technologies, except for weapons. It is part of being independent from needing anything we can't make ourselves. For me to say I own one of these twenty-first century monster machines would have driven her right up the wall." Ghost Wind's smile faded, and Kita saw the hint of tears before the younger woman turned her face away.

"Your teachers aren't here, so let's get going," Kita said. "Down here, we use every resource we can get our hands on."

****

It took them less than an hour to reach the spot Eli had suggested was the most likely route of Axyl and his Indie kilabykers. The choke point for the ambush was south of the junction of old SR 97 and Hwy 126, just a short way before what was left of the city of Redmond.

An old Ecar station on one side of the road was still standing, charging stations rusting in the February chill. On the opposite side, junipers and sagebrush had taken over empty lots that had stood awaiting development for the last twenty-seven years.

"Listen carefully," Kita said, looking at her too small assortment of warriors. "These people have joined, even if temporarily, with the Road Shark Gang. That makes them our sworn enemies and they're on their way to take over the compound and maybe kill the people we trade with. Good people, people who in years to come will probably be our relations, one way or another and we have to make sure that these assholes don't just pay dearly, but are in no position to cause us trouble again. It is essential that we destroy as many of them as possible before their leaders realize they are under attack."

"We won't let you down, Sensei." A short blond man named Blue spoke up.

"You all know the stakes, both for our friends and ourselves. We HAVE to win here."

Ghost Wind carefully positioned each member of the ambush team, putting the best archers farther back along the road, to take the enemy from behind. The scout then carefully gave each person a *makeover*, consisting of dust, ash charcoal and various foliage pieces. By the time she was done, most of them couldn't be seen at ten paces unless they moved. She hurried to Kita's spot at the old E-station and settled next to where the older woman had positioned herself to shoot.

"That's about the best we're going to get. If the archers can take out enough of the group before the people in front catch on, we might just have a chance."

Kita looked at her, skepticism on her face. "This is a Hail Mary strategy." When the younger woman looked at her blankly, she explained, "We are terribly outnumbered and I don't have high hopes for a clean victory, if we have a victory at all. The people we're ambushing are very used to violence, and many of my people are not. I pray that their training carries them through this."

"If Axyl is leading them, I worry that they'll just blow through and make a run for New Hope. You and I, Mort and Roger over there on the other side of the road may be the last chance to thin their numbers to where they're not going to be that much use to the Road Sharks."

"If they get past us, I've got one more little surprise," Kita said, checking the old AR rifle she carried for the tenth time, "Something Eli picked up for us, once. Hopefully it still works. In the meantime though I want you down the road with the archers."

"What? You need me here! If it comes to hand to hand, this is where I can be the most help, and you need as many fighters to pick off the remainder..."

"You must be a decent archer, and I want as many of these men dead BEFORE they get to me as possible. There will be nine archers and eight gunners. If most of them are still kicking when they get this far, we'll have little chance of stopping them."

CHAPTER THIRTY
New Hope Redux

Just before sunrise, Eli calmly drove up to the gates of New Hope. He had
entertained the idea of trying to use some of his admittedly rusty original
infiltration skills to sneak through the Road Sharks line, but thought better of
it. He had instead covered the well-known markings of the Terror, rolled in the
dirt for a while and then covered his face with a head wrap and goggles. He'd
toyed with the idea of trying to emulate the piquant smell associated with his
enemies, but decided that was a step too far.

The earliness of the hour worked for him as he approached the compound.
A couple of the still sleepy Sharks had stumbled from out of concealment and
tried to wave him off.

"Damn fool! You're gonna let 'em know!" a craggy dirty biker yelled. Eli
just waved and rode past them, leaving the men jumping up and down with
frustration.

Now the problem was to get the folks of New Hope to not shoot him as
he rode up to the gate. Eli whipped out the oversized and only slightly dirty
pillow case he carried and frantically waved it as he approached. A figure on
the parapet aimed a rifle at him, and another knocked it upward.

"Hold on Ted," Horace's voice drifted down, "We ain't so far gone as we
need to shoot a lone man wavin' a white flag."

"Horace!" Eli half yelled, his voice strained as he pulled the head wrap
down from his face, "It's me, Eli! Let me in before I catch a bullet in the
back!"

Horace looked down at him for a moment, then looked behind the wall,
"Open it. Be ready for trouble."

Eli rode the Terror through the triple sheet metal doorway and it was
swinging shut almost before he cleared it. Eli realized he was sweating
profusely in the February morning.

"Man, my back is still crawlin'. Thanks for letting me in on short notice,
Horace."

"What's up with covering everything up so's we can't recognize ya, son?
It's pretty lucky I was near the wall when the alarm was raised or Ted here
might'a shot you in your front side."

"What's up, my old friend, is that you have a hell of a problem outside your walls," Eli said, climbing the ladder to the parapet. "You have about fifty or so Road Sharks hiding out in the junipers all around the place, waiting for the signal to blow out one of your walls with charges and to come streaming in."

"Shit, Eli," the older man said, looking nervously over the outer landscape, "I hope to hell this is some kind of joke. The Sharks would have to throw just about everything they have at us for such a venture, as well as come up with something to blow through three layers of sheet metal."

"From what Ghost Wind told me, they've managed to get their grimy little paws on some C-4 and either have, or are going to plant it at some weak spot in your wall."

"Ghost Wind? That gal you brung in here? How'd she get so knowledgable as to the plans o' them vicious sacks of filth?"

Eli's face went hard and tight. "They captured her. Tortured her. But they weren't too careful about what their prisoners heard and she escaped."

Horace's face was horrified for a moment, then slipped into his own mask of stoic endurance. The Road Sharks were a scourge on the area, and everyone he knew had problems with them or had been hurt or damaged by them in some way. He liked the young woman Eli had brought with him and the thought of her in the hands of those awful vermin made his blood run cold.

"Goddamn it, Eli. You were supposed to get her somewhere safe. How the hell did you let that happen!?"

Eli looked down at the decking underneath them. "She had a tiff with Kita, which was no surprise, and stormed off. She's damn good at covering her tracks and I lost her. Somehow the Sharks found her and beat her up pretty badly. But there's one thing you should know, Horace. I think she's changed the game."

"What the hell does that mean?"

Eli looked Horace straight in the eye, "If what she told me is true, she's managed to cripple Darwin Shell."

"What? Cripple the Road Sharks? Then how the hell do I supposedly have a small army of them on my doorstep?"

"Not the Sharks, at least not directly, she's actually managed to break Darwin Shell's spine. I don't think she'd lie about this, and if Shell's crippled, then most likely, that dandy boy Axe Man is in charge of the group." Eli waited for that to sink in, then continued, "Axyl may be a charismatic guy to rally his troops, but he's NOT what I would call a deep thinker."

****

Earl and Ballsy, the two Road Sharks that had tried to wave Eli off were sitting and eating a breakfast of corn mush and MRE crackers. They were both stung that they had not shot the unknown rider off his bike, but with all the Indie riders who were supposed to be helping them, they both agreed "how were they to know?" They had both also agreed to keep the incident to themselves. If they told anyone they'd be sure to get shit for it in one form or another, and it was just one guy. Big whoop.

However, they were in no way reassured when they heard the sound of a man laughing with delight coming from the stockade they were watching.

CHAPTER THIRTY-ONE
Hammer Time

Axyl had headed directly up the main highway. Even though the group of psychos, bastards and scungeballs he was leading weren't officially Road Sharks, they were riding under Shark colors and Sharks didn't skulk around on the backroads when there was serious shit being done.

The night before at the old museum hadn't been a walk in the park. Some of these yahoos were such marginal excuses for human beings that even the Sharks didn't want them around on a regular basis, and that was saying something.

This was why he realized he still needed Shell, if he could wean the man off being stoned all the time. Even in a wheelchair, Shell could, using that buttered brass low voice of his, charm even shit-for-brains animals like these. He preferred to let Axyl do most of the talking to the lower life forms but when he needed to, Shell could sell the shit.

Axyl had managed to convince only twenty-six of the forty-five kilabykers who had shown up to join the cause of taking New Hope. The rest had simply walked away or, to add insult to the ol' injury, flipped him off or mooned him as they left. Not one of the Red Slavers had joined, the useless parasites.

"Yeah," he growled to himself, "Someday, gonna take the Sharks on a hunting trip for all those fuckers, and they're gonna die bad." The very thought improved his sour mood.

But even with just twenty-six, that boosted the forces they had surrounding New Hope to over seventy and that was pretty damn good against a bunch of farmers, a third of whom were women and kids. He just hoped it was enough for an easy victory. This job wasn't without its risks and if he lost enough Sharks, the balance of power in the area could shift. He looked back at the Indies he was leading. They were allies today, but you never knew about tomorrow.

"Yeah," he said to himself, "I think you boys are gonna get the most dangerous jobs for sure. Losing you... I could live with that."

They were approaching an old business park, slowly returning to nature and Axyl was daydreaming that he could have been probably a big man in the Beforetime, the soft time. Well he was going to be a big man anyway and...

What the hell was that noise?

Axyl glanced over his shoulder, and to his horror, saw two of his 'tail-end Charlies' lose control of their bikes and crash on the broken weed-filled pavement. His adrenaline spiked even higher when he realized that two more of his crew were down even farther back, probably causing the original noise he had heard when they smashed up.

"Ambush!" he said, standing up on his bike and screaming at the top of his lungs, "Fucking ambush! Gun it! Full throttle!" He rammed his own throttle to the max, making the decades-old bike vibrate as it jumped forward. Not all the men following heard him over the noise of the road, but his wave forward and the speed at which he accelerated told them enough. All jumped to full speed according to their various reaction times and states of repair. Rifle shots broke out all around them and Axyl felt something hit his bike.

Axyl glanced over at Big Mo, riding just behind him on the right as the man grabbed his leg and lost control of his ride. Axyl was horrified to see an arrow sticking out of the man's thigh.

Fucking Ghost Wind! It's gotta be!

Riding past an old service station, Axyl felt a bullet ping off the front of his bike, just below the windscreen and tried to will the elderly cycle to faster speeds. He heard more gunshots over the wind and whine of the fusion-bike and heard a crash behind him but didn't look back. It was every man for himself at this point, and any of his people who hadn't figured out the situation by this point were too stupid to live anyway.

The shooting had just died down when he noticed something smoking on a tree and recognized an elderly Claymore mine fizzing and sparking.

"Go! Go! Go! Booby trap!" he screamed and anyone who wasn't at full throttle definitely moved there.

They were well down the road when the explosion came, missing everyone. Axyl looked back and a quick headcount told him he had lost six.

"Someone's gonna pay for this someday, but for now let's get the fuck outta here!"

None of his motley crew objected.

****

The strategy had not really survived contact with the enemy.

Ghost Wind, shooting arrows as fast as she could pull them from the ground they were stuck in, hit three of the kilabykers as they zoomed through, and someone had hit a fourth before their enemies had figured out their danger. But most of her archers had missed. Flat out missed.

Two of her targets had been dead before their bikes had went down and the third was leaving this world quickly. The fourth died in hail of arrows, Kita's students actually being able to hit a target if it wasn't moving.

She turned towards where Axyl and the rest of his men were tearing up the road, dropped her bow and grabbed the elderly AR rifle at her side. She began firing as fast as she could and thought she had hit another man though he didn't crash his bike. For a moment, the crowd of bikes shifted and she had a clear shot at the back of the Axe Man's head only to hear a disconcerting click when she pulled the trigger of the elderly rifle.

"Shit!" she screamed, trying to clear the jam. "Damn you, Axyl!" Looking up, she saw that the enemy had put the pedal to the metal and were rapidly moving out of range. It was a forlorn hope that she would get a shot at him now, but she started limping up the road while trying to get the jammed cartridge to eject out of the chamber.

"C'mon, Kita! Fire that Claymore!" she growled, only to see the enemy bikers blow through the booby trap with no casualties. "Oh for the love! You people have brought new meaning to the word FUBAR!"

Two more bikers were down in the road ahead, and one of them had propped himself behind his machine and was exchanging shots with Roger and Mort, evidently hoping for a chance to make a break for it. The other was a huge man and the arrow in his thigh hardly seemed to bother him. He had seen Kita emerge from the building she had used and was advancing on her with a sawed off shotgun in one hand and a spiked baseball bat in the other. He'd started to raise the gun towards Kita, when the older woman shot him in the stomach. He doubled over for a moment, and dropped the shotgun, putting his hand over the wound. Ghost Wind could hear the click of an empty magazine as Kita tried to shoot him again and was stunned when the kilabyker raised his head and charged the older woman.

"Kita!" she screamed, trying to break into a painful trot. "Run!"

Kita however, watching as the man picked up speed and raised his horrific club, simply waited for him with a disdainful expression on her face. As the huge man reached her he screamed and swung his awful weapon at the diminutive teacher but his club met only empty air. Kita took what looked like a tiny step to the man's left, pulled the sword she wore from its wooden scabbard and cut, seemingly with her entire body.

The result was instantaneous. Her opponent went down without any other conscious movement, his head flopping loosely. Half a second later, a jet of blood erupted from his half severed neck and Kita stepped back to avoid the spray. She then pulled a piece of paper from her pocket and folding the paper to each side of the blade cleaned it in one sliding movement. She released the bloody paper to flutter down on her dead enemy like a falling cherry blossom.

A few more shots rang out and the remaining biker went down under the bullets of Roger and Mort. As Kita looked down at the man she had killed, the mine she had planted finally blew, showering steel shards all over the empty road. Axyl and most of his men disappeared over a rise in the road, too far to reach.

They had failed.

CHAPTER THIRTY-TWO
Honey, I'm Home

The bodies had been dragged from the road and their fusion cycles had been hidden inside the old recharging station. Ghost Wind had resolutely kept her mouth shut, though she had wanted to yell at Kita for not training her warriors to shoot better in respect to moving targets. There was no need of course, the lack in their education was readily apparent, and Kita and all her students were well aware of their shortcomings.

"We'd better get after them." Kita said, "Maybe we can thin them down a little if we can catch them. I don't relish the idea of pursuing men who live on their motorcycles with people who only ride occasionally, but we need to do something."

"No," Ghost Wind replied, "That would be a huge mistake, and probably cost many, if not all of your people here."

"Explain yourself," Kita said harshly, stung by the bluntness of the words.

"Axyl's group just blew through our ambush with minimal losses. He knows someone is trying to take them down and that someone failed. The same someone is now behind him, and if they are determined, what is the first thing his ambushers are likely to do?"

The older woman thought for a moment. "Either give up, or more likely, to pursue the kilabykers and try to do a more thorough job the second time around."

"And we're just about to do the latter. Axyl may not be the sharpest tool in the shed, but he's got a lot of time 'til the attack tonight, so I'd guess he's going to pull over a little way up the road and see if he can turn the tables on us. My guess is that within the next five to ten miles you'd run into a firestorm from both sides of the road and it would look like Custer's last stand."

The whole group looked at her, horrified at the thought.

"What do you suggest?"

"I was a scout of the Clan of the Hawk. The way of the scout is to always do the unexpected. Always. I suggest we take one of these back roads that lead to New Hope, and make contact with Eli. If we can find the explosive they're going to use to blow the wall of the compound, we'll know where most of them are going to attack and can concentrate defense in that area."

"How will we be able to reach Eli, if he's in the compound, much less move about the outside of the wall looking for explosives?"

"That," Ghost Wind said, looking over the broken grassy concrete, "is my personal specialty."

****

"Maybe we could have done more," Roger, one of Kita's more experienced students said.

They had parked almost five miles from the compound, not wanting to have any unexpected encounters with the Sharks. Ghost Wind looked over the small crew of would-be warriors and realized there was little that they could do until they had more information.

The group stashed their cycles and gear in the low-lying juniper forest and came together to discuss what they were going to do.

"Maybe we should have tried to get ahead of the Axe Man and set up another ambush just before they reached the compound," Roger said, his long brown beard drooping in the chill of the February day. "Maybe we could have got another shot at those turds and done some real damage this time."

"We would have been too close to the Road Sharks that are here already," Kita told him, "We were outnumbered in the original ambush, and if we were caught between the two groups, it's unlikely we'd last long."

"So what do we do? Just go home?" The question was asked by Tara, a short muscular girl with flawless skin the color of onyx. "I want to do something to help the people of New Hope! I know people there! I have friends there!"

"You will have your chance," Ghost Wind said, looking into the faces of the entire group, one by one, "but for now, I have to go alone to warn Eli about our earlier failure and to see if I can find where they've got the explosives planted."

"How in the name of God do you plan to get to Eli, if he's in that compound and get past all the Road Sharks that must be around the place?"

"When I was there, I noticed small gaps in a few places in the metal wall they've put up, gaps at the base where gullies were. They've tried to fill them in, but I could see it was mostly loose dirt and rock in a few of them." She touched the big rough knife at her belt. "With a little digging, I think I can wiggle through. The people of New Hope have also not been as diligent as they should be about keeping the weeds and brush trimmed at the base of their walls. It gives me a little cover to work, and a little cover is all a warrior scout needs."

She moved toward a small spring, the reason she had signaled them to stop and park their motorcycles. Ghost Wind sat on her knees Japanese style, and started digging up grayish mud and algae from the water. She applied the gooey mess to her face, making a base layer of grays and greens, then took a piece of campfire charcoal she had retrieved on the way and began to work shadows and highlights into the mix.

"You gals always gotta get made up 'fore you go out on a date, don't cha?" Mort chuckled. Ghost Wind's face at this point would have made any Beforetime special forces operative proud.

"We always like to look our best for the men-folk. Besides, I'd like to cover up this black eye anyway." Ghost Wind said, smiling white teeth standing out in the stone-mud texture of her face. Her face obscured, she started to work on the wool coat when she noticed Roger's old gray-tone camouflage military jacket. "Roger, will you switch coats with me? I'll be getting yours a bit dirty…"

"Hell yeah!" Roger exclaimed as he took the field jacket off. "Not a problem."

As Ghost Wind pulled off Shell's overlarge wool coat, the group went silent. It was not the sight of a half-naked muscular woman that shocked them; it was the battered condition of her body. The scout's skin was covered in purple bruises, scrapes, and scratches. The women's faces were stony, and the men's faces showed straight up outrage.

"Damn, girl, what did they do to you?" Tara asked. "What did those bastards do?"

"Not as much as they had planned or threatened," Ghost Wind growled, feeling her own blush under the mud. "And they paid for what they did do with their leader's spine. Kita? Can you wrap my ankle? It's been giving me trouble all day."

"Er... um…" Roger reached into his pack and pulled out a pair of baggy old jeans. He blushed as he said, "It might be easier for you if you wore these too. The brush here is notoriously stickery."

"Thank you. I appreciate that. Can you hand me my haversack, Mort?"

"Sure, here you go. I sure would like to give those fucks some payback. Harm our friends, get treated like the rats you are," Mort said, voice thick with emotion. "Whatever happens here, I'm glad and proud of anything we can do to monkey wrench these… these…"

"Yes," Kita said quietly as she tightly wrapped Ghost Wind's ankle. 'We all feel this, Mort. They have hurt one of our own." She looked up into Ghost Wind's eyes.

Ghost Wind stared at the older woman, confused. "Wha.. what?"

"You heard me, young lady. And I mean it. So try not to get killed so that perhaps I can…" she sighed as she said it, "..make amends."

The group wasn't quite certain what had just happened, but they saw the young scout doing her best to not let her tears show.

"Here now, honey," Mort said quietly, "you're gonna make your makeup run."

The white smile on the muddy face flashed for a second again. Then Ghost Wind went to work on her clothes.

****

As she ghosted between the junipers, Ghost Wind chuckled to herself at the amazement of the group when she had finished her camouflage. She had moved into cover as she left, and she could tell they lost sight of her quickly.

She had covered two miles before signs of her enemies began to show. The Road Sharks had people all around near New Hope to keep an eye on their objective, but the majority of their troops were farther back, to avoid any of the stupider members of the gang letting themselves be seen. As she moved forwards, it wasn't that hard to detect them before she ever saw them. Aside from the stink, most of the more idiotic members couldn't seem to realize talking to each other wasn't the best way to remain hidden. Whoever had moved these boneheads to the rear had known what they were doing.

"Gaw'damn I am tired o' sittin' on my ass out here in the dust, George." A particularly piquant gentleman opined. "Not sure that fuckin' Axe Man knows what the hell he's doin'."

"Well Norv, he's over there in the vicinity of the front gate with all them Indies he brung. Whyn't ya just go on over an' ask 'im?"

Another voice interrupted, "I heard someone tried to jack Axyl and his bunch on the way up here. I wonder if them sodbusters know we're plannin' somethin'?"

"Not unless they's somehow resurrected the cell phones them Beforetimers used to use. Someone might know, but I don't see how they could tell the folks inside. We got the area sealed up tight. A lizard couldn't get through if we didn't want it to."

Ghost Wind smiled wryly as she crawled past their position.

A hundred yards farther, she started encountering the more alert members of the gang and started moving lower to the ground. There were points where she had to move forward by doing a push-up and rocking forward, careful to lower herself back to the ground noiselessly. To try and crawl in spots like this would have made too much noise in the dry juniper needles and dried grass. Mud and dirt stuck to her clothing, but Scouts felt safest when they were covered in muck.

A half hour later, she saw one of New Hope's walls before her as she lay at the base of a large patch of sagebrush. She shook her head. As well as brush and dried grass at the base of the walls, the previous year's growth of weeds had not been removed almost the whole distance between the wall and the low-lying juniper forest.

It's good for me, but if we live through this, I'm going to have a talk and demonstration for Horace and his people about sloppiness.

So much had happened this day that it was hard to believe it was still early afternoon. This was a good thing. She still had to find where the Sharks had placed their breaching explosives, make her way into the compound and convince Horace and Eli the plan that was forming in her head was a good one.

CHAPTER THIRTY-THREE
You're Kidding, Right?

Eli was getting worried.

There had been no indication that Axe Man's group had arrived intact, but there had also been no indication that his group had been waylaid either. The suspense of not knowing if his plan was responsible for the deaths of Ghost Wind, Kita, and all the dojo warriors was driving him crazy. Part of him wanted to jump the walls with a machete and a rifle and take out as many of the Road Sharks as he could before they managed to kill him.

"You're gettin' mighty jumpy there, son," Horace said, climbing the ladder to the walkway. "You're starting to worry everyone that we're in big-ass trouble."

"We ARE in big-ass trouble! I thought I made that quite plain," Eli said, glaring toward the low afternoon sun.

Horace's eyes widened for a moment, and he signaled Eli to walk down the wall away from the others at the gate with them.

"Eli, these people are terrified. They're farmers, not fighters. I'd appreciate it if'n you could try to put on a good face, even if it's hopeless. We can't have them just givin' up before a shot's fired."

"Sorry, Horace," Eli said, looking down at his boots, "I'm just worried my little plan may have backfired and gotten her killed."

"Ghost Wind?"

"Her, and Kita, and how many other of Kita's students went along with them. Most of those people had only ever fought in a dojo, and they were trying to take out people who spent most of their lives doin' violence to others. It was an ill-conceived plan and if it failed, their deaths are my doing."

They were silent a moment before Horace spoke again. "You don't know that anyone is dead. Right now, you've taken on the responsibility, God help ya, of tryin' to get our group outta the shitstorm we find ourselves in. It could very well be that the ambush was a success, or that they didn't get there in time to set it or that Frankenstein's monster came and killed everyone involved. Ya don't know and coming up with wild scenarios and freakin' out about 'em will probably only wind up getting the people HERE killed. Pull it together, Eli."

Eli couldn't help the slight grin that appeared on his face, "Frankenstein's monster? Really?"

"Just as possible a scenario as that Miss Ghost Wind was killed by Axle."

"I suppose so."

"Damn straight! That gal will probably outlive us both."

"I need to get out. If I can remember some of my old sneakin' skills, I can find where on the wall those boys have planted the C-4. Do you have a priest hole kind of escape tunnel out of this place?"

"Kinda sorta. We could have it clear of dirt in about ten minutes."

****

The day was starting to cool as they grew close to clearing the hidden tunnel under the southeast wall of the compound. Eli had rummaged through his gear on the Terror, and come up with an antique camouflage kit, military surplus from the Beforetime that he had found in a derelict surplus store. He currently sported several shades of green, dark brown, ochre and gray and had changed into an old Marine Corp battle dress uniform that he kept for just such occasions.

"We about there, Horace?" he asked, carefully stowing his pistol in his waistband, under his untucked shirt. "Day's not getting any younger."

"We're there. Time for you to start crawlin'."

Eli dropped down and started to wiggle carefully face first into the hole when he realized the way was blocked.

"Dammit, Horace, there's still a big ol' rock in the way! How the hell am I supposed to—"

"Oh, you are going to pay for that, Eli," the rock said.

"Ghost Wind! I'm glad ta see you alive, sweetie!" Horace crowed as she climbed out of the tunnel Eli had just vacated.

"Glad to see you too, Horace," she said, looking over at Eli.

"I... uh..." The tall man stammered. "You're okay!"

"Yes. Yes, I am. Thank you for noticing Eli."

"I was so worried... I thought I had sent you and the others to your deaths. I couldn't..." Choking up, Eli was unable to finish the sentence.

"We took no losses," she said, looking at him with concern. "However, Kita's people were... they... all right, let me be blunt. They were piss poor ambushers. Axyl and twenty of his people got through. We only took down six."

Eli had gained control of himself as he answered. "I had assumed about forty, so if there's only half that many, it's a good thing."

"Yes, it IS a good thing, because if Kita's group had been trying to ambush forty kilabykers, I'm pretty sure we would have been slaughtered. Had the twenty turned around and charged us, and Axyl not been such a chickenshit, we might all be dead too. Your plan vastly over-rated Kita's students ability in actual combat."

Eli was silent for a moment.

"Don't worry, Eli, perhaps Kita and I can strengthen their abilities later on. She and her people are about five miles out in the junipers, ready to help if they can, but I have a plan that might make the need to use them moot."

"Do tell," Horace said, "we could really use a plan right about now."

"I noticed last time I was here you have lots of building materials stockpiled, specifically, more of the sheet metal you used to build these walls, right?"

"You never know when you're going to need to replace or expand the walls, so we snapped up every piece we could find in a twenty mile radius. Whatcha got in mind, miss?"

"Let's look at them and I'll tell you, but first, you might want to store these someplace cool." Ghost Wind opened the canvas haversack she'd been carrying.

Inside were several charges of C-4 explosive and several detonator spikes.

"Nice work!" Eli said, admiring the contents of the canvas bag. "I was about to try to do the same thing. I doubt I'd have done it with the ease that you accomplished it though."

"Oh my," Horace said, grinning. "Guess they won't be comin' in through the wall after all."

"Actually, Horace, if my plan works, they will be. It's just that they won't be expecting what's on the other side."

"Hunh?"

"I want another look at these building materials of yours," she said, limping towards the sheds. "We need to make sure that as few Road Sharks get out of this as we can. Attrition will make them weak."

Eli and Horace looked at each other, then at the woman walking off.

"Damn," Horace whispered, "force o' nature, that one."

"Amen, brother."

CHAPTER THIRTY-FOUR
Let's Grind 'Em

Axyl was tired. Tired of waiting to put the plan in place, tired of sitting out here in the pines and tired of smelly assholes questioning every other damn command he gave.

"I'm tellin' ya, Axe," Sky Rider said, looking toward the metal walls of New Hope, "if we just went at two a.m. instead of midnight, they'd all be asleep for sure, probably even whatever sentries they might have posted. Midnight, they might just be windin' down. Two a.m. and they'll be deep asleep."

"Goddamn it, Rider! The problem with your idea is that these goons we're assaulting the place with are never awake at two a.m. and even now, are probably sneaking drags from whatever bottles of hootch they smuggled with them when we rode up here. At midnight we might be able to hit the walls with most of our force still ready to rumble, but by two a.m. I can tell you, half of them will be worthless."

"Heh. Most of them are worthless, sober or smashed, Axe."

"Yeah. But hear me, Rider. Neither you nor I are great strategists here. Darwin Shell was… er.. is! This is his plan, and we're gonna follow it, if we want any fuckin' chance of pulling this off. Sabé?"

"Yeah, yeah I gotcha."

"You're sure no one has been through here, today? I don't want these farm boys to know what we're planning ahead of time. Surprise will make this a whole hell'uva lot easier."

"I had Earl and ol' Ballsy stationed not fifty yards from the main gate…"

"Oh! Ballsy! There's a paragon of alertness," Axyl growled.

"Well, maybe he ain't the best of our people, but there's no damn way they could've missed anyone. If anyone had gone through there, we'd know and they'd probably have never made it to within sight of the gate, Axe."

"You better hope so, man. If not, this night is gonna be a lot hairier that we expect it to be."

****

It was almost half past eleven p.m. and the troops were getting restless. Axyl, Shadow Rider, and a few of the more intelligent Road Sharks had been carefully trying to get the remainder into a semblance of a strike force and it was proving to be a bit more difficult than planned. Shell, before his accident, was fond of quoting a Beforetime comedy guy who said, "You can't fix stupid" and Axyl was inclined to agree. The hardest thing was to get some of the more dense members of the group to simply shut their mouths. Many had nothing resembling impulse control, and only learned to rein in their useless comments when they were given enough pain to let the lesson sink in.

"Fuck it, Axe," Rider said. "This is the first time we've really tried a strategy different than 'ride in and do mayhem' and honestly, I'm not sure half these shit-for-brains are gonna be equal to the task!"

"With these farmers, you can be sure some of them will be ready to shoot when we come through, which means we're probably going to lose some men. I think we should choose pretty carefully who goes in first, once the wall is blown. You know who the assholes are in the Indies, and we both know the Road Sharks that tend to lower the IQ curve."

"Yeah. What're ya thinkin'?"

"Let's stack the strike force so the people we like least are in the front of the pack when we go through. If the whole thing don't work like Shell thought, at least we'll have cleaned up the gang's gene pool a little." Axyl looked at the Rider, to make sure there were no objections. He needn't have worried.

"Oh hell, yeah." The old man grinned, "Some o' these uppity assholes been making life unpleasant for everyone and not respectin' their elders. I'll be happy to herd 'em to the place in line they'll be most likely to catch a bullet!"

"Good. And Rider? As the two smartest men out here, I think you and I should come in last, so we can see and discourage any excesses we see. Shell wants these farmers, if not happy, at least not fuming for revenge, so we need to come down hard on any unneeded brutality or rapes. Come down HARD."

"I ain't gonna argue about goin' in last. Less chance of takin' a bullet. That's what our cannon fodder is for."

Axyl smiled his white shiny smile. "I'm so glad we had this talk."

****

The explosion at midnight was not as big as Axyl had expected. There was the flash and the bang, but he suspected the elderly explosives had lost some of their oomph in the decades passing. Nonetheless, the effect was as desired. The big sheet metal wall, instead of flying into the air in a million pieces simply teetered and fell inward in a cloud of smoke.

"Now! Charge!" Axyl screamed, and the ragged column of men began to move forward into the smoke. He hoped that a few of the defenders that were awake had been on that section of wall, but that was probably wishful thinking.

"We got 'em moving, Rider, let's keep 'em moving!"

The attackers picked up speed, and began pouring through the breach and Axyl knew he couldn't wait too long to stick his head in. He was at the rear, but his own adrenaline was so jacked up that if someone ran up to him to tell him something right now, he'd probably shoot them.

He would have to do some serious crowd control on his own men, or they'd have an empty compound filled with dead farmers. He was still behind the last of his crew to enter, only so many could go through at once and had just stopped for a moment to listen to what was going on in the smoke, when a horrendous tightly-coordinated series of shots rang out. Screams followed immediately.

"Shit! Rider, we gotta get in there! They're slaughtering the farmers!" Axyl looked for the older man, and was surprised to see him standing ten paces to his rear. There was something about the biker's expression that didn't seem right.

"Axe, I don't think that shooting was us!" Shadow Rider yelled to him, "Those shots were too controlled to be our guys! I got a bad feeling--"

The Rider never finished the sentence. Another volley of shots rang out and in that instant Axyl recognized some of the screams as coming from men he knew. A road flare went flying into his group from inside the compound and Axyl saw that large numbers of his forces were lying on the ground in front of a second wall.

A huge body knocked him aside, and to his horror, he realized his troops were in full retreat. He tried to stumble to his feet when another volley went off, and he felt an impact graze the outside of his left shoulder that could have only been a bullet. Fearless Leader Axyl was immediately replaced by Save Yer Ass Axyl and as he glanced toward the compound, he saw the inner wall was actually three walls built like a cattle pen to hold his men. There were a lot of bodies lying in the kill zone.

"Get to the bikes! Back to the base! Every fucker for himself!" Axyl screamed. And the pro-tem leader of the Road Sharks took to his heels.

****

Ghost Wind slipped over the wall after the first set of shots rang out. She hoped Kita's people had stayed hidden and were ready to pick off stragglers as they went by. There could be no mercy allowed. If they wanted to have a Road Shark free future, they needed to teach these vermin a lesson that any survivors would NEVER forget.

She hugged the wall, mindful that the people of New Hope were still at the trap point, shooting anything still moving. She slipped into the darkness carefully, not wanting any of the sentries to shoot her, thinking she was a kilabyker in the dark.

Ghost Wind went hunting.

Once out in the junipers and pines, she could see shapes moving in various stages of panic, and she silently cursed herself for not having Kita's fighters working on destroying the Road Shark bikes. It was too late to worry about it, now.

"Shit!" She went down. Ghost Wind was not accustomed to tripping over things and reached out, to feel a body under her hand. A quick investigation found an arrow in his back and she was reminded, that in the dark, she could catch an arrow also. She resolved to move more carefully.

She trotted, keeping low and staying silent, and had no trouble finding the main body of Sharks stumbling and yelling to each other. They were totally disorganized, a perfect setup for a wolves-on-deer attack scenario. Ghost Wind had only killed one man in the time before she was banished, a brutal mountain man that had gone cannibal back in Clan of the Hawk territory. She had done what she had to, but it had left its mark on her soul.

But now, somehow, she didn't feel all that guilty about what she was about to do. Maybe it was the threats, beatings, and humiliation she had endured at their hands. She loosened her big Khukri from its makeshift sheath and pulled it out.

"Where are the fucking bikes?" a voice screeched out of the darkness and a man trotted towards her. A flare went off, coming from New Hope and she saw a big man with an even bigger beard coming her way. "George! Is that you? Where the hell are the goddamn bikes, man?"

"Norv!" a voice yelled to the left, "over this way!"

The big man started, looked to his left and looked back at her. Realizing that he was coming up on the wrong person, he tried to see which fellow Road Shark was in front of him when Ghost Wind swung the big knife in a glittering arc at him. The lower half of Norv's beard fell away and he grabbed at his throat. He went to his knees, blood flowing between his fingers.

Ghost Wind whirled away from the dying man, hearing footsteps coming up behind her and saw a lean skinny kilabyker aiming his rifle at her. There was no way she could cover the distance in time or get her pistol out and she readied herself for the bullet's impact. Just as the man's finger tightened on the trigger, another shape appeared behind him and knocked the rifle aside and the shot went wild. A punch too fast to see hit the man and he doubled over, another blow loudly broke his neck.

"Lovely night for an ambush, wouldn't you say, dear?" Eli whispered.

"That was close, thank you."

A noise behind her caused her to whirl, but it was only Norv, finishing up dying and falling on his face. The majority of the Road Sharks were still ahead of them and Eli pointed where they had gone.

"I'm not a man who likes slaughter, but we'd better take as many of these idiots out as we can while we have the chance. I want them dead or terrified."

Ghost Wind felt no pity for the Road Sharks, remembering their plans for her when they had her helpless and in their power.

"I'd prefer the former." She said.

****

We're so screwed.

Axyl's self-preservation instincts and youthful muscularity had put him at the front of the retreat towards the bikes, and he sought to outdo himself for speed as he ran. Shadow Rider had fallen far back after a brief run, the old man not able to keep up with the younger Axyl, or in fact even most of his fellow Sharks.

"Good luck, Rider, wherever the hell you are," Axyl breathed. To say this night had not gone according to plan, would have been the understatement of the Aftertime, and he had little idea what they'd do after this. The understanding hit him that he needed to keep as much of his army alive as he could, and he started to slow, to rally the troops when a young thickly mustached Shark a few feet from him stiffened and fell to the ground. Looking at the body, he saw an arrow sticking out of the man's back.

Ghost Wind! She's out there! I'm out here! With her!

He looked wildly around, and realized most of his men had passed him, and were starting to mount their motorcycles. He was near the end of the pack.

"Screw this! If they ain't made it to the bikes by now, they're on their own!" he said, once more breaking into a sprint. He had made it another thirty feet when something flashed by him right in front of his nose. He heard a hefty 'thunk' as bark exploded from the tree just to his right. He looked and saw a huge curved knife stuck in the wood, a knife he recognized. He turned and looked where the blade had come from, and she was there.

"Axyyyyl!" her scream of rage and hate sounded like a hawk on the attack. The Axe Man, in a panic, fumbled for the old .45 automatic pistol he had taken to wearing and finally got it loose from its holster. As he looked up again, she was gone.

"Fuck!" he screamed, firing several times at the area where she had been. Axyl turned and sprinted again, beating any speed records he's previously held by a wide margin. He was jumping on his bike when the first pistol shot rang out to his left, shattering his windscreen. He always insisted that his bike be given the best maintenance, and old Willard, understanding where the power in the Sharks lay, made sure it ran like a dream.

The fusion engine fired first try and the bike leapt ahead, just as another shot tore the seat just behind him. He looked back and saw her in the fading light of the flare taking aim with her pistol again and he began to ride a serpentine path. He heard two more shots, and felt a burn along his right side.

He hit a turn in the road, faster than he should have and the bike slewed for a moment but he quickly regained control. Axyl had been riding the metal beasts since he was fourteen years old and Shell had taken him in, and it was his learned instincts that made him lay the bike over on its side in a slide as something went flying over him.

He used the motorcycle's momentum to throw it upright again, and looked at what had just missed him. It was the dark outline of a man rolling to his feet.

Eli! Shit!

Adrenaline dumped into his bloodstream and Axyl gunned the throttle, throwing dust behind him. The bike surged forward but as he looked back he saw the big man run out of the dust, chasing him faster than any human had a right to move. He turned the throttle to full, knowing there was no way Eli could catch him now. He looked back.

The bastard's still coming!

His long duster drifting to the ground behind him, Eli was sprinting full out, and he was gaining on the fusion cycle!

Impossible!

Eli was getting close when Axyl remembered his side arm, drew it and began wildly shooting behind him. His pursuer turned, ducked and ran off the road into the junipers and Axyl tore off hell-bent for leather down the road.

The Axe Man kept looking over his shoulder all the way back to Bend.

CHAPTER THIRTY-FIVE
Pushing It

"We can't stop now."

Ghost Wind turned from Kita to Eli in the fading gloom of the pre-sunrise morning. "Eli, surely you see we need to put the pressure on them now, while they're reeling. This is scout psychology beginner stuff. Don't let your enemy regroup or dig in."

"We've cut their number in half," Kita broke in, "but it hasn't been without cost. Horace has lost three people, and we lost…" She had to stop for a moment. "We lost Mort."

The pang of grief that Ghost Wind felt at that news surprised her. She had known the older man less than a day, but he had been kind, and he had been a brave fighter.

"Well, I don't want to seem callous, and I liked ol' Mort too, but I think we need to look at the bigger picture," Horace said. "I think the wolf-girl here is right. We need to press 'em, to make them even sorrier they ever got into the bein' an asshole business."

"I'd like nothing better than to be done with all this too," Eli said, looking at Kita, "But Axyl got away with at least thirty men and bikes. That's still a sizeable enough force to be a thorn in everyone else's side, not only that, but he'll probably, if left alone, decide he wants revenge. At that point, they'll be actively hunting anyone they can catch and probably making raids based purely on malice."

"That's nothing new," Kita replied.

"Actually, it is," Eli said, looking at the row of captured fusion cycles. "Before, as much as those sadists might like to hurt people they catch alone and unprotected, their coordinated efforts always revolved around profit in one form or another. Now, they'll be coordinating on just giving everyone they think wronged them a very bad day. These jack holes need to be given the gift of fear."

"I agree," Horace said.

"I don't want to lose any more of my people," Kita told him. "We have so few as it is."

"Same with New Hope, Kita. And you may think they'll only come after us, but eventually, somebody in that bunch will find a way to Yama No Matsu, and you'll be wishin' that we'd dealt them boys a death blow when it happens."

Reluctantly, Kita nodded. "Let me get my people, and we'll form a plan."

Axyl arrived back in the big municipal garage fifteen minutes after sunrise, and he was in no mood to take anything off anybody.

"Boss! What we gonna do? Half our guys didn't come back."

"Back off." He told a grimy biker who had a splatter of blood on his face. "You want to make yourself useful? You want to know what to do? Go tell Cook we all need food and drink and to get her ass on it. Then go find me Cord and anyone else that stayed behind and tell them I want them guarding our perimeter."

The shell-shocked biker looked at him for a moment too long and Axyl grabbed him by the collar, pulling him close. "Why the fuck are you still standing there? Didn't I just give you a fucking order?" Released, the man turned and ran to do Axyl's bidding. Axyl watched him go, a sneer on his handsome face.

"Shadow Rider! Where's Rider? He and I need to strategize!" Axyl yelled.

"I.. ain't sure he made it, Axe." One of the burlier Sharks carefully walked up to him. "Last time I seen him, he was on all fours wheezin' and coughing. He was a pretty old dude, and I don't think he could run far. I'd guess he's probably worm food by now."

Uneasy, Axyl remembered how he'd left the old man in his dust as he fled the ambush. He also remembered he had said "every man for himself" and if the old fart couldn't keep up, that was his own fault for getting so old.

"I'm goin' to wake up Shell. I'll see if he's able to form coherent sentences this early in the morning before he's had his meds. Have Cook send my breakfast up to the new office."

Axyl took the stairs to the third floor two at a time. When he reached the main hallway, he saw Doc Mullins leaving the office where Shell's bed was.

"Doc. Is he awake? Is he remotely sober?"

"Yes, I was just going back downstairs to get his meds…"

"He gets pot only, from now on. You sabé? He'll use up every painkiller we got otherwise. Shell ain't a man to suffer the slightest discomfort."

"His back is fractured, Axyl, his discomfort is more than slight."

"He'll have to deal, Doc. We might need them meds down the line."

The doctor just nodded and walked towards the stairwell.

"Doc!"

"Yes?" Mullins said, turning back toward the younger man.

"We've got those three solar electric vans, and they're supposed to be charged up. I want you to pack up your sickbay and get it in one of those vans."

"We going somewhere?"

"The raid went off the rails, badly. We lost a lot of guys. I'm thinkin' it might be prudent to take the remainder south to the ranch, 'til we can regroup and maybe do some recruiting. So get your stuff ready to go mobile, clear?"

"Like glass," the doctor said, and turned back to the stairwell.

As he headed to Shell's room, Axyl knew he was not going to admit the real reason he wanted to take the remaining Sharks to their southern hideout. The truth of the matter was simply this: he wanted to go because Ghost Wind was on the loose.

And she knew where he lived.

****

Mullins was carrying a load of medical supplies down the far north stairwell when Cord appeared below him on the stairs.

"Got a minute, Doc?" the dark haired man asked, leaning against the cool concrete wall.

"For you, Cord, I can take a quick break." Cord was one of the few Road Sharks that seemed to have anything resembling a conscience, and they had both engaged in mutual bitch sessions about being conscripted by the kilabyker gang.

"Doc, I can't help but notice you're packing up the med room. Goin' somewhere?"

"Axyl is planning on pulling out and going to the Nevada ranch. I guess you've heard that the Sharks plan went awry?"

"I heard they got their asses handed to them." Cord half laughed. "Glad I wasn't there! Looks like they lost over half the gang, and I can't say I'm sorry."

"Indeed. Axyl has decided it would be a good idea to get some distance from reprisals and is loading up everything the Sharks need to take with them. Including me."

"Yeah, about that..." Cord looked up and down the stairwell, making sure they were alone. "They're hurt, they're disorganized and they've got a lot less people to watch the roads. Doc, I think we're not going to get a better opportunity."

"To do what?"

"To get the fuck out of here, away from the barbarian horde. To have our lives back. Me, my boys, and the four women from the slave pen are going to fade like a cool breeze in August. I thought you might like to join us."

"If it was that easy, I'd have left a long time ago, Cord. They've watched us fairly closely all this time, knowing we're not really onboard with them and their evil God-awful ways."

"Well, they ain't watching real close at the moment."

Mullins stood there for a while, staring at the ground deep in thought. He finally looked up at Cord and asked, "What do I have to do?"

"Me and the boys've been sneaking supplies, parts and guns into the

Happy Bend Bakery solar van. If you're supposed to load your med stuff into one of the vans, why not that one?" Cord said, looking the older man straight in the eye. "As soon as you're done, we head out, saying Axyl's told us to get the van on the way to this Nevada ranch. When we get out, then we head north, and see if some of these people they attacked might be willing to listen to our side of the story."

"That sounds pretty risky, son."

"Doc, me and the boys feel we'd rather risk our lives to get free than risk having our souls destroyed by being part of this any longer. If I die today, just trying, I figure it's a risk I'm willing to take."

Mullins stood a moment longer in thought. He looked up. "When?"

"Soon as you've got sickbay loaded, we make a break for it."

"All right. If you help me load, we'll be out that much faster."

CHAPTER THIRTY-SIX
Learn to Shut Up

"So, you screwed up the plan, didn't you, Axyl?" Shell's dry voice rasped out and Axyl's irritation at being verbally waylaid by his crippled mentor was just on the sparking edge of fury.

He had done everything according to the plan as it was laid out by the very man who was road-rashing him, and the main reason it hadn't worked could be described in two words.

Ghost Wind.

"Shell," Axyl said quietly, with little of the respect he had shown his former boss in happier times, "They knew we were coming. They had two different ambushes ready for us and I should have pulled the plug at the first one. And YOU know HOW they knew we were coming."

"We don't know—"

"SHE told them! Yes! Ghost Wind! The one I told you to forgo all your stinking rape threats and just shoot her between her fucking eyes! Little Miss Death on a Stick!" Axyl looked down at Shell's paralyzed legs. "Bet you wish you'd listened for once, instead of craving the sound of your own voice, am I right?"

Shell's face reddened with anger. "I gave you a foolproof plan, you young moron, and you can't get around the fact you couldn't pull it off!"

Axyl hit his tipping point. He wanted, for a moment, to just put his boot into Shell's face, but Shell was a thinking man and the way to express things in a way to kick the older man's ass was to put them into words.

"Dude. You don't get it. You can sit there, and call me names and say it's my fault, when your busted-ass plan failed, but you've sent others to do your dirty work for so long you don't remember what it's actually like out there" Axyl looked grimly at Shell. "But NONE of that matters. None of it!"

"And why is that?"

"I'm taking the remainder of the Sharks, and as much gear and food as we can carry, and we're headin' to the ranch in Nevada." Axyl paused for effect, "Guess which liability ain't goin' with us?"

"Now Axyl," Shell's voice became fatherly and conciliatory. "There's no need to go off half-cocked..."

"That would be you! Mr. Dead from the Waist Down! You can stay here and be our night watchman and run off all the mean people when they come in to loot what's left!"

"Axyl, I can still be very useful! There's no need to be like this!"

"Yeah? Hey, y'know what? When I came in here, I was working out how we were going to get your cripple-ass self down there, how much in the way of supplies we'd need to leave behind to get you in one of the solar vans," Axyl started grinning in a way that did the name of his gang proud. "Now? Problem solved! I'm already sending guys and stuff south man, and by late, late tonight, you can have the entire place to yourself. Then you can bitch at me all you want without my fucking size twelves leaving their imprint on your broken old butt."

He started toward the door and Shell tried to roll his wheel chair after him. It caught on the rucked up rug near the door, spilling him out onto the floor.

"Axyl!" he nearly screamed. "Wait!"

The younger man looked back at him, no trace of pity anywhere to be seen. He flipped off the man lying on the floor, and walked down the hallway.

"H'asta la vista, asshole."

****

"Honest, boss! I didn't know!" Ballsy hysterically reported. "You said we was all goin' to the ranch! Cord said they was goin' to the ranch, so I thought you'd sent 'em!"

"Fucking, Cord!" Axyl snarled. "Why on God's green Earth would I send that backstabber off with his boys by themselves? Particularly with Doc and all our medical supplies! You can't trust that bastard. He's just been with us to save his skin, only now he doesn't have to worry about it, does he, Ballsy?"

Ballsy started to shake. For a moment, Axyl was tempted to pull his pistol from its behind-the-back sheath and just end this shit-for-brains. He mastered his anger, remembering that his forces had just been cut in half, and instead focused on the problem at hand.

Was it worth it to send some boys after them? To catch them, retrieve Doc, and to shoot Cord and his boys down like the unfaithful dogs they were? Not in the shape the Road Sharks were currently in.

"What's done is done. We don't know which side road they may have taken, which direction they went or what their true destination is. Or if they're going to get themselves some help." Axyl said to the man quaking before him. "I think we'll just have to write it off for now, and see if we can replace the drugs, and find us a new medic."

"Sure, Axe! We'll find someone!"

"Oh, Ballsy?"

"Yeah, boss?" Ballsy tensed, knowing Axyl's habit of speaking softly before beating the living shit out of someone.

"If you're not sure of something, make sure to come and ask me next time. You're the one who's gonna have to do the extra scrounging for med supplies from now on," Axyl said calmly. "Oh, and Ballsy?"

"Yeah… boss?"

"Don't fuck up like this again."

"I won't, boss! No worries!"

"Oh man," Axyl said as he walked away, "we've GOT worries, plenty of them now. No fucking way around that."

CHAPTER THIRTY-SEVEN
Atonement

"I think this as close as we can get with the truck," Kita said.

They'd been moving south as carefully as possible with an untrained force, bringing the remainder of the mountain apprentices and twenty of the farmers, both male and female. There would be no bows and arrows this time for most of them, they were instead carrying the best firearms of both villages could muster for the assault on the Road Sharks. The only exceptions to this were Kita and Ghost Wind, who carried both guns and bows.

They drove to within five miles of the administration building, and then left the fusion cycles and the big farm truck, powered by homemade bio-diesel, hidden in derelict structures out of sight. Fortunately, the Road Sharks had done little to clear their lanes of sight from the natural world's encroachment of trees and bushes. Even the large parking lots had young trees growing through cracked pavement.

Ghost Wind and Eli helped all their followers find hiding places and sat to wait 'til darkness fell. No one wanted to assault what was in effect a citadel in broad daylight. They kept their distance.

Sitting in the shade of a partially collapsed electronics store, Ghost Wind was staring at the dead computers, stream boxes and tablets without really seeing them. Contemplating her possible future, she let her mind concentrate on what had been said earlier. If Kita was serious, then Ghost Wind was one of their own, a member of the village.

I might actually have a place with these people.

The back of her mind was trying to tell her something...

I might actually have friends.

The little voice inside of her suddenly over-rode her roaming thoughts and her awareness realized she was hearing vehicles approaching.

"Dammit!" Ghost Wind looked down the street, and saw Eli. He had noticed she was up and moving. "I'm supposed to be on point here and I let my..."

She immediately stopped thinking about her error, and went into action, signaling Eli that they were about to have visitors. Eli's dark skin allowed him to simply slip back, disappearing into the shadows and moving to tell the others. Ghost Wind moved forward to get a look at who was coming and saw five bikers and a dirty white van approaching. By the time they reached her position, every gun Kita's people had would be trained on them.

No one went through these rubble-strewn side streets of old Bend fast, unless they wanted to lose a tire and leave skin behind. The approaching group was carefully weaving between debris, derelict cars and young trees growing through the deteriorating asphalt. Looking more closely, she saw the man leading them on a large fusion cycle.

Cord.

In a few moments, they would be in the kill box, and she doubted the farmers would be likely to show much mercy. It was also doubtful the riders would have a chance in hell of surviving. She looked into the front window of the van, and saw an older man, seated next to a Latino woman, who looked very much like the one Ghost Wind had shared a cell with.

She heard Jannelle's voice in her head clearly. *Stop them. Save them.*

Ghost Wind stepped out in front of their convoy.

****

Eli had quickly lined up the hidden 'troops' into a passible ambush, and was waiting for just the right moment to spring the trap on this contingent of Road Sharks when Ghost Wind stepped directly into his line of fire.

"Goddamn it, woman! What the hell are you doing!?" Eli watched as the small convoy stopped in front of her. "Everyone get your fingers off your triggers unless I tell you to shoot!"

The big dark-haired Road Shark in the lead stopped his fusion cycle, and slowly got off. Infinitely slowly he picked up the rifle attached to the bike, handling it by the barrel and walked forward to meet her.

"Oh no you don't, you son of a bitch!" Eli growled and raised his own weapon, sighting down on the man. He felt a hand on his shoulder, and looked over to see Kita looking at him.

"Wait, Eli. Watch."

Looking at the scene before him, he saw the man place the weapon at Ghost Wind's feet, take five steps back, and kneel in the dust, placing his hands on his head. The man turned his head and yelled something to the bikers behind him, and they each dismounted and walked forward with their hands up. Each kneeled in the dust beside their leader.

"Eli! Kita! Horace!" Ghost Wind called to them. "Please come down here and join me."

Horace and Kita stood, dusting themselves off and began to walk towards her, an action that Eli very strongly disagreed with. He was out-voted, so he followed them, rifle on the men kneeling on the dilapidated street.

****

Ghost Wind stood, arms crossed, looking down at the men kneeling before her. As Eli and the others slowly came to her position in the street, all eyes were on her, expectant as to her thoughts on this turn of events.

"Cord, isn't it?" she said, looking the man kneeling in front of her directly in the eye.

"It is. And I understand if you want to shoot us all, but there's women and a half-wit kid and a couple of old guys in the van, and one of 'em is a doctor. If you're gonna kill us, I'd ask that you spare them, those folks're all just Road Shark victims."

"Yet, here you are, wearing Road Shark colors."

Cord looked down at the vest he was wearing and cursed. "Damn it, I forgot when we snuck out we were still wearing these pieces o' shit." Not caring how many rifles were on him, he stood, shrugged out of the vest, threw it to the ground and stomped on it with vehemence.

"Boys! Lose them vests. If were gonna die, I'd prefer not to do it wearing the colors of the asshole army," he said, hatred in his voice.

"Oh, that's reeeeaall convincing," Eli said, his voice dripping with sarcasm. "I'm so damn impressed with your change of heart."

"Cord, I remember you from the interrogation," Ghost Wind said. "I remember that—"

Eli cut her off. "You were one of the animals that tortured her? One of the ones who were going to rape her!" The rage coming off the big man was like the heat of the summer sun radiating from an old blacktop road.

Ghost Wind reached over and grabbed the barrel of his rifle, slowly pushing it skyward. "Eli, he was the one who stopped another man from abusing me."

"He saved us all, too!" a woman's voice yelled to them. It was the woman Ghost Wind had spoken to in the slave pen. "He and these others slipped in, cold-cocked our guard and took us with them. They coulda been caught tryin' to help us, but they did it anyway. Don't shoot!"

Reason returned to Eli's eyes. "What do you want, then?"

"The old fella is a bona-fide doctor of medicine, and he needs a new place to practice. The boy… well, he needs a place where people will be kind to someone whose brain ain't up to speed and these ladies and ol' Willard, they've got nowhere to go now. We all heard there was civilized people to the north and hoped we could be part of that." Cord kneeled back down in the dust. "As for me and my boys here, we was hopin' to join up with Eli."

"What!?" Eli exclaimed, confusion in his tone.

"Everyone knows how you've been lone-wolfin' up and down the territory, trying to be the guy who brings some sanity and law back to the area." Cord replied, "Whether you think of it this way or not, you're the sheriff around here. Sheriffs needs deputies."

The silence on the dusty street was impressive. Only the sounds of a few birds in the pavement-breaking trees wafted through the air. Somewhere, a cricket chirped.

Cord continued, "I know. We were Road Sharks but goddamn it, we was drafted. Me and my boys rode into their territory and they caught us and gave us the choice of joinin' up or havin' our throats slit. We're kinda fond of our necks, but now, after ridin' with the Sharks for a while, we're not all that sure we made the right choice."

"So why should I work with you?" Eli growled.

"We need to atone. You need help." Cord looked down at the dirty asphalt between his knees. "I'm asking you, please let us be good guys again."

All of Cord's men nodded their heads, expressions miserable.

Ghost Wind looked at Eli and raised her eyebrow. Eli glowered at her a moment and looked at the others. They all looked back at him expressionless. He was stuck making the call.

"I've talked a lot with this man, when he wasn't stuck sitting out at some Shark checkpoint," the older man, the doctor, spoke up, walking from the side of the van to where the men kneeled in the dust, "Everyone here was forced to be with the Road Sharks. No one liked it and none of us wanted to be there, but we weren't given any choice. It was quite literally do or die for us."

Eli ran his hand over his face. "Horace? Can you have two of your people ride with the women, the kid and the doctor back to New Hope?"

"Sure!" The long-bearded farmer replied. Ghost Wind wasn't surprised. A doctor, medical supplies plus four new females was a treasure to the small farming community.

"Kita," Ghost Wind said, "if I'm not mistaken, Willard here is a fusion cycle mechanic?" The older man nodded. "Maybe there might be a place for him with us."

"What about us?" Cord asked. Ghost Wind turned to Eli, who reached deep into an outer pocket of his duster. His hand came out with a ragged and dog-eared map of old Oregon and he took it to Cord.

"Get up," he said. Eli pointed to a spot on the map. "Up here, near the Columbia River, there's an old farmhouse, about a quarter mile east of this bridge. You'll know it because the front door had a little shotgun accident. Get whatever food you need from what you got from the Sharks. These others will be well taken care of, so don't worry 'bout them. I will show up at the farmhouse in a week, week and a half. If you're there, we can discuss if you can be of real help or not." Eli's face grew bleak. "If you're not there, well... best stay out of my territory from now on, as I'll assume you'll play me false from then on."

"We WILL be there, Eli," Cord said. "We WILL!"

"Then get your guns and gear and get the hell going."

****

The van drove off, and Cord and his men were preparing to leave, when the dark haired man walked over to Ghost Wind and Eli.

"Looks like you're going to get some payback on the Sharks. I drew up a little map of their building while I was there. I needed to know all the quick exit points and places to stash stuff I pilfered from that bunch." He handed the much-folded piece of old sketch paper to her. "If you need some more guns, me and the boys—"

"If you're going to follow my orders, then follow orders," Eli said gruffly.

"Yeah. Guess I deserved that," Cord said. "Just so you know, Axyl, is packing up, intending to go somewhere in Nevada to lick his wounds. They're probably leavin' tonight. I strongly doubt they'll be taking the back roads south. You might want to think on that" With that, he walked over, got on his fusion cycle and rode north.

CHAPTER THIRTY-EIGHT
Pay the Piper

It was getting dark, and Kita was still positioning people.

Ghost Wind had spent the last ten years of her fairly young life working mostly alone, finding and spying on the enemies of the Clan of the Hawk. All this coordinating with an untrained group was starting to chafe at her. In addition, her aching body and tired eyes were screaming at her that she at least needed a catnap. She told Eli where she was going to be and told him to wake her when all was ready.

She had hidden herself under a pine tree that had been a small ornamental when it had been planted and now was a good thirty feet tall. She wiggled down into the needles as she leaned against the base, and watched the Road Shark base. She fully intended to watch for activity, for signs the Sharks were headed out and did so right until the moment her chin found her chest.

"Wake up."

She looked up, was it time move already? Looking around, she realized she wasn't under the pine tree. She was on a huge rock spur, with a deep cave at the top, looking over a peaceful river valley.

Fear spiked through her. She wasn't in the decaying city of Bend any more, she was several hundred miles north, at the Roost, the scout base where she had lived and trained. She was in Clan of the Hawk territory, and the banishment of the clan was nothing to be taken lightly. She had been banished on "pain of death."

"Ghost Wind." She looked up. Jannelle Longwalker sat across a small campfire, looking at her with concern.

"Sifu!" Ghost Wind looked around warily. "How did I get here? I'm not supposed to be here!"

"This only looks like the Roost," Jannelle replied. "You're safe for the moment. I need to tell you something."

"You're alive! I can hear you! Oh, Sifu! I had a terrible dream!"

"No," her teacher bluntly said, "you didn't have a dream. You ARE having a dream now."

"What?"

"This is the only way I can get through to you other than in tiny fits and starts. Had someone paid more attention to their meditation and shaman studies, I wouldn't have to resort to waiting 'til you fell asleep!'"

"Oh Sifu, I've wanted to tell you for so long how sorry I am about what Axyl—"

"Yes, yes, I know all that." Jannelle told her, "You're forgiven for being a very young and foolish girl dammit, so let it be! This is important, and Eli is about to wake you. Listen to me, I must tell you two things!"

"But—"

"SHHH!!" Ghost Wind's teacher raised the well-known finger of silence, "Listen! I can't say much, so listen closely! You want so badly to kill the snake by destroying the body, but you must cut off its head! Also, your dealings with the Clan of the Hawk are not done, so be on your guard."

"But what are you talking…"

"That's all I can say to you…"

"Ghost Wind, wake up!"

Ghost Wind's head snapped up, Eli was lightly shaking her.

"Ghost Wind, you were out, girl!" he said. "It's time to move."

****

Had it been a dream? Or had she actually had a moment with the spirit of her teacher? Ghost Wind's confusion mixed with hope until Eli tapped her shoulder. He pointed across a wide broken parking lot to a lighted building. It was go time.

She had expected getting close would have been a lot harder.

As Ghost Wind and Eli crawled through the big parking lot to the old municipal building, she could see the Sharks guarding the place were spread thinly. None of the guards looked that focused on their jobs either, often looking back at the building with worried expressions.

As close as they were to the river, the untrimmed vegetation ran riot, and the Road Sharks were too arrogant to realize that their lack of care could be used against them. The scouts reached the edge of the north wall, and moved silently into a tangle of ornamental shrubs being overtaken by weeds and maples.

"Is it just me, or do those guards look like they want to be somewhere else?" Eli breathed into Ghost Wind's ear.

"They're getting ready to leave their base and move into an unknown future." Ghost Wind's voice was more quiet than the slightest breeze. "Some of them are probably thinking Axyl is crazy to leave this fortress for someplace in the middle of Nevada."

"Yeah, and no one likes to leave their home, even these vermin."

"I think we can convince them otherwise," Ghost Wind said, a grim expression on her muddy face. "It will be full dark soon, then you and I can sneak in and cause them enough damage that they'll panic and hopefully run south into Kita's ambush."

Eli patted the satchel he had dragged with him. "Not to mention make sure they're never gonna use this place again."

They sat, leaning against the wall and watching the light slowly leave the western sky in varying shades of pink and purple. It was so beautiful. Ghost Wind thought that everything always looked better before a battle, before danger. Things usually ordinary took on a special meaning simply because she didn't know if they'd ever be seen again.

"Look, Eli. The guards."

Both of the men they could see were growing more agitated, as if they could somehow sense trouble was coming and things were going to go bad for them. The man to the north began a slow walk toward his compatriot to the south, and in a few minutes they were standing only a few yards from the hidden infiltrators.

One of the guards, a short stocky man whose jeans had enough holes in them to qualify as a net, looked at his fellow guard, a Latino looking man with a scar that made his mouth turn down in a permanent sneer.

"Jorgé, all that activity inside there, we really leavin' the place?"

"That's what ol' Axe Man says, Frank." The Latino had a surprisingly boyish voice for such a large man. "I can't see how we're gonna take even half our stuff with us, though, with just our bikes and them three vans."

"You didn't hear? Cord and his boys took off with the bakery van, and half our parts and all the meds. Doc Mullins went with him. Took the slave girls too!" Frank told him. "Best try not to get injured, now. We got no one to patch us up."

"And no one to screw either."

"Oh, I dunno. There was that little piece Shell's got chained in his bedroom. I'm thinking' she's still there, and Shell sure as hell ain't got any use for her. Nice and young and tender."

"We could go up, do her and be back here before Axe even knows we been gone. Be fun to give it to the boss man's chica." Jorgé grinned an evil grin.

"Then why the fuck are we still standing' here? I call first, man!" Frank returned the vile grin.

"You'll take sloppy—" Jorgé's eyes opened wide.

His fellow shark looked at him curiously, "Dude? What's wrong?"

Jorge fell forward on his face. Looking up from his comrade, Frank saw the woman standing behind him, covered in dirt and leaves, bloody knife in her fist.

"Shit!" He started to raise his rifle when a huge shape exploded from the weeds, knocked the gun from his hands and grabbed him by his chin and the back of his head. "Eli?" he said, terrified.

The last thing the Road Shark heard was the sound of his own neck snapping.

****

"Well," Eli said, "I guess we're starting our attack a bit early then."

He let the body of the guard fall to the ground and walked over to where Ghost Wind was starting to clean the blood from her knife on some broad mullein leaves.

"You'll pardon me," she said, "If I'm a little intolerant of men planning to rape someone. Anyway, that's two less we have to worry about."

"If we could catch them two at a time like this," Eli said, looking down at the two bodies, "we could get rid of the whole nest. Unfortunately, I'm pretty sure they're concentrated around the garage at the moment. We're probably not going to get more than a few unless we're willing to take some huge risks."

"That's not the plan. We stick to the plan."

"Yep. We just need to terrorize them a bit. That's where that C-4 I brought comes in. We'll make them believe it's time to run, and in a hurry. They zoom out, into Kita's ambush and maybe the Road Sharks won't ever threaten anyone ever again."

"I've been through an ambush with Kita," Ghost Wind said, slipping back into the grass and brush, "I'm not as confident that her part-time warriors will be able to get the job done. Either way, we'll deprive them of their best base up here in this area."

They slipped from their hidden position, and carefully moved around the side of the building away from the main entrance. Twenty yards down on the south side, they found a rusty fire door, the lock corroded and the handle hanging loosely.

"No… it can't be this easy," Eli said. "Hell, it even swings inward!"

"Give it a try, QUIETLY."

"Uh, yeah. I got that."

Eli began to slowly exert pressure on the elderly door, and it moved forward, inch by painful inch.

"What the hell is stacked against this thing?" he growled.

Ghost Wind carefully peeked through the open crack.

"There's about a dozen pieces of large furniture stacked against…" She paused. "Hold it. Wire."

"Relaxing tension, or tightening?"

"Tightening. Push that door much farther and something bad is likely to happen."

"Can you cut it? I have side cutters in my coat pocket."

"As long as we don't increase the tension, I can disarm it," she said, reaching into Eli's pocket. She stuck her arm into the narrow opening and with great care snipped the wire. Nothing happened and they both breathed out in relief. He pushed the door in a few more inches and she stuck her head in, moving it from high to low.

"I don't see anything else. Just be careful sliding the door in or something will fall over. Noisily."

Eli slowly slid the door far enough and Ghost Wind wiggled over a desk, slid off and rolled to her feet. Eli followed and they both stood in a dark hallway, coated with dust and cobwebs.

"They don't seem to use this exit a whole lot," Eli said.

"Hopefully no one will come down here now." Ghost Wind noted, pointing down at the tracks they were leaving in the floor's half-inch thick dust.

The pair moved carefully down the hallway, and the growing twilight, coming in from dirty ground floor windows did little to give them away. They occasionally came to lit areas where old LED solar lights had been scavenged and repurposed as interior lights, but these were fairly few and far between. The people of 2057 A.D. were used to low or no lighting after dark, and areas that were not used much had only the light from the darkening sky.

Approaching a junction of hallways, Eli kneeled and gave the old republic military signal to stop. Ghost Wind dropped down beside him noiselessly. Ahead, she heard voices, many voices, all sounding very stressed and busy.

"They're getting ready to leave," she said. "We need to figure out a way to give them some incentive."

Eli hefted the haversack he carried. "Oh, I might have sumpthin'…"

"It's too bad we don't have enough to bring down the building." Ghost Wind eyed the pack as if it was at fault for its lack of destructive power. "I think, though, if we can take out one main support, it will make the whole building too risky to use."

"We'll have to do it in the basement level or maybe the ground level might work, but ground level has a lot of Sharks scurrying around," Eli replied.

"Basement it is, then."

****

The basement was not well guarded, in fact it wasn't guarded at all.

In an odd way, that made sense. No one was likely to attack them from the basement, other than maybe the rats and mice, and the door was unlocked. As Ghost Wind and Eli descended the dark stairwell, Eli pulled a small device from his thigh pocket, and handed it to Ghost Wind.

"It looks like it gets pitch black father down, take this, and spin this little handle clockwise," he said.

Ghost Wind did so, and as she cranked the near silent little motor, a soft glow began at one end. As she turned the crank a little faster, the glow became a dim beam of light.

"Beforetime tech, I guess. Thank you, Eli." she said, "But won't you need this?"

"Not really. I can see pretty well in the dark."

"How well?"

He hesitated a moment, "Well, a cat's got nothing on me."

"Part of your big secret?"

He nodded, and started down the stairs. Ghost Wind noted the stairs had no dust to speak of.

"Looks like they come down here on a regular basis; let's watch out."

They reached a large fire door at the bottom, marked appropriately enough *basement,* and they entered. The room had been used more than they believed it would be. Piles of cordwood lay all around, and the large HVAC units had been ripped out and stuffed to one side. In their place was a very elderly, very battered furnace that had obviously been brought in from somewhere else.

"So that's how they keep warm in the winter! Using the air ducts as chimneys, I bet," Eli told her, looking at the battered furnace. He opened the unit's door and saw only slightly glowing coals, about to burn out. "So much for modern technology."

"Must be horribly smoky," Ghost Wind said.

"Depends if they could get the vents to draw or not. Either way, beats freezin'. Looks like they're not keeping it going now that they're buggin' out."

"You'd think in a city this size they would have found a fusion generator to power the place."

"Those things are finicky. Keeping a motorcycle gen running is a lot different from keeping one of the big generators functioning. The furnace at least would be easier for men of lesser intelligence to keep operating."

"Look! The main load bearing support is just behind the furnace, Eli. We can not only make the building unsafe, but also unheatable."

"I love a two-fer," he said, smiling grimly. Eli took the three remaining C-4 charges and carefully placed them at the base of the support pylon. With exceptional care, he stuck a detonator in each then pulled out his remote to make sure the power light was still lit. "We're green. We can be a quarter mile away and still detonate."

"And this will take out the pylon?"

"Yep, right at the base, and then this end of the building will be unsupported. It may not collapse right away, but it WILL collapse, at least on this end. Be pretty unsafe to live in after that, but if the Sharks want to try, it's fine with me!"

Ghost Wind smiled in a bit of a shark-like manner herself. "Let's see if we can find that girl they were talking about and get her out of here. Maybe the blast will catch a few of the Sharks before they decide to take off."

CHAPTER THIRTY-NINE
Guard This

"God, I hate this!"

Gordon truly did hate waiting around, so normally he wasn't very good at guard duty. With everyone else stuffing their pockets and saddlebags, (everyone but him that was), he was terrible at it.

He knew that a lot of the things he should be stuffing in his pockets as they fled this building, (and make no mistake, he realized they were fleeing) was winding up in the pockets of the bastards he sometimes called friends.

He was supposed to guard the area around the mess and sick bay, to make sure Cook wouldn't escape and what remained of the meds weren't taken. He was also tasked with keeping an eye on the one unblocked stairwell to the upper levels. Axe had given him strict orders not to move, and not to let anyone go upstairs to talk to Shell. Gordon, being a little smarter than the average Road Shark, figured Axe had offed the old fart and wanted to keep it secret.

"Like anyone would give rat's ass," he grumbled. "Everyone knows Shell's a cripple, an' I can't really see anyone in this bunch wantin' to play nursemaid to him. Dude's better off dead."

He was wondering if there was someway he could leverage Axe Man with this theory, get a little extra to stay quiet and realized that he would need to actually see the body.

He looked out toward the garage. He could be up the stair and into Shell's room and back down the stairs in five minutes, and Axe Man was way too busy to check on him. If he took some of Shell's swag with him, well, that was only common sense!

He moved quickly, though he wasn't that concerned that anyone would see him. The others were either guarding outside or were frantically loading the last of the supplies into the two solar vans they still had.

"I see anyone," he mused, "I'll just say Axyl told me to take a turn around the place every fifteen minutes. No worries, I am the fucking guard after all!"

Emerging onto the third floor, Gordon moved quickly to Shell's room to see the bodily evidence. When he opened the door, however, he found the Shark's former leader, not on the floor with a bullet in his head, but quite alive and being eased into his wheelchair by a huge black dude covered in camouflage.

"Eli! Shit!" His eyes went wide, and he began to raise the old carbine he carried. He had it half way to his shoulder when he felt a huge impact to his back, driving him into the big man in front of him. Eli deftly plucked the rifle from his hands and shoved him backwards so hard his feet went above his head and he hit the floor very hard.

As if the stars he was seeing weren't enough, the air was driven out of his lungs by a knee, one connected to the muddiest woman he had ever seen. She put a huge, very sharp knife to his throat.

"Would you like to live, little shark?" she asked him, her eyes just a little too open to be completely sane. "Just nod if you would."

Gordon nodded so hard he heard his neck pop.

"Good for you. Flip over, I'm going to tie your hands."

He felt his hands bound, and he could tell after fewer than ten seconds the woman knew how to tie things. He couldn't move his hands or his lower arms. She placed a foot against him and shoved him onto his back.

Eli reached under his arms and lifted him to his feet like he was a four-year-old. Gordon knew the guy was strong, but seeing this, he was glad he was already captured. Maybe they wouldn't hurt him too bad.

"So. You want to live, and we need something from you. Seems like a good opportunity to make a deal to me, how about you?" Eli said.

"Yeah. I'll deal, man."

"Good lad. I simply want you to give Axyl a message when they find you tied up. You can do that for me can't you... I'm sorry, what was your name?"

"Uh.. Gordon. What message do I give?"

"It's so simple anyone can remember it Gordon. Just tell Axyl that Ghost Wind and I are in the house and there will be more booms to come."

"What...booms?"

"Not for you to worry your furry little head about, Gord. When the time comes, we'll put you where they can find you and you tell Axe Man what I just said. For that, we won't cut your throat. So... deal?"

"Yeah. Deal. I said I'd deal, man."

"Good. Go sit against that wall and do NOT move. Shenanigans will constitute a breach of contract, and you know what happens then, right?"

"Yeah." Gordon went and sat against the wall. To his surprise, he saw Cook hovering behind the woman, Ghost Wind. The scrawny woman looked like she didn't want to get left behind when her new benefactors left and Gordon wanted to say something to her, something sarcastic, but he saw Ghost Wind's eyes on him and there was little room for mercy in them.

Gordon shut his trap as the two women moved on down the hall and Eli wheeled Shell to the doorway.

****

Ghost Wind moved off the carpeted hall to the room Shell had pointed out, with the silent woman known only as Cook, right behind her. The scout carefully and slowly opened the door, thinking their captive might have set a guard on his room and not mentioned it but she found no one around.

"I tell ya, the girl's in there. They's a room in the back where he keeps 'em," Cook told her. "Gets him a new one when the others get to the point they don't cry enough. Sends the previous girls off to them slavers to the east, or sometime gives 'em to his men. They don't tend to last long."

"Wait here 'til I call you," Ghost Wind quietly told her. She silently glided into the room, moving to the side of the doorframe once in. She noted that Shell was a man who liked the best that the old world could still offer. Fancy sheets and blankets were on the huge bed, with its fancy carved headboard and posts. To a person used to sleeping in wild places it looked ridiculous. Old sports team equipment covered the walls, much of it signed by long-dead athletes.

She had moved to the side of the bed and was edging toward the second door when she noted it was ajar. She just had enough time to get fully to her feet when a huge bearded man burst from the room and tackled her. He straddled her and his massive hands found her throat.

"Goddamn," he growled at her, "a man just tries to sneak away for a little fun, and someone's always gotta interrupt. It was pain enough to sneak past that stupid shit Gordo, now I got mud people gettin' in my way!"

Ghost Wind began to see spots in front of her eyes, and jabbed stiffened fingers towards his eyes. The Road Shark was not so easily taken, and ducked his head so that she only scratched his forehead. The world began to go dark.

She heard a heavy impact, and the big hands loosened from her throat. She slammed her elbow into his forearms and tore loose from his grip when she heard another heavy impact and her attacker fell off her. Looking up, she saw Cook standing over her with a baseball bat, signed illegibly in black ink sometime decades before. With a snarling grimace on her face the thin woman began using the wounded Road Shark for batting practice, putting everything she had into each blow.

"Where's my dinner?" she screamed. "Well here it is, bitch! Here's your goddamned supper. How's it taste?"

The big man tried to cover his head and her next blow connected mightily with his knee. When he reached for his shattered knee, the next blow went heavily to his forehead. He went down.

Ghost Wind had made it to her feet, coughing and still a little dizzy when Eli came running through the door. He looked at the snarling woman batter with surprise and started towards her as she continued to rain blows on the kilabyker.

"I wouldn't," Ghost Wind rasped out. "I sense issues here and we'd be wise not to get in the way of her resolution. Let her run down, he won't be getting up again."

"He sure as shit won't," Eli replied, a slightly nauseated look on his face. "You okay?"

"I will be. Don't let our prisoners get away."

Eli looked back toward the hall with an irritated expression and went out the door.

Cook had started to run down, and the blows she was raining on the remains of Ghost Wind's attacker were getting weaker and slower. The scout walked over to her and gently removed the bloody and cracked bat from her shaking hand.

"Thanks for saving me. We need to see what he's done to the girl."

Cook nodded, breathing heavily from her exertions and followed Ghost Wind through the door. The girl was chained naked to the back wall, and seemed to be unconscious. It didn't appear that she'd been raped, but the warrior woman noted that she had a water bowl in front of her, bone dry and the bare remains of a meal sat on a plate against the wall. If this had been the last meal she'd had, it had been some time ago.

"Were you the one who was feeding her?"

"I made her food, but ol' Shell would get it and hand feed her himself."

"I don't think I even want to know what that was about. Can you find her some water on this floor? She looks dehydrated and half starved." Ghost Wind said, "While you do that, I'll find away to break or open these links."

Cook went out in search of water and Ghost Wind took a close look at the chains. They weren't thick, almost ornamental looking, but considering how thin and frail the girl looked she doubted much heavier ones would have been needed. A good chop with the big knife would probably bite through them, and the gold leafed shackles could come off later.

"Hey! Wake up. You in there?" Ghost Wind shook the girl lightly and the young one's eye's snapped open, terrified. She tried to curl up in a the fetal position but her bonds got in the way.

"Please... please don't hurt me..." Tears leaked from her eyes.

"Okay. Was actually planning on getting you out of here. How does that sound?" Ghost Wind said. She saw a slight glimmer of hope in the girl's eyes. "What's your name?"

"Carly," the girl replied, watching Ghost Wind search around the room.

"I'm Ghost Wind. Ah! Just what I need!" Ghost Wind held up a lacquered wooden tray with the words "Made in China" written on the bottom .

Moving back to the chains, Ghost Wind carefully held it against the wall with one hand and drew her big Khukri knife. The girl cringed.

"Oh, for the love... this is not for you. Hold your hand up here. Good, that's the spot." Holding one part of the chain in the hand that steadied the tray, she raised the big knife in the other and chopped down. The mild steel links parted like butter cut with a hot knife. A few more blows and the girl was dressed only in shackles with a few dangling lengths.

"I found some water," Cook said, re-entering with a pitcher of lukewarm liquid.

"Great. Get Carly here hydrated and dressed as best as possible." Ghost Wind pulled the older woman aside. "I'll toss a sheet over handsome out there on the floor. Don't linger there. I'll be at the other end of the hall with Eli so bring her when she's ready, but don't take long." Cook nodded.

Eli and Shell were waiting at the head of the stairs, with Gordon sitting against a wall.

"You two are quite mad, if you think you're going to make it out of here without my help," Shell told them, quite calmly. "No one could sneak out past that garage without being seen."

"I seem to remember doing that very thing on the way up, Darwin," Eli said. "And as I remember, there was an actual guard on duty."

"That's debatable." Shell looked with disdain at Gordon.

Ghost Wind looked back toward the room and saw Cook and Carly coming down the hallway. The girl was dressed in a man's suit pants that only stayed up because of the belt of rope from the bed decoration. She also wore a baggy black dress shirt with fancy rose embroidering, the shirt hanging on her like a tent. Cook carried her bloody bat.

"That's my best shirt!" Shell yelled.

"Go ahead, make noise, Darwin," Eli told him, "Die quick."

"Sorry, sorry," Shell said cringing slightly. "I'm just not used to my new station in life. Axyl was going to leave me here to fend for myself and I find I must throw myself upon the mercy of strangers."

Ghost Wind and Eli exchanged a flat skeptical look.

"Gordon." The guard looked up at Ghost Wind's call. "Up. Over here."

"Okay, lady. What do you want me to do?"

"Open your mouth." She took a perfumed handkerchief, one of several she had pilfered on the way out of Shell's room, wadded it up and stuffed it in Gordon's mouth. "Eli, you have that tape?"

Eli pulled the remains of a roll of military tape from his pocket, peeled off a short section and carefully laid it over Gordon's lips. The Road Shark's pained expression said volumes about how that felt.

"Be glad you're still alive, dipstick," Eli told him. "Now, walk with Ghost Wind to the bottom of those stairs. You make a break for it, or do anything to make us nervous, and you know what happens, right?"

Gordon nodded, and started down the stair. He stopped when he felt a sting on his throat and looked down. Ghost Wind's knife was pressed against it.

"Just so we understand each other, Road Shark," she said. Gordon started down VERY carefully.

"You're next, Darwin," Eli said.

"How am I supposed to get this damned..." Shell shut up as Eli lifted him chair and all, and began to follow Ghost Wind down the stairs. The two women followed.

At the bottom of the stairs, the warrior scout already had Gordon tied to the railing and was peeking out the doorway. Her eyes were calculating and as she turned back to Eli she gestured towards Shell's mouth.

"I assure you, that the Road Sharks have thrown me over for Axyl, I have no reason to…" His sentence was cut short as Eli slapped more tape over his mouth.

"Darwin, you do ANYTHING to give us away, and I'll turn Ghost Wind over there loose on you with her big knife. You dig me?" Like Gordon, Shell nodded.

"Good. Most people like to think they're brave, but facing grisly death usually disabuses them of that notion." Eli looked at Ghost Wind, who gestured for him to roll Shell out the door. He glanced out, saw there was no one in the section they were in.

Moving across the floor, they came to a side door leading back to the way they had come in. When they reached the blocked fire door, Eli quickly moved much of the furniture out of the way and rolled the former Shark boss into the darkening twilight.

"I think we're done here," he said as Ghost Wind joined him.

"Not quite," she told him as she reached into his pocket. She pulled out the detonator, and led the group through the broken remains of the parking lot. They reached the cover of an adjoining building, one that has been half destroyed by fire at some time and she turned back to look at the Road Shark's headquarters.

"Mind if I do the honors, Eli?"

"Please, be my guest."

****

Axyl was thinking to himself that thirty men was still a fairly formidable force at the moment when Hell came to Sharktown.

The first indication that anything was wrong was a tremendous BOOM from the other end of the building, and he and most of his men were knocked off their feet. The follow-up to that was the sound of windows breaking and bricks and debris falling off the building.

"What the FUCK!" he screamed, as everyone began to get to their feet, looking apprehensively at the ceiling of the garage. The building rocked as if in the aftershock of an earthquake and everyone looked upward as a slow moving fissure made its was steadily across the ceiling.

"Ballsy! Take Skunk and Beau and find out what the hell just happened. It came from the other end of the building. Move! Everyone else, finish gettin' your shit together, that ceiling don't look too stable," Axyl commanded. "Cooler, get out and tell the guards to get in here and get ready to roll. We leave in a half hour!"

Axyl put the last few items worth taking into his saddle bag and was stopped in his haste for a moment by thoughts of Shell. The old man was probably laying up there in his own filth, and Axyl began to have second thoughts about leaving him there. The old man had taken him in when he was just a punk and Axyl had once thought him the smartest dude alive.

"Not so fuckin' smart lately though," he said to himself. "Couldn't listen to me when I gave him some good life-saving advice. And he shouldn't have been such an a-hole when he was the one that caused most of our problems."

He looked at the two vans, now filled with food, parts and supplies, realizing to take Shell now would mean dumping a load of stuff. His second thoughts ended at that moment.

"Axe!"

Axyl looked up to see Ballsy bringing Gordon down from the far end of the garage, the guard looked worse for wear. Then he saw the man's hands were still tied behind him and felt a chill down his spine.

"Gord, why the fuck are you tied up?"

"It was that Ghost Wind, Axe!" Gordon whined, "Her and that damn Eli said to tell you they're still in the building and to expect more booms."

Axyl stood for a moment, staring at the wall while his men waited with varying degrees of patience for him to give them orders. Men like these needed orders to do anything besides their baseline debauchery, and their leader's lack of leadership was making them very nervous.

"Hey," Ballsy said, "Anyone smell smoke?"

"Shit!" someone yelled, "There's smoke comin' from the stairwell! We're on fire!"

Axyl's head snapped up. "Everyone on their bikes! Anyone not ready in five gets left behind."

"Looks like Shell is staying here," Axy thought. *"Tough break, old man."*

CHAPTER FORTY
H'ast la Vista

Ghost Wind watched as the north end of the building developed a decided sag and began settling. Pieces of building, glass and brick and plaster fell out of empty window sills and exterior facades crumbled. She noticed one more thing. There seemed to be smoke coming from where the bomb had gone off.

"The C4 somehow set all that cordwood afire," Eli said softly. "Ain't NO one gonna be using that headquarters again." Ghost Wind didn't answer. He saw she had retrieved her carbine and was gripping it tightly, her expression intense.

"If you take a shot at Axyl when they run, they might veer off on a side road and miss Kita's ambush all together."

She turned to him, deep anger on her face, but she didn't reply.

"Take the shot." Shell told her, with his mouth tape none to gently pulled off he was in an even more foul mood. "Little shit was going to leave me there to starve in an empty building. Give the bastard what he deserves!"

She lowered the rifle. "Were I you, I would be cautious about speaking of what people deserve. I intend to see you get what YOU deserve, and it won't be kind or pretty."

"Isn't it enough that you've made me a cripple for life? I'm stuck in this wheelchair for the rest of my miserable days."

She walked over to where he sat and placed her face inches from his. He looked into her rage blazing eyes for only a moment before having to look away. Suddenly, Shell found he couldn't stop shivering.

"I wouldn't invest too much time," she said very softly, "into planning the rest of your days."

****

"C'mon, dammit!" Axyl screeched, "Get on your fucking bikes! We are leaving now!" The Axe Man was a true expert when it came to looking out for his own ass, and the last minute loading of crap on to bikes had exhausted his patience. He gave the signal to the drivers of the vans, and aimed his fusion cycle for the front garage door. "Guess we won't need to close that this time."

Gordon jumped on his bike just as the group roared up the ramp onto the road leading to the highway. He was last leaving the burning building and Axyl was in the lead, the two vans right behind him. The remaining Road Sharks spread out in front of the abused guard, all likely wondering what their future was going to be and how things had gone so wrong so fast.

Gordon, who was Tail-End Charlie, was feeling very bitter indeed. He'd had only a very short time to gather belongings, and compared to the bulging saddlebags and packs that other 'brothers' carried he had only a few items and half full saddlebags. He was not a happy camper.

"Fucking Axyl. If he hadn't fucked things up so bad, we wouldn't be in this predicament," he growled to himself. "If Shell hadn't been knocked down so far, we'd still be on top. Now we gotta run like a buncha pussies from some stupid-ass farmers and we got young Shit for Brains in charge. We're so screwed."

They had just reached the intersection with the main highway when he learned how screwed they actually were.

Gordon actually heard the whine and the thwack as his fellow rider, Cooler, seemed to leap sideways from his bike and rolled on the ground. Gordon veered to miss him and looked down as he passed. Cooler's bike was still rolling but Cooler himself actually had flopped to a halt, a large bloody hole in his chest.

"Ambush!" was the last thing he said, screaming it out at the top of his lungs. The next moment, he felt a burning impact in his ribs that caused him to hunch over in pain, losing control of his bike. He hit the pavement hard, the heavy machine on his leg and realized he couldn't get a breath in. He looked down his body and saw a growing pool of blood, and it was spreading fast.

"Oh... no... please..." he said, as the darkness claimed him.

****

Axyl realized something was wrong the second he heard the yell of 'ambush!' His hands gunned the throttle before he even thought to look back.

The van that had been following him veered suddenly to the left, impacting an old Volvo rusting on the street. The larger vehicle seemed still intact, except for a few crumples on the left fender...

And a windshield full of new bullet holes.

"Gun it! Go! Go! Go!" he screamed. This was the third ambush he'd been in today and each had only made his survival reflexes faster. It seemed to have improved the timing of many of his men as well. The remaining van almost popped a wheelie as it jumped forward, and it was all Axyl could do to get out of the way. The remaining Sharks didn't hesitate to open up their throttles as well.

Speed wasn't going to save all of them though. He glanced back and saw fusion cycles going down left and right. The ambushers were doing a hella better job leading their targets now that they were using firearms.

"Move it! Unless you want to stay here forever!" he yelled and turned back to the front. He narrowly missed a small tree and rolled up on the right sidewalk. As he jumped the cycle back onto the street, he heard a large thump and felt a shock wave pass him and looking back and saw that the entire north end of the garage was on fire. Something must have been flammable, explosive or both.

That home was a goner.

"Goddamn it! I WILL be back, and you fuckers will PAY!" he screamed. He looked back and what he saw dismayed him. They had cleared the ambush and were heading south on old 97, the ones that were left anyway.

A quick head count of his remaining men told him he now had one-quarter the manpower he'd started the day with. Anyone who'd gone down in that last barrage of bullets, even if only wounded would probably never be seen again. The Sharks had been yanking the people of this area's chain for a long, long time. They tore down the now-empty highway, leaving their dead and wounded to their fate.

Axyl noted, even in the dim light of the headlights, some of his men were directing semi-covert looks at him, and the looks were not kind. The men knew since he'd taken over everything had gone to piss and he was sure some of them were going to try to make trouble over it.

"Better sharpen my axes when we stop," he said. "May have to do some culling."

The pitiful remnants of the once mighty Road Sharks zoomed south through the night and their pitiful leader thought dark thoughts all the way.

CHAPTER FORTY-ONE
Justice?

They watched the building burn with deep satisfaction.

Ghost Wind made sure to roll Shell's wheelchair to a clear vantage point so the Road Shark's former leader could see not only the end of his former base of operations, but also the bodies lying in the street in front of the burning building.

"It's all gone." His voice was bitter with regret. "Everything I built, everything I worked for. Goddamn it! So fucking unfair!"

She looked at the pathetic creature beside her, complaining of the unfairness of his life and anger came up from her chest like magma.

"Unfair? UNFAIR!?" she snarled at him. "If you want to know what unfair is, ask that poor young girl you had chained to your wall so you could rape her whenever the mood took you. Ask the people whose lives you ruined when you sent them off to be slaves! Ask everyone who had to worry every moment of their lives when your bunch was going to come along and destroy everything THEY worked for!"

She leaned close and Shell tried to move back in his chair, ignoring the shooting pain in his vertebrae. Her hand went to the big knife at her belt and for a moment, he thought she was going to decapitate him. But he saw Ghost Wind master herself, slide the half-exposed blade back into its sheath, take a deep breath and look with cold fury into his eyes.

"Perhaps you should ask me," she said, oh so quietly, "the woman you hung from chains in a room filled with men ready to rape and sodomize me at your bidding. I could tell you what unfair is like."

Shell looked away at the ground, unable to face her any longer.

"Ghost Wind," Horace walked up and looked at their captive with contempt. "You gonna put one in his brainpan, or will ya be a sweetheart and let me do it for ya?"

"Well, that would be quick for him, wouldn't it?" she said. "Oh no Horace, I have plans for Mr. Shell. None of them involve quick."

****

The elderly bio-diesel truck moved slowly up the old logging road.

They were high in the Cascades now, on a road that had been graveled and oiled years ago, somewhat retarding the number of small trees in the way. The huge tires rolled over the smaller ones and the larger trees were far enough apart to weave around.

"You sure you want to do this?" Eli asked.

"Yes. Sure." Ghost Wind's answer was terse.

They sat on opposite sides of the open back of the big truck, Shell and his wheelchair, tied to the truck with extensive rope-work, sat between them.

"What are you going to do to me?" Shell whined. "You can't just take me out and execute me like a mad dog! It's inhuman. Your soul will suffer, I promise you!"

He'd been going on in this vein for approximately the last hour. Eli and Ghost Wind ignored him.

"I got no problem with shootin' him. It's not like there's a judge and jury here. I do however, have a problem with sitting there and torturing the man, human vermin that he is." Eli looked very pointedly at Shell as he said this.

"I have skills! I CAN be useful!" the man began lightly crying.

"I don't intend that you, myself, or Horace will lay a hand upon him," Ghost Wind said. She banged on the back of the truck's cab and the big diesel came to a stop. She jumped down from the back and walked up to where Horace sat in the driver seat, Kita next to him on the passenger side. Horace rolled down the window.

"Well, miss! This where you want to give the old boy a new hole in his head?"

Ghost Wind looked up the road. "There's a wide spot just ahead where you can turn the truck around. Eli can help me get him down."

Eli didn't really need her help to get Shell from the truck. Once untied, Shell's chair with Shell in it, seemed to be no more trouble than the fusion cycle he had carried earlier. Less in fact. Once on the ground, he began to push, but Ghost Wind gently elbowed him out of the way.

"I'll do this." she told him.

"You don't have to do it alone."

"Come if you wish, but I will do this deed."

Eli looked at her grim countenance, beautiful even with its huge scar and relented. As much trouble as Shell had caused the people here, none of them could hold a candle to what Ghost Wind had been through, even before she came here. He nodded and walked beside her as she wheeled the chair up the rough surface of the old road. He didn't try to assist when the going became difficult and simply walked on, listening to Shell try to bargain for his life.

"Now look. you two, be reasonable," Shell whined. "I know we've had our differences, but this was a simple case of conflicting visions of what could be. I wanted to unify this region under one government, much like the old republic, but you can't make the ol' omelet without breaking eggs."

"Godamighty," Eli laughed, "That stale analogy has been used for more fucking atrocities than any other in the history of man. Shell, just be honest, you were the king of assholes, man. This is Karma, Your Royal Highness, and Karma likes to eat the arrogant. Shut up and take your medicine like a man."

"You do not understand what you're throwing away here, Eli. I have a lot to offer you people! I'm a skilled tactician and planner! I can manage people! I have a lot of Beforetime knowledge that will be fucking LOST if you do this! All I want in return is a place to live and people to help me get along. I'm not asking for much. PLEASE! See reason!"

"Not my call, man," Eli said, looking at Ghost Wind. Her face was a stony mask and Eli was glad he wasn't her enemy at that moment.

She stopped, then walked a little ways farther, leaving Shell and Eli to wait. She kneeled, looking at something in the road. She nodded with seeming satisfaction then walked back. Pushing their enemy again, she moved toward what looked like a wide turnout in the old road. As they advanced, Eli looked at what she had kneeled to see. A grim smile came to his face.

"This is the spot," she said. "This will do."

She had pushed Shell near the edge of the slope. The view over the valley below was stunningly beautiful. She stood looking out at the view, but Shell could only watch her, trembling.

"Please, you can't just dump me down this hill like trash. It's inhuman!"

"I have no intention of doing so," she said, still admiring the vista before her.

"Well, if you're going to shoot me goddamn it, just get it over with!"

"Not that either. Nor knife, nor fist, nor club." Ghost Wind heard something up the hill behind her and turned to look. Eli saw some birds fly up from the brush up there and when he looked back at the wolf woman, she had a small, slightly satisfied smile on her face.

"Let's go," she said.

Eli might have argued earlier, but just nodded. Shell watched them walk away.

"You're just leaving me here!?" he yelled.

"Remember the lesson of Karma," Eli yelled over his shoulder. "Or simple cause and effect. You caused this, and this is the effect. Goodbye Shell."

****

Darwin Shell, former leader of the Road Sharks, looked out over the valley and wondered what the hell had just happened. He had no illusions that this was supposed to be mercy, being left out here to freeze to death, but Darwin Fucking Shell did not intend to go out like that.

He laboriously turned the wheelchair and pushed himself down the road. After about twenty yards, he was breathing hard and the part of his lower back he could still feel throbbed. Surviving this might be harder than he thought. If this had been the Beforetime, he'd still be in a hospital bed and maybe have a chance of at least a partial recovery.

He really hated this new age.

"Don't know what I'm gonna do when I get to the bottom of this road, but I sure as shit don't want to die out here in the ass-end of nowhere."

He passed over what Ghost Wind had seen on the ground without noticing. This wasn't surprising. Shell was the kind of man who noticed if his potato didn't have enough butter or if his home brew was too warm. He wasn't the sort of man to take much interest in marks on the ground.

He'd been hearing small birds nearby, but didn't really notice their song until it stopped completely. He ceased straining at the wheels of his chair for a moment, and looked around. He, of course, saw nothing. Nonetheless, he instinctively knew something wasn't right. He tried to ignore it.

"They think they can just leave me to die of the cold out here, well Mama Shell's little boy won't be going down without a fight. Who knows, I get to the main road, and find someone who'll take pity on a man in a wheelchair. Might take me south, maybe to Nevada!"

He knew this was unlikely, in this age of wide open spaces with few people. You could go for days, weeks even and not see another person but Shell had to hang his hope somewhere.

"Goddamn it, I AM going to make it, and Axyl, and that bitch will be damn sorry when I do!"

It was as he pushed over a particularly stubborn hump that he heard growling behind him.

Shell's bladder, none to steady since his injury, emptied and he smelled the pee that ran down his leg.

The growling grew louder and he heard a twig break a short way behind his chair. He stared straight ahead, frozen. He was too afraid to look over his shoulder.

When the impact came, it was over much more quickly than his enemies might have liked.

****

As they rode back down the hill in the truck, Eli looked over at Ghost Wind's stoic face.

"I guess he thought you were being merciful."

She looked away and grimaced. "I gave him all the mercy he deserved."

"I saw the tracks."

Ghost Wind returned Eli's stare. "He had to be punished, and her tracks said she was getting old. Probably having difficulty making her kills. I was just going to leave him to die alone in the cold, but two birds, one stone."

"Death by big cat?"

"No less than he deserved." Ghost Wind looked back over the passing landscape, and her thoughts for the rest of the trip were her own.

CHAPTER FORTY-TWO
Going Home

The next day started with a cool spring morning. Ghost Wind stood on the small plateau were her shelter had been built a couple of days before and looked out over the incredibly beautiful sunrise view. She had spent the last two nights alone, asking Eli to drop her off near where she had originally been captured, so she could just sit and think for a while.

In the past week, she had killed several men (though she felt she was using the term *men* quite loosely) and the thought weighed on her. Without empathy, those men destroyed others and she did not want to walk that path. She didn't want to be one who killed without remorse, to truly walk into darkness. She had no sympathy for the Road Sharks; she just didn't want to become one.

"It had to be done, Go-Go. If the Road Sharks hadn't been broken, they would have continued to grow like a cancer in this area." She told her small companion.

She packed everything including the stuffed bear, broke down her camp and spent time making all traces of her having been there disappear.

It was time to go.

****

At mid-afternoon she walked up on the concrete building at the old hatchery, and a slight whiff of smoke told her the hibachi was going.

"Hello the house!" she called out, mindful of the appropriate way to approach these things. "This is the entire Road Shark gang. Permission to pass?"

She felt a tug of happiness when Kenji walked out and saw her. He broke into a quick run, dashing up to give her a quick hug, then fell back a little, embarrassed at his own audacity.

"Ghost Wind! You finally came! Eli told me to watch carefully for you and he told me you're coming to live with us. It's AWESOME!" Kenji sang the last word and started a little dance, obviously of his own design. It took every resource Ghost Wind had not to start laughing.

"It seems that I am, Kenji. The thought of it makes me happy too."

"This is so great! Here, let me escort you to the village."

Ghost Wind simply looked at him.

"I know I'm on lookout, but you all trashed the Road Sharks, so being on lookout isn't as important…"

She continued to look at him.

"Oh. Well… I suppose I probably shouldn't leave my post anyway…." He said, disappointment in his voice.

"I'll see you when your shift is done Kenji." She patted him on the shoulder. "Or sooner, if they kick me out again."

"They won't do that!"

Ghost Wind grinned and continued up the path to Yama No Matsu. Then she stopped, went back and kissed him on the cheek. Kenji blushed.

As she came to the main "street," she realized everyone was looking at her. Ghost Wind halted for a moment, ready to turn and bolt for the nearby forest, when she saw that many of them were smiling. Many walked up to her, saying variations of "welcome" and she soon found herself overwhelmed by names, handshakes and attempted conversations about the village. She was surrounded by more people than she had seen in many a year.

"People, people!" Eli pushed through the crowd. "She's new, she's a forest elf, not a schmoozer. Let's give her a little time to adjust and get used to us before we rush her en mass."

"Sorry 'bout that." Eli led her away from the group. "Everyone has heard about your part in subduing the Sharks and they're stoked to meet you."

"I…" she said dazed, "I just did what needed to be done. There's no need to treat me like some sort of hero."

"So said by the most heroic, usually." Eli smiled that big smile at her. "I want to show you your new digs. Kita's going to meet us there."

"Digs?"

"We had just built a new cabin for the Sheffields. It's kinda small but it has a stove and some solar." Eli grew quiet for a moment. "The Sheffields are moving into Mort's cabin. It's larger, and Mort was a bachelor with no kin. So, we have a cabin ready for you, and as a bonus, it backs up to the forest."

When they reached the cabin, she saw it was small, around six hundred square feet, but for someone who had never had a house of their own, it was a palace. It was new log construction with the usual slightly rusty roof and covered front porch. On the porch sat a rustic newly-made wooden bench, built with an angled backrest. A steel bucket sat to one side.

"That bucket is for hauling water," Eli told her. "We need to scrounge some more Ultraflex pipe before we can get something running from the creek system we're using. Sorry 'bout that."

"I don't mind. I don't mind at all. It's… wonderful!"

"Good. I felt a little bad we hadn't gotten that done for you. Lack of materials…" Eli opened the cabin's rough-hewn plank door for her.

There was furniture inside, obviously handmade also. The bed was wooden framed with a grid work of leather straps taking the place of a mattress. There was a table and two chairs that looked to have been Beforetime products and a squat wood stove sat on bricks in one corner. Next to a slightly worse for wear loveseat, she saw the wonder of wonders, a handmade bookshelf. It was almost half full of books.

"The books," Eli said, noting the stars in her eyes as she looked at it, "were donated by the townsfolk. I told them about your taking the books from the farmhouse, and they stepped up to the plate and helped start your library."

"It's great!"

"Now, if you go scoutin' around and find some books, you can bring 'em back, if they're in decent condition," Eli said. She smiled at him. It was all too wonderful to take in. Nothing could spoil this moment.

A knock came at the door. It was Kita.

"I see you have finally come," The older woman said formally. "Do you find your accommodations to be satisfactory?"

"I do." Ghost Wind adopted the same formality. "It is a very nice place to live. I thank you."

"I want to say this to you. You are officially a member of this township. We welcome you and you will want to read our laws in the common cabin. Everyone here contributes and as elected leader of these people, I am informing you that we have a job for you. Actually more than one."

"I see," Ghost Wind said, envisioning all sorts of demeaning "break in the new girl" jobs. Whatever came, she was willing to do her best, no matter how irritating. "What do you want me to do?"

"Other than Eli, we have no scouts. We didn't know how much we needed them. Being one is your first job. Your second job will be to train apprentices in your arts, both those of the scout and the empty hand fighting."

"But," Ghost Wind said, almost stuttering, "I'm a mere scout, and I've only been one a couple of years. Normally, apprentices are trained by Master Scouts in the Clan of the Hawk. It would be presumptuous—"

"I don't know if you've noticed," Eli said dryly, "but this ain't the Clan of the Hawk and around here, you're the best there is. So, Kita, shall we promote her, on our vested authority, to the rank of Master Scout?"

"Done and done'" Kita replied. "Besides, we need to have SOMEONE who will train the next generation following. Certainly the only other person here who might be considered a scout hasn't seemed to have much interest in that."

"Now, Kita," Eli said, "You know I'm trying to cover a huge area and…"

In a most formal manner, Kita slowly turned her head towards him and stuck her tongue out. Ghost Wind did her best to hide a smile.

"So, Master Scout, do you accept your position?" Kita asked.

"I will do this job to the best of my ability. I so swear. But who do you have in mind to study my arts?"

"Certain young people who have been impressed with you. Kenji, Tara, and Arianna. Roger would also like to train with you. For some reason they're fascinated by you and what you do. Take that and mold them into the warriors they can become, for the good of this village."

"I will, but it won't be easy for them."

"I should hope not," Kita said. "Now, when you get settled in, come see me. I have a wood-heated hot tub that might help ease some of those aches and pains of yours. I would also like to take a look at some of those injuries to make sure none become permanent." Kita's tone made it clear this was not a request.

"Yes, Kita." Ghost Wind inclined her head. She was smart enough to pick her battles and the thought of a tub of hot water was actually a very enticing one.

"Good. Come then, Eli, let's give our Master Scout a little time to get settled in to her new home. Eli? Are you coming?"

Eli looked like he didn't really want to leave, Ghost Wind noticed, but he turned and moved through the front door. As he and Kita walked away, the newly minted Master Scout couldn't help but notice how narrow his hips were, and how incredibly broad his shoulders were. She shook herself.

"Enough of that kind of thinking, girl," she said to herself.

"Ghost Wind!" Eli's bass rumble actually made her tingle. "I'll see you later, OK?"

She gave a big smile and said, "In a village this size, Eli, I don't see how you can avoid it."

He smiled and they walked on. Ghost Wind was alone in her own home, and realized she still carried her pack and rifle. She set them down and pulled Go-Go Bear from the blanket roll, setting him on a shelf above the bed.

"We have... a home, Go-Go! I... thought..." She couldn't finish the sentence.

She went out to the porch and sat on the bench. She gazed at a stand of quaking aspen down the hill from her cabin.

Home. I have a home. I have people who care whether I live or die. I really thought I would die alone, unloved, unmourned. Tears started from her eyes.

As if to interrupt this good moment, she felt that old sense of someone seeking her and remembered what Jannelle had said about the Clan of the Hawk, and their unfinished business. Her eyes narrowed.

"Come then, whoever you are. You will find Ghost Wind ready for you. Knowing you are out there will keep me sharp."

As she moved back to unpack her meager belongings, she thought to herself, *I have a place to stand, a future and friends to defend. And I WILL defend them.*

She looked out over the world she had come from, smiled, and went inside.

End.

Acknowledgements

If this is the first time that you've been exposed to the post-apocalyptic world of The AfterTime, you many not know Ghost Wind's origins. She was a secondary character in my long running (15 years to date!) online webcomic, The Wandering Ones (wanderingones.com). Ghost Wind is the sister of the main character of that comic, Ravenwing, and in that comic, they have some big differences with each other. (but that's ten years into Ghost Wind's future)

Note: If you liked this book you'll probably like the Wandering Ones, (and it's free to read) but you might want to pack a lunch. I mean... fifteen years...

I can safely say, without the kindness and support of my Wandering Ones fans, not only would this book not exist, but I might well have given up on my creative endeavors some years ago.

So, let's raise a glass to all those fans, past and present!

I'd also like to thank the people who in one way or another helped me with this book.

My wife and fellow author Suzette (Suzie) Hollingsworth, who encouraged, badgered, cajoled and quite agressively beta-read for me.

Daniela Moreschalchi for much needed encouragement when I was needing help. J.S. Brady for looking at the raw book and giving me much needed early feedback. Richard Van Fossen and Michael Kay for helping me not make a complete idiot of myself when it comes to rifles and C4. (Hint: Hollywood doesn't always get it right, and should not be your sole source of information)

Thanks also to my editors, Tina Winograd and Michele Carter for helping me not look like an uneducated ape. Ladies, you at least partially succeeded.

NOVELS BY CLINT HOLLINGSWORTH

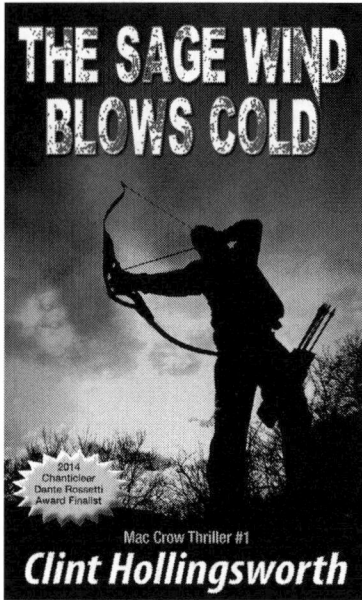

THE SAGE WIND BLOWS COLD

2014
Chanticleer
Dante Rossetti
Award Finalist

Mac Crow Thriller #1
Clint Hollingsworth

The Sage Wind Blows Cold

Bagging a killer should have been the end of it, but it was only the beginning.

Young tracker Mackenzie Crow, working at his uncle's bounty hunting business, is ambivalent when an old flame pleads for help. Mac's conscience won't allow him to say 'no' to finding a lost child in the woods.

Mac, in his element, within a short time has found the child's trail. He also finds something completely unexpected: a strange set of tracks following the girl. It's clearly the day for unwanted surprises.

Deep in the woods, desperately following the trail, Mac comes upon an SAR volunteer face down in the forest with an arrow in his back. Little does Mac know, this is just the beginning of his problems.

Available from Amazon.com

GRAPHIC NOVELS

Wandering Ones 3: The Mission

2066 AD: In a Post Apocalyptic Pacific Northwest, Clan of the Hawk scout/ tracker Ravenwing moves deep into the territory of the brutal Farnham's Empire to find the man she loves.

Forced to go on a mission by their supposed ally, The Western Alliance, Max Thorson and Jack Crow travel east to a final confrontation with the Empire that will mean their end, unless Raven-wing can find them and rescue them!

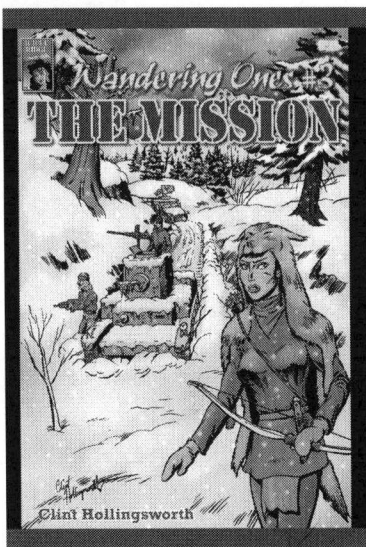

200 page print editon in black and white, with a color cover.

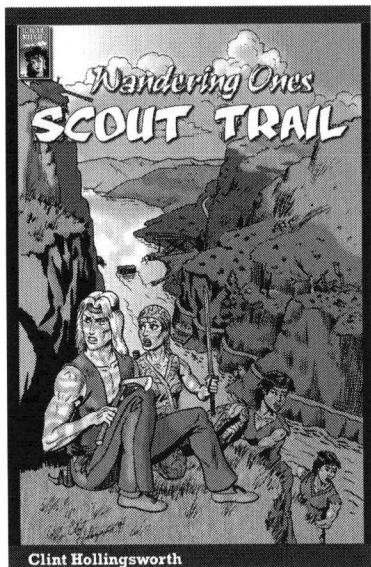

Wandering Ones: Scout Trail

All new, never before seen story of the Warrior scouts of post-apocalyptic 2066a.d.

Young Clan of the Hawk scout apprentice Wolfrun must withstand the Scout test to end his apprenticeship and become a full-fledged scout warrior.

This first *full color* Wandering Ones adventure takes 4 young heroes through the stark landscape of the deserts and river basin of the mighty Columbia River to a meeting with an old enemy.

Available for both Kindle and print from Amazon.com

Clint Hollingsworth has studied tracking under Tom Brown, Jr., consultant on "The Hunted", and is a black belt in Goju Ryu karate.

Having spent a good deal of his time in the woods growing up, Hollingsworth developed a certain sensitivity to the natural environment. In 1990, he became a student of Brown's Tracker School, learning wilderness survival and tracking. This led the author to more advanced training from naturalist Jon Young in tracking and awareness and survival with Frank and Karen Sherwood of Earthwalk Northwest. These skills have saved his life on at least one occasion in the far back country.

Hollingsworth holds a 4th degree black belt in Sho Rei Shobu Kan Okinawan Goju Ryu. He co-authored *Wolves in Street Clothing,* a non-fiction book on situational awareness, with judo and martial arts expert Kris Wilder, and is the author/artist/creator of the long running post-apocalyptic webcomic (and its attending books) The Wandering Ones at wanderingones.com with over 20,000 readers across the world.

He lives in the beautiful Cascade Mountains in Washington state with his lovely wife Suzette, author of *Sherlock Holmes and the Case of the Sword Princess.*

You can find more about Clint at his website;

clinthollingsworth.com

Thank you for reading this novel. An honest review is much appreciated on Amazon, which enables the author to reach a wider audience, and consequently, to continue writing for a living.
:D